SURVIVORS

THE ENDLESS LAKE

OMEN OF THE STARS

Book One: *The Fourth Apprentice*
Book Two: *Fading Echoes*
Book Three: *Night Whispers*
Book Four: *Sign of the Moon*
Book Five: *The Forgotten Warrior*
Book Six: *The Last Hope*

DAWN OF THE CLANS

Book One: *The Sun Trail*
Book Two: *Thunder Rising*
Book Three: *The First Battle*

EXPLORE THE WARRIORS WORLD

Warriors Super Edition: Firestar's Quest
Warriors Super Edition: Bluestar's Prophecy
Warriors Super Edition: SkyClan's Destiny
Warriors Super Edition: Crookedstar's Promise
Warriors Super Edition: Yellowfang's Secret
Warriors Super Edition: Tallstar's Revenge
Warriors Field Guide: Secrets of the Clans
Warriors: Cats of the Clans
Warriors: Code of the Clans
Warriors: Battles of the Clans
Warriors: Enter the Clans
Warriors: The Ultimate Guide
Warriors: The Untold Stories

MANGA

The Lost Warrior
Warrior's Refuge
Warrior's Return
The Rise of Scourge
Tigerstar and Sasha #1: Into the Woods

NOVELLAS

SEEKERS

RETURN TO THE WILD

MANGA

SURVIVORS

THE ENDLESS LAKE

ERIN HUNTER

HARPER

An Imprint of HarperCollinsPublishers

Special thanks to Inbali Iserles

The Endless Lake
Copyright © 2014 by Working Partners Limited
Series created by Working Partners Limited
Endpaper art © 2014 by Frank Riccio
For information address HarperCollins Children's Books,
a division of HarperCollins Publishers,
10 East 53rd Street, New York, NY 10022.
www.harpercollinschildrens.com

Library of Congress Cataloging-in-Publication Data
Hunter, Erin.
 The Endless Lake / Erin Hunter. — First edition.
   pages cm. — (Survivors ; #5)
 Summary: "Lucky and his Pack must learn to survive in their new home, at the edge of a strange
lake that seems to go on forever"— Provided by publisher.
   ISBN 978-0-06-210272-0 (hardback) — ISBN 978-0-06-210273-7 (library)
   [1. Dogs—Fiction. 2. Wild dogs—Fiction. 3. Survival—Fiction. 4. Adventure and adventurers—
Fiction. 5. Fantasy.] I. Title.
 PZ7.H916625En 2014   2013047944
 [Fic]—dc23   CIP
                                                                      AC

Typography based on a design by Hilary Zarycky
14 15 16 17 18 CG/RRDH 10 9 8 7 6 5 4 3 2 1
❖
First Edition

For Teresa Sanderson Concejo and Grace Vasco-Jarvis

PACK LIST

WILD PACK (IN ORDER OF RANK)

ALPHA:

huge half wolf with gray-and-white fur and yellow eyes

BETA:

small swift-dog with short gray fur (also known as Sweet)

HUNTERS:

FIERY—massive brown male with long ears and shaggy fur

SNAP—small female with tan-and-white fur

SPRING—tan female hunt-dog with black patches

LUCKY—gold-and-white thick-furred male

BRUNO—large thick-furred brown male Fight Dog with a hard face

BELLA—gold-and-white thick-furred female

MICKEY—sleek black-and-white Farm Dog

PATROL DOGS:

MOON—black-and-white female Farm Dog

DART—lean brown-and-white female chase-dog

MARTHA—giant thick-furred black female with a broad head

DAISY—small white-furred female with a brown tail

WHINE—small, black, oddly shaped dog with tiny ears and a wrinkled face

LANCE—black-and-tan male

ARROW—young black-and-tan male

OMEGA:

smaller black-and-brown male (also known as Bullet)

PUPS:

FANG—brown-and-tan male

LONE DOGS

OLD HUNTER—big and stocky male with a blunt muzzle

TWITCH—tan chase-dog with black patches and a lame foot

PROLOGUE

The pups wrestled to be the first outside. Yap beat his small paws against the clear-stone door, yipping. The longpaw stalked through the room, stepping between them with the same amused growl he made every sunup.

Yap's litter-sister Squeak butted him with her golden muzzle and he gave her a playful shove.

"Be patient," scolded their Mother-Dog. "You're not little pups anymore."

Yap fell back immediately, sucking in his chest and raising his head.

The Sun-Dog bounded over the sky, touching the clear-stone with his dazzling light. Yap blinked at it, reminding himself that he had a proper name now—Lucky—even if he wasn't used to it yet, and he had to act like a grown-up dog. He watched without making a sound as the longpaw reached over them.

I'll be quiet and patient, just like Mother-Dog said, thought Yap. He fought the urge to hop and bark like his littermates. But as the clear-stone door flew open, he surged out with the rest of the puppies.

"Race you!" yipped Squeak, charging across the backyard.

Yap started after her but halted in his tracks. The ground was frozen and glittered white like shiny claws. It crunched under his paws and felt rough and cold.

Mother-Dog stepped up behind him. "This is frost. It's quite safe."

Squeak was turning slow circles in the grass, her little tail pointing straight behind her. The other pups were tapping the ground with their paws and turning back to their Mother-Dog, wide-eyed.

Yap took a nervous sniff of the grass. "It's so cold."

Mother-Dog gave his ear a reassuring lick. "Cold, but not dangerous. It can't do you any harm."

This made Yap feel better. He reminded himself that he was almost a grown dog, not a scared little puppy. He pulled away from his Mother-Dog and started nosing the crunchy grass. It tickled his whiskers as he lowered his muzzle. He was surprised to find that the usual scents of the yard had vanished beneath its damp chill. There was no hint of the thick, dark soil beneath the grass or the bitter tang of insects. He inhaled deeply. A ripple of excitement ran over his fur. He could smell something just beneath the frost, the tracks of a warm body.

Something small and tasty passed through here not long ago.

Yap's tail began to wag but he willed it to still. The rest of the Pup-Pack was chasing one another near the door to the yard, bouncing and yipping noisily. Yap ignored them. Prey had been creeping around beneath the frost and he was going to find it! He would prove to his Mother-Dog that he wasn't a little pup anymore. But he would need some help.

He stiffened a moment, his head dipped. How would his Mother-Dog say it?

O Forest-Dog, protector of hunters, who is clever, quick, and brave, please guide me to the animal that lives beneath the frost. Yap gave his forepaw a satisfied lick—that had sounded good. Hopefully the Spirit Dog would be impressed.

Almost immediately the whiff of the warm body seemed to rise on the air. *The Forest-Dog has answered me!* Yap wasted no time tracking the scent. He trod over the crunchy grass until he reached a small longpaw building made of wood at the end of the yard. To his dismay, the smell vanished at the building. Yap sniffed urgently.

Where is it? Where's the prey-creature?

The scent returned and he licked his chops—it was close now; he was sure of it. He blocked out the yips of his littermates, focusing only on the scent. It seemed to be coming from beneath the small longpaw building. Yap nosed the wood. He would have to get *under* it somehow. He scrabbled with his paws but the tangle of frosted grass made it impossible to dig at the earth beneath the building. A low growl escaped his throat before he swallowed it down.

To be a good hunter, you must have patience. Mother-Dog had taught him that.

Yap took a deep breath and started again. He was sure that the scent was coming from beneath the wood. There had to be a way to reach it. . . . He tracked around the building. The scent grew stronger and Yap's tail twitched with excitement. There was a hole down there! The creature must have dug a passage underneath the longpaw building.

"Yap, what are you doing?" barked Mother-Dog, standing by the clear-stone door.

"Nothing, I won't be long!" *I'll surprise her with the prey; she'll be so proud of me!* He took a quick look in her direction. Squeak was bounding around their Mother-Dog, pulling at her tail. That ought to distract her for a while. *I just need a bit of time to get to the creature....*

He nudged his head into the hole. It wasn't very wide inside but the smell of the creature was much stronger now, sweet and salty all at once, and Yap's mouth filled with saliva. He shoved his muzzle deeper into the hole, working in his head. The passage seemed to channel directly beneath the wooden building. The creature had to be down there, probably sleeping—there was no hum from the ground, no movement, and its salty-sweet scent was growing stronger.

Yap squeezed one paw alongside his head and started to dig. The soil was hard and icy. It took all his energy to draw both legs in front of him and ease his way down into the hole. Now that his forepaws were leading, it became easier to work a path through the earth. As shards of sunshine shone down, Yap saw that he was right—the hole was a sort of passageway that sank beneath the ground under the longpaw building. He shoved his paws against icy soil, thrashing and digging as the scent of the warm body grew. He eased himself deeper, only his hind legs aboveground.

A hush above his head made him stop in his tracks. He wasn't moving a muscle but suddenly his paws were sinking. He tried to rear up aboveground but the dry soil came showering over him, plunging him into darkness. The barks of his littermates faded away.

"Help!" cried Yap, taking in mouthfuls of dirt as his body sank deeper down the hole. Choking on soil he tried again, barking frantically, but his voice was stifled by the Earth-Dog.

Imprisoned by the cold earth, Yap could scarcely tell which way was up. Panic thrummed in his ears. He fought with his paws but every movement just seemed to pitch him deeper into the hole. When he paused to catch his breath it was dark and quiet, and even the smell of the creature had gone. Heart thumping in his chest, he remembered Squeak telling him that the Earth-Dog gobbled up dogs when she was hungry. He hadn't believed his litter-sister at the time—how would *she* know? Now he wasn't so sure. . . . He panted and gasped, whining for his Mother-Dog. The more he thrashed about, the worse he felt. The air was thin and his head grew light.

Please, Earth-Dog! he silently willed. *Please let me go!* He pictured her as a great black beast, as vast as the whole world. Strangely this thought seemed to still his terror, and his breathing eased. Then he heard something.

"It's okay, Yap! I'm right here."

It was his Mother-Dog! Her voice was muffled by the soil.

She sounded impossibly far above his head.

"Can you hear me? Stay calm and come to me. Move slowly."

All he could manage was a strangled whine.

"I'm here, Yap, just here."

Very carefully he shifted his weight onto his right forepaw. The soil around him trembled but didn't sink. Yap pressed onto his left forepaw, shuffling his back legs up to his body. With slow steps, he started to ease himself toward the Mother-Dog's voice.

"That's it, Yap, just a little bit farther."

Her voice sounded closer now. Resisting the urge to leap ahead, Yap took a small step toward the voice, and then another, pushing his body upward. A moment later his muzzle burst through the soil and he gasped great gulps of air.

His littermates yipped as Mother-Dog reached into the hole and closed her jaw around his scruff. With a stiff tug she yanked Yap out and set him down by her side.

The pups pounced on Yap, licking and nipping him.

"My foolish brother!" yipped Squeak, nuzzling him. "I thought we'd lost you forever!"

"Let him breathe!" snapped their Mother-Dog, and the pups fell back as she cleaned the dirt from Yap's face. She pressed her muzzle close to his. "Never do that again!" she growled. Then her voice softened. "I can't lose you, my pup."

He shut his eyes and allowed the relief to wash over him.

"I was scared," he murmured to his Mother-Dog. "I thought the Earth-Dog had swallowed me up and I'd never get out. I tried to fight her but it only made things worse. It was when I stopped fighting that the fear went away."

He opened his eyes.

Mother-Dog was gazing down at him lovingly. "You don't need to fight her. Earth-Dog takes us when we die," she reminded him. "Until then, she protects us and gives us strength. She watches over us night and day—when you need her, she will help you." The words rolled about Yap's mind as his Pup-Pack gathered around and licked the soil from his coat.

When you need her, she will help you. . . .

CHAPTER ONE

Lucky awoke with a shiver to a cloudless night. The dogs were by the riverbank, huddled together beneath a bush. The warmth of their bodies wasn't enough to keep out the freezing wind. It whipped over the water, burrowing under Lucky's golden fur.

He looked about him. Bella's head was resting on Martha's huge black flank, and Lick—no, she was *Storm* now—was nestled between the water-dog's paws. *Oh, Storm, why did you have to choose that name?* Lucky's stomach clenched. He couldn't shake the feeling that her choice was an omen of some kind. Could the young Fierce Dog have a part to play in the gruesome battle that haunted Lucky's dreams?

The Storm of Dogs?

He still didn't know exactly what it was, or when it would happen . . . but it *was* real. He sensed the chaos, the frenzy of snapping teeth. His tail drooped against his flank. Storm looked so

9

peaceful with her head resting on her brown forepaws, her ears flopping back. But Lucky couldn't forget the savagery with which she'd attacked Terror, the crazed leader of Twitch's Pack.

Twitch was sleeping on his side, revealing the stump where one of his forelegs had been. Moon slept with her back against Lucky, her paws covering her eyes. The Farm Dog's lip trembled, revealing one fang, and she whined softly. "Fiery, I'm here . . . . I'm here. . . ."

She must have been dreaming of her mate. Maybe in her dreams, the great hunter had survived.

If only they were back with the Wild Pack already. Fiery's illness and death had left Lucky feeling exposed. His mind returned to the Dog-Garden, where black-faced, yellow-furred longpaws had built a Trap House in a giant loudcage. The dogs had found Fiery locked inside, along with other animals. Foxes, rabbits, a coyote . . . even a ginger sharpclaw. And every creature was sick.

The dogs had managed to free them all, escaping with Fiery into the forest, only to come across Terror's Pack.

Lucky shuddered. Fiery had been such a powerful fighter, but his time in the Trap House had left him as feeble as a pup. He hadn't been able to defend himself. Lucky whined softly as he remembered the gaunt dog with watery eyes that the once-mighty Fiery had become.

He smelled bad too. . . . His blood was foul, like the poisoned river.

By the time they'd found him, it had been too late. Poor Fiery . . .

The dogs had formed a circle around Moon when they'd settled down for the night, as though they could protect her from her loss, as well as the bitter wind. Lucky rose carefully so as not to disturb her, and trod over Twitch's tail, stepping out from beneath the bush. Frost clung to the small green leaves and sparkled on each blade of grass. Even Lucky's fur was stiff beneath its icy touch.

He edged around the bush, looking out across overgrown fields that rose and fell in peaks and valleys. He turned back to the river, crunching over the frozen grass to the bank. The water hadn't turned to ice, but it was so cold it scalded his tongue, and he drank only a little.

Lucky smelled salt on the chill night air. It had grown more powerful as the dogs had wandered downstream, but he couldn't work out where it was coming from. Lowering his muzzle, he caught the scent they'd been following: Alpha, Sweet, and the rest of the Pack must have passed this way. They couldn't be far ahead—a day at most. It still stung that Sweet had gone with the dog-wolf, refusing to look for Fiery after the yellow longpaws had captured him. But Lucky was grateful that Sweet had left careful scent-marks along the way, just as she had promised.

Moon and the others would be happier among more dogs. And Lucky had been feeling isolated since the battle with Terror and his Pack—if a brave, powerful dog like Fiery could fall so easily . . . He lowered his head. That crazed Pack was still out there somewhere, as were the Fierce Dogs. He and his companions would be safer once they were reunited with the Wild Pack.

The cold was also worrying. Red Leaf had passed and Ice Wind was taking hold. He'd lived through Ice Wind before, but that was in the city, where the longpaws' tall buildings blocked the worst of the gusts. Here they seemed to cut through Lucky's fur to chill his blood. Lucky's Mother-Dog had assured him as a pup that frost was harmless, but even in the city that wasn't always true. Lucky remembered Ferret Tooth, a Lone Dog who had begged for scraps outside the Food House. On a bitter night, he'd curled up in the park and never got up again. Lucky hadn't seen him, but he'd heard that the old dog had grown as hard and cold as the frost. Mother-Dog was very wise, but Lucky had to admit that she hadn't known everything. . . .

He shook his head to clear away the sad memories, the same way he would shake rain from his fur. He looked around. They were still in the territory of Terror's Pack. Standing at the bank of the river, Lucky detected faint traces of those dogs on the wind. Glancing back at the long-eared dog among the heap of sleeping bodies, he couldn't help but be impressed. Twitch had walked out on Alpha's Pack, lost a leg, and joined another Pack. The lame chase-dog had somehow managed to stay alive and keep his wits despite Terror's unpredictable fury.

Terror's Pack lacked order and discipline. How would the Pack react to their Alpha's death? Lucky hoped they would stick together and form a gentler Pack, rather than seek out more fights.

Lucky sat down on the frosty grass with a shake of his head.

Where would Twitch fit in now? He was brave and determined—he'd helped the rescue party find Fiery and finally defeat Terror. Twitch deserved some rest and comfort. *He should be with the Wild Pack, with his litter-sister, Spring. He would be safe there.*

Lucky scratched his ear with a hindpaw. Alpha would never let Twitch return. He had branded him a traitor and told him he was no longer welcome. But Twitch could hardly return to the Pack whose Alpha he'd helped destroy. Perhaps he was destined to be a

Lone Dog, as he had been when Lucky had seen him in the forest.

I was a Lone Dog myself before the Big Growl, thought Lucky. It felt like a lifetime ago.

He turned to gaze over the river. The Moon-Dog hung in the sky, growing full. Her reflection floated on the still water. The faintest hint of dawn light touched the far bank.

With a sigh, Lucky trod over to the sleeping dogs. "Time to get up," he murmured, tapping each on the nose.

Storm blinked and threw back her head in a yawn, revealing her sharp white teeth. "But it's still dark. . . ."

"The Pack will start moving at sunup. We have to leave now to have a chance of catching up with them."

Storm stood up without further protest. Twitch was stretching and rising onto his three paws.

Bella shivered. "So cold."

Lucky nodded.

"Try exercising your legs," said Moon. "Like this." She started hopping from paw to paw, shaking off the frost.

Bella copied her, shaking her fur vigorously, and Lucky joined in. Moon had been a Wild Dog all her life and she had ways of dealing with the cold.

Storm tried to hop about like the other dogs. Her forepaws

crossed and she lost her footing, stumbling and righting herself. Moon nosed her, gave the pup a lick to the ear, and repeated her hopping action. "Don't do it too fast if it makes you feel dizzy. Just a gentle motion, back and forth. Martha, give yourself a good shake to get rid of the ice."

Lucky watched Storm try again with more success and was touched by how Moon tried to help the others, licking the frost off their fur and encouraging them to hop about. *Poor Moon, she already lost one of her pups. It's good that she has something to do besides grieve for her mate.*

"I do feel a bit better now," said Bella, licking her paws and following Moon down to the riverbank. The dogs drank the icy water. Martha tapped it with one huge, black paw but seemed to think better of taking a dip. The great dog plodded along the bank, stretching her legs, as tall as a loudcage.

Bella craned her head. "That salty smell is getting stronger."

Twitch sniffed the air. "What do you think it is?"

"I'm not sure. . . ." Bella shut her eyes a moment. "It's familiar, though. Reminds me a bit of some food I used to eat as a Leashed Dog."

Twitch didn't look convinced. "It doesn't smell like food to me."

"I think it does," yipped Storm. "Salty . . . like blood."

Lucky felt a wrinkle of unease as the pup ran her tongue over her sharp little teeth. He quickly changed the subject, turning to Martha. "You were a Leashed Dog before the Big Growl. What do you think?"

Martha paused, gazing over the dark water. "I don't know. But I agree with Bella: It's somehow familiar."

He heard a low rumbling and his ears pricked up. It was Storm's belly. She dropped her head and gazed up at him guiltily. "I can't help it."

"I know how you feel. We'll find something soon." Lucky looked about him. As the weather grew colder it was becoming harder to find prey. They'd managed to catch two young rabbits yesterday, but the meal hadn't lasted long when it'd been split between all of them. "We need to find something before we set off to follow the Pack's trail."

Storm nodded with relief.

The dogs began to stalk along the edge of the river, sniffing the frosty earth and looking for signs of prey.

Lucky moved slowly, trying his best to stay quiet, but his paws crunched on the frozen grass with every step. The wind rose over the river, bringing with it a fresh wave of salty air that masked other scents. Lucky sighed. *We'll never find prey-creatures here.*

"Look! In the water." Martha's low growl startled him. Lucky turned to see an animal bobbing up on the surface of the river, spinning around and ducking out of sight.

"Is it a fish?" whispered Storm.

Lucky shook his head. What he'd seen had been covered in fur.

The dogs watched in wonder as the creature turned loops in the silvery water. The Sun-Dog's whiskers glanced off its coat, and it shimmered as it threw back its head in a lazy yawn.

Bella spoke with authority, breaking the spell. "It's a river rabbit. I've heard of them."

Lucky cocked his head at his litter-sister—he wasn't sure about that. Rabbits lived in burrows underground; he'd never heard of them swimming. He was about to say so when the animal bobbed up again. Its round face and short muzzle looked more like a sharpclaw's than a rabbit's, and its ears were very small. Its body was long and muscular and as it splashed about in the water Lucky spotted a long, pointed tail. He watched as it flipped onto its back and floated with clawed paws in the air, easily riding the gentle current.

"We need to keep downwind and stay quiet," warned Moon. She began to stalk along the bank, Martha and Lucky close behind her. Twitch, Bella, and Storm held back. It was common hunting practice to circle the prey, with dogs behind to flush it out and others up ahead to stop it in its tracks. Lucky wasn't sure how that would work with the prey swimming free in the river, but what choice did they have? The water was too cold for a dog, even Martha. None of them would be quick enough to swim after the animal anyway. Their only hope was that it came on land, but there was nothing to stop it from climbing onto the far bank, where it would be out of reach.

Moon, Martha, and Lucky sank behind a tussock of grass by the riverside. They watched in silence, licking their chops, as the river rabbit splashed about in the first glow of sunup. Then the animal flipped onto its belly and made for the near bank. To Lucky's amazement, it floated toward the spot where the dogs were crouching, just where Martha's black pelt rose over the tussock. Martha and Moon exchanged looks as it slid effortlessly onto the frosty grass and shook out its fur. Martha sprang, throwing her weight on the creature, which struggled and squealed ferociously. It slipped out of her grasp and bounded along the bank with Martha, Moon, and Lucky in pursuit. Lucky was right—it was slower on land than the dogs. Spinning on its short legs it started back toward the water, perhaps understanding that was its only hope. Lucky pounced in its path. The animal reared back with a furious screech and Martha dived at it, this time throwing it to the ground with her huge paws and locking her jaws around its long neck.

The dogs stretched along a jumble of brambles, picking the last morsels of meat from their claws.

"River rabbit is delicious!" yawned Storm.

"Like regular rabbit but more fatty and rich," Bella agreed. "I could get used to this."

Well, don't, thought Lucky. They were fortunate to have caught it. There weren't any rabbits around, not even mice. . . . *I hope the Pack is heading somewhere with more prey.* At least the dogs were cheerful now that they had eaten. He watched as Martha approached the riverbank and murmured her thanks to the River-Dog.

"We are grateful for this delicious meal, bountiful and kind Spirit Dog." She dipped her head respectfully.

Lucky waited until she had finished and rose to his paws. The Sun-Dog was bounding over the water, starting his slow climb into the sky. "We should get going. Alpha and the others will be on the move now." Who knew how far the dog-wolf would go in order to escape Blade's Pack?

Martha came back from the river's edge. "I know we have to get away from the Fierce Dogs, but that can't be the only reason to keep moving. Where are we going? What are we heading to?"

Lucky had no answer to that. He started along the river path, keen to get moving. The others followed.

It was Bella who spoke. "Somewhere we can live safely. A quiet, peaceful spot with lots of rabbits and fresh water."

Storm's tail gave a wag as she gamboled alongside them. "Will Alpha have found a place like that?"

"I hope so," Lucky replied, though in his heart he knew that it wouldn't be easy. Looking at Storm, he saw a large, playful pup. He felt a swell of protectiveness toward her. He would go a very long way to avoid her breedmates—to be certain that they wouldn't come looking for her and try to take her away by force ever again.

They passed some shrubs with whiskery thorns that clutched at their coats. Lucky shook his fur, his nose twitching. He gave a small yelp. What was that scent? His haunches rose, his tail stiff behind him.

"There's a dog here!"

Bella and Moon looked around with their ears pricked, immediately on alert. With another sniff, Lucky realized it wasn't a Fierce Dog. There was nothing of their rage or aggression in the odor that wafted on the cold breeze.

Twitch stepped forward and barked toward the bramblebush. "Splash, is that you?"

Lucky heard a rustling, and a small, wiry-furred, black dog crept out from under the bush. Six others followed cautiously and shook the leaves from their fur.

It was Terror's Pack! Lucky took a step closer to Twitch, and Bella moved to his other side, flanking him protectively. Lucky sensed the reassuring scents of Martha, Moon, and Storm just behind them.

But Twitch didn't look like he needed protection. The black dog skipped up to him, throwing his forepaws on the ground, wagging his tail, and dipping his head submissively. His Packmates followed his gesture, nervous but friendly. Twitch approached his former Packmates and touched his nose to theirs, his feathered tail lashing the air.

The wind shrilled over the water and the dog called Splash snapped his head around with a start. Lucky watched his quick, nervous movements. He recognized this dog—he had seen Terror bully him as he'd watched the Pack from a distance.

All the dogs seemed malnourished and fearful. Under Terror's rule they had been vicious. *They must have been driven to it,* thought

Lucky. He stole a glance at Storm, remembering how he'd found her by the body of the dying Alpha. Had she killed him in an act of mercy, or was it bloodlust? Lucky pushed the thought away.

Twitch turned to the members of the Wild Pack. "This is Splash. I guess you could say he was Terror's Beta."

"Terror didn't really have a Beta," Splash murmured, dipping his head humbly as he greeted them. He turned back to Twitch. "We followed you because we . . ." He glanced back at a couple of the others. "We think you should stay here."

Lucky looked to Twitch. The long-eared dog cocked his head thoughtfully.

"You belong with us," yipped a skinny gray dog, pawing the ground.

Lucky was startled to hear a small growl. Twitch's former Packmates fell back instantly as Storm pressed between Bella and Lucky. Her forepaws were slightly splayed, giving her a dense, stocky appearance. Her head was dropped to shoulder height and her lips peeled back to reveal her fangs.

"You tried to hurt me and my friends!" she snarled. "You won't take Twitch! I won't let you!"

Splash backed away, startled, his tail curling between his

legs. This seemed to feed Storm's confidence and she took a step toward him, her voice rising furiously. "I'm sick of dogs trying to make decisions for everyone else! He wants to stay here; leave him alone!"

She thinks he's just like Blade, trying to force Twitch to go with them, Lucky realized with a sinking feeling. It troubled him that Storm seemed to think a dog was either good or bad, friend or enemy. It wasn't always so simple. Splash was asking Twitch to stay with them, not forcing him. Lucky ran his eyes over the lean, anxious faces of Twitch's old Pack. They seemed pathetic now, but he remembered how wildly they had fought under Terror. It wasn't wise to provoke them.

Splash licked his chops nervously, his ears flat against his head.

Lucky tensed, preparing to defend Storm if the mad dog's Pack lurched at her.

But it was Twitch who stepped between Storm and the little black dog. Turning to the Fierce Dog pup, he gave a quick wag of his tail in a gesture of appeasement. "Thank you, Storm. I am glad that you want to protect me, but Splash is right."

Storm stared at him. Her body relaxed and she sat down on the grass, but didn't speak.

Twitch glanced back at Lucky and Bella, trailing his eyes over Storm, Martha, and Moon. "I'm sorry, I don't want to desert you. But I've been thinking about this a lot. These dogs . . ." He turned to them and their tails wagged hopefully. "They are my Pack now. It's like Splash said: I belong with them."

CHAPTER TWO

Moon rushed to Twitch's side. The wind blew back her long coat, more white than black, fanning it about her face. "Are you sure you want to go with them?" she whined, nudging him with her snout. "You've only been with this Pack a few circles of the Moon-Dog. You belong with *us*."

"I used to," Twitch agreed. "But it stopped feeling that way when I injured my paw. Every dog looked at me with pity. I couldn't stand it. Anyway, you saw how Alpha reacted when I came back. He'll never let me rejoin the Pack."

Moon looked crestfallen. "Please don't go. . . . Spring will be so disappointed when she hears."

Twitch hesitated. Mention of his litter-sister seemed to give him pause. "I don't know," he murmured. "We were so close as pups, but we've drifted apart. . . ."

Lucky thought it was a bit cruel of Moon to use Spring like

that, but then he remembered what she'd been through. *I'm only a recent member of the Wild Pack. The same goes for Bella, Martha, and Storm. I can't blame Moon for wanting an old friend by her side until we find the others. But it isn't fair to Twitch—not when coming with us means risking his life.*

Lucky lowered his head. "I think you should stay with this Pack, Twitch." Moon's ears flicked back and a look of betrayal crossed her face, but Lucky continued. "Even if Alpha lets you return, he'll make your life miserable. I don't think you should risk it—not when you already have a Pack."

The black-and-white Farm Dog wasn't prepared to give up so easily. "We could talk to Alpha! We could convince him that Twitch should stay."

Bella's muzzle wrinkled. "And when has that ever worked in the past?"

Lucky's litter-sister was right—Alpha wasn't exactly quick to forgive. Lucky remembered how close the half wolf had come to branding him with a nasty bite. The hairs along his back still rose like spikes at the thought.

Twitch sighed. "Lucky's right. I remember Alpha well enough. . . . He was hardly friendly when I came to find you. Nothing you could do would convince him." He took a step toward Splash. "My choice is clear. I will stay with my new Pack."

"At least let us *try* to talk to Alpha," Moon urged.

"It isn't just Alpha. I want to stay here, where I'm helpful. If I come with you I'll only be a burden. The river rabbit was delicious, but we were very lucky to catch it. Food is scarce; you don't need another mouth to feed on the journey."

Moon looked doubtful, then seemed to understand. She sank down onto the grass. "We'll miss you, Twitch."

He leaned over and licked her on the nose. "I'll miss you too."

Lucky noticed Bella giving Splash a hard look. The little black dog seemed calmer now that Twitch had said he would stay. His tail wagged slowly and the rest of his Pack hung back.

Bella took a step toward Twitch. "I don't think it's safe for you to come with us, but that doesn't mean you have to stay here either. These dogs were our enemies only a few days ago."

Splash bowed his head. "Terror goaded us and forced us to fight with any dog we met. He's gone now, and we have the chance to become a real Pack, not just a group of mad dogs."

Several of his Packmates whined their agreement and he turned to them, as though seeking reassurance before continuing. "To be a real Pack, we need an Alpha. We're all agreed. . . . We think Twitch should be our Alpha."

Martha and Bella exchanged glances.

Twitch seemed as surprised as they were. "I'm not really Alpha material, am I?"

"And he's only got three legs," Storm piped up. Lucky cringed. He had been thinking the same thing, but it wasn't tactful to say it out loud.

Splash eyed the Fierce Dog warily. "There's no rule that an Alpha has to look a certain way. Twitch is a capable hunter and fighter. And he always stood up to Terror better than the rest of us. He's smart; he knows how to survive." The rest of the Pack yipped their agreement.

Twitch's tail wagged cheerfully. He shook his head, tossing up his long ears, his tongue lolling out of the side of his mouth. Lucky didn't think he'd ever seen him looking so pleased.

"So what do you think?" pressed Splash.

Twitch bowed shyly. "If you're sure . . ."

Moon rose to her paws. "Wait! This is not how it's done. A Pack doesn't *choose* an Alpha!"

Twitch, Splash, and the other dogs stared at her.

"But we want Twitch!" yipped a scruffy little ginger-furred mongrel.

Moon stared down her nose at her. "That doesn't matter. There must be honorable combat. It's the Wild Dogs' way."

Splash shifted nervously from paw to paw. "It's true. . . ." He drew a deep breath, raised his muzzle, and puffed out his chest. "Twitch of the Wild Pack, I challenge you to a fight!"

Twitch's tail stopped wagging and he stood quite still. Lucky tensed—was Twitch really going to fight this dog? He watched as Twitch drew himself up to his full height and pulled back his lips.

Storm yapped in shock, turning to Lucky. "That doesn't make any sense. They have no quarrel. They don't even disagree about who should be Alpha!"

Lucky didn't know what to say. Twitch and Splash were fronting up to each other, treading a slow circle as the other dogs stepped back to give them space.

Storm grew more agitated. She pawed Lucky's leg. "Are you letting them do this? They're going to fight just for the sake of fighting! I thought it was supposed to be a last resort!"

Lucky frowned. "Storm's right. Twitch, this is madness."

The long-eared dog did not respond, his eyes locked on Splash, who had drawn to a halt opposite him. Silence fell among the group of dogs as Twitch lowered onto his haunches, preparing to pounce.

Without warning, Splash dropped to the ground and rolled onto his back with his legs in the air.

Twitch nodded in understanding before hopping up so that his one front paw rested on Splash's belly. "I accept your submission." He dropped back and licked his forepaw.

Splash climbed to his feet. "Thank you, Alpha."

Martha had been watching at a distance. Now she stepped forward, tail wagging. "Well done, Twitch." At this, all the dogs surged toward him, bowing and yapping their congratulations.

Lucky held back a moment. He was happy that there'd been no fight, and his tail swished, but the challenge left him puzzled. He had always imagined that a battle for Alpha would be a violent one. He couldn't picture the Wild Pack's Alpha giving up power without a fight.

Watching Splash and the other dogs in Twitch's new Pack, Lucky decided that the odd bunch was no longer dangerous. The ritual may have been pointless, but it clearly pleased Twitch's Pack, who were nuzzling him and barking.

Lucky went to join them. "Good luck, Twitch."

The long-eared dog nodded. "You too. Please tell Spring that I'm sorry. I hope I will see her again one day."

Lucky tapped Twitch's nose with his own. "Of course," he murmured.

Moon was the last to say good-bye. "You are a loyal and

resilient dog, Twitch, and you'll make a great leader. May the Spirit Dogs be with you always." She turned, her tail low, and made her way back to the riverbank. The Wild Dogs joined her, sniffing for traces of their Pack. Trailing at the rear, Lucky could still hear the yips of excitement from Twitch's Pack as they fell out of sight beyond the bramblebush.

Lucky trod along the riverbank, shaking the mud from his paws. He had drifted to the lead and was tracking the path of the Wild Pack on the salty air. His nose crinkled. *Why does the wind smell so strange? And it's growing stronger. . . .*

Looking over his shoulder, he saw Bella and Moon lagging behind him, just ahead of Martha and Storm. The dogs walked in silence as the Sun-Dog climbed over the river. *Fiery led the hunting party. Now it's like we have no leader. And even Twitch has left us. . . .* His head dipped as he walked, and his tail hung behind him. He knew that Twitch was right to stay with Terror's old Pack, but he couldn't help feeling abandoned. His eyes trailed over the rugged grass and the valley beyond it. The world seemed very large and dangerous.

Unlike the dogs, the river charged along restlessly, swelling and growing more turbulent. With a shudder, Lucky saw a leaf fall on the surface of the water, spinning before it sank from view in a curl of white froth.

Distracted by the leaf, Lucky stumbled on a pebble. He yelped and examined his forepaw. It wasn't hurt, but he cocked his head to one side as he saw that tiny yellow-and-white grains had become buried beneath his claws and clung to his paw pad. He looked up. The ground was changing, growing harder, and there were piles of the grains between the rocks and the plants.

Bella drew alongside him. "It's sand."

Lucky gnawed at the small grains. It was hard to get rid of them. "Yes . . . you don't usually find it at a riverbank, do you?"

Bella scratched at the ground, etching shallow grooves. "I don't know; I've only seen it in the Leashed pup place when my longpaws took me to the dog park. There's so much of it here. . . ."

Lucky wrinkled his nose. "And the smell. It's really salty." It seemed to be coming in waves, rising on the freezing wind.

As the dogs advanced along the riverbank, the peaks and valleys that ran alongside them became steadily duller. The earth was no longer coated in a rich green pelt. Long, scraggy grass burst through bald patches of yellow earth. Lucky could only see a couple of low trees in the distance.

Gazing up, he saw that the sky was a twisting mass of pale gray clouds.

"Where are the birds?" asked Martha.

Lucky frowned. The water-dog was right; it was silent overhead. He didn't like it. . . . It felt eerie without their constant twitter.

"Moon, you grew up as a Wild Dog," said Bella. "Have you ever been somewhere like this before?"

The Farm Dog shook her silky head. "Nowhere like it," she murmured.

A high-pitched whickering made them jump. Lucky spun around, ears pricked up.

Storm's hackles were raised, her eyes bulging and her teeth bared. "What was that?" she snarled.

No dog replied. They stood low to the bank, preparing to run.

Martha's dark eyes glittered. "It doesn't sound angry. . . ."

Lucky lowered himself to the ground. He could feel the faint tremors of hard paws drumming against the earth. "Whatever it is, it's coming closer."

A huge brown creature galloped over the scraggy grasses. It

was even taller than Martha, with bony legs, a muscular body, and a narrow face. Its fur was short and glossy, except for the billowing hair that ran down its long neck and its tail, which swished in the salty wind. Its ears twisted forward and backward as it stopped at the edge of the river, blowing steam from its flaring nostrils. Despite the sharp cold, streams of sweat ran over its flanks. It sank its great head to drink.

The scent of its peppery fur carried on the air. Lucky's belly rumbled.

"It smells delicious," whispered Bella, as though reading his thoughts.

Storm nodded, her tongue hanging out. "Maybe we could catch it."

Unlikely! thought Lucky. *It could easily outrun us.*

Moon looked doubtful. "It looks a bit like an enormous deer, and deer are hard to catch even in the forest. Look at the size of it—we'd never be able to bring it down."

Martha licked her chops. "But such a feast. I don't think it's a meat eater. It smells . . . grassy. Like rabbit, but richer somehow. Even its ears look a little rabbitlike. I bet it would be tasty!"

Lucky's eyes trailed down the animal's bony legs. "It does smell delicious. But it looks powerful. . . . I bet it could give a mighty kick." The dogs took in the creature's muscular thighs, its firm legs, and its stumpy, round paws, which seemed to be cut from rock.

"We'd be okay," Storm yipped. "We're fast, and we work as a team."

Martha gave the young dog a calming lick. "I think Lucky's right: Those paws look deadly. And did you see the speed it came over the valley? It's much quicker than we are."

Storm snorted but didn't reply. The strange animal had finished drinking and was pulling up mouthfuls of scraggy grass with square teeth. Its rabbit ears swiveled around. A large brown eye rested on the dogs, and it reared with a whicker, turning to gallop downstream along the riverbank. It kicked up the grainy earth with its paws, masking its legs in a cloud of sand. Soon it had loped behind a small hill and vanished from view.

"Let's get it!" howled Storm, springing forward and racing along the bank.

"Wait!" snapped Bella. "Martha's right: We could never catch it."

Storm ignored her, disappearing around the hill.

"Storm!" barked Lucky, sprinting after her. His fur rose along his back and his lip twitched with anger. *Can't that pup ever listen?*

Does she have to go charging off every time? A sharp nip is what she needs! When I catch her—

Lucky rounded the hill and scrambled to a stop. Storm was standing just ahead, body stiff and head cocked. The giant animal was already a distant dot on the horizon. Lucky looked beyond it with a shocked gasp. *What is this place?*

All traces of soil had disappeared from the grainy earth, which fanned out in all directions in soft yellow waves. The tang of salt stung his nostrils and he sneezed.

Storm's tail hung down between her legs. "The sand . . . it just goes on and on."

Lucky nodded, his frustration at the young Fierce Dog forgotten. He had never seen anything like it. There were no trees here, no fields or flowers. *Maybe we've reached the end of the world . . . a place beyond the reach of the Forest-Dog. Maybe even the Earth-Dog has no power here. Has every Spirit Dog abandoned us?* His tail wound around his flank guiltily. Was it fair to lose faith in the Spirit Dogs after all they had done for him?

Martha appeared over the hill with Bella and Moon just behind her. "Look!" she barked. She was peering past Lucky. "In the distance."

Lucky blinked. At first he couldn't see anything but sand.

Then he noticed movement. It was a shifting mass of blue.

Martha's black tail swished uncertainly. "The river ran into . . . a lake."

Moon took a step forward, her black-and-white paws sinking on the soft ground. "Not just a lake . . . It isn't like any others I've ever seen. It looks endless. . . ."

With a quiver of fear, Lucky realized Moon was right. No land could be seen beyond the shimmering blue. At the bottom of the hill, great waves crashed angrily over the sand. Then they sprang from the bank in a burst of froth and rolled away forever.

CHAPTER THREE

The dogs made their way to the waterfront. Lucky struggled to take in the strange, salty world of the Endless Lake. His paws sank against sand that clung to his fur and between his paw pads. Large white birds looped over the water, screeching as they rode the icy wind. Below them surged white-capped waves, dissolving into the sky.

"What *is* this place?" whined Moon. Her black-and-white ears twitched nervously, her brown eyes wide.

Lucky sniffed the sand. All he could smell was salt. *The end of the world . . . a place beyond the reach of the Spirit Dogs.* He thought better of sharing his fears. It would only scare them, and Moon had been through enough already. "I'm not sure," he said instead. It was true.

The Endless Lake sprawled in all directions. The giant ripples that ran over its surface reminded Lucky of those on the lake where the Wild and Leashed Dogs had set up camp the first night the Packs had come together. But these were much more powerful, rising and falling by some invisible force. His ears flicked back at the crash and roar of the waves.

The ground along the bank was dark and sodden, even harder to walk on than the dry yellow hills. Storm pranced along it, leaving imprints of her small, round paws.

"Careful, Storm, not too close," warned Lucky.

A moment later, the water burst over the sand and Storm leaped back. It ran over her paws with a hiss of white foam and slid away, sucking a layer of sodden sand as it went. Storm scampered onto the dry earth. She licked her paws and spat out the yellow grains with a grimace. No trace of her paw prints remained on the wet sand.

Martha approached the bank and stood gazing out over the Endless Lake, letting the icy water flow over her paws. Lucky wondered if she was trying to connect with the River-Dog. Lucky doubted even she could control this much water.

If she is even here . . .

Bella shook out her fur. "Well, the Pack must be close!" she declared with a cheerful wag of her tail.

Moon's ears pricked up. "Really, you think so?"

"I do! Why wouldn't they settle by an endless source of water?"

She dipped her muzzle to drink and pulled away with a whine. "It's horrible! Salty, undrinkable!"

Lucky stepped alongside her and sniffed the water gingerly. His whiskers bristled. He didn't think it was poisoned like the river near the longpaw city, but it was far too salty to drink. Watching the frothy, white water draw back from the sand, he noticed that the ground was beginning to freeze. The wet sand glistened with frost, growing brittle, reminding Lucky that they had to find somewhere warmer and drier to avoid getting sick from the cold.

He turned to the others. "We should keep moving."

"I can't smell the Pack anymore," whined Moon. "I can't smell *anything* except salt!"

Lucky took a deep sniff. Moon was right: The air that rose off the Endless Lake masked everything. He tried again. *Got it!* He'd caught a faint whiff of Alpha's musky scent. "This way!" Lucky barked.

As the dogs clambered over the sandy earth, Lucky picked up a sweet scent that made his whiskers tingle and his chest fill with warmth. His tail gave a quick, involuntary wag. It would be great to see the Pack again, Lucky told himself. He tried to picture his old friend Mickey and his Leashed companions. He reminded himself of the original Wild Dogs like Snap and Spring. He thought of Moon's pups, Thorn and Beetle, with their bright, eager eyes.

But it was Sweet he pictured as he climbed a sand dune, his fur bristling with anticipation.

"The air off the water is freezing," murmured Bella.

Lucky snapped out of his thoughts. It was true. The icy wind rushed over the Endless Lake and seemed to slip beneath his coat to chill his blood. They trailed along the bank of the Endless Lake, where the sand was flatter. Water surged and fell to one side of them; on the other the sand rose in sweeping hills.

Moon's tail shot straight behind her. "What's that?"

Lucky gazed into the distance. A metal pole jutted out of the sand with a jumble of snaking wires. He couldn't imagine what purpose it had once served. He spotted one of the hard objects that longpaws liked to sit on. It was covered in sand and one of its four thin legs had collapsed in on itself. "It's like the city," he whined as the dogs approached. There was even a loudcage, over-turned on its back in the middle of a sand dune. Water, perhaps from the Endless Lake, had gathered behind its clear-stone eyes, and its body was caked in the fine yellow grains.

Lucky was puzzled. "There's probably a longpaw camp nearby. A city or something like it." He couldn't understand how these longpaw objects had found their way onto the sand. They must have been thrown a long way by the force of the Big Growl.

As they padded along the sand, the contours of a town appeared on the horizon, just as Lucky had predicted. Running along its outskirts was a longpaw camp, but it wasn't like any that Lucky had seen before. It was built on a huge wooden platform that overhung the Endless Lake. Broken buildings ran along it, strange angles against the bright, cold sky.

The dogs stopped to stare.

"What are those twisty things?" asked Storm.

Giant metal loops spun behind the buildings at the far end of the wooden platform, ridged like tracks.

"Are those loudcages?" asked Martha.

Lucky squinted. Martha was right: Small loudcages clung to the metal tracks. "They remind me of those giant loudcages that traveled back and forth over part of the city," he told her. He tried to remember. "They moved about on tracks and longpaws climbed in and out of them when they stopped."

"I've never heard of anything like that," said Bella, throwing him a questioning look.

Martha cocked her head. "These tracks don't *go* anywhere. . . . I don't see why a longpaw would want to move around and around in circles."

"Circles in the sky!" yelped Bella. "Maybe they were hunting birds up there. Have you seen those huge white birds above us?"

Lucky looked up. It was true: There were several enormous white birds flying over the water of the Endless Lake. He felt a pang of hunger, but the birds were higher than any dog could jump. They'd never catch one unless it landed right in front of them. Storm's eyes rose to the birds too, and she smacked her lips.

Moon looked at Bella quizzically. "It doesn't make much sense. But then, nothing the longpaws were up to ever did."

Bella sniffed haughtily. "I'm not sure about that. Just because you don't understand why somebody does something doesn't mean there's no reason for their actions. The longpaws were good hunters. I never had to find any food for myself back when I was a Leashed Dog. If longpaws were riding their loudcages in the sky, there must have been a good reason."

Moon didn't respond, but her tail stiffened and her ears flattened. Lucky could guess what she was thinking: *Once a Leashed Dog, always a Leashed Dog.* He watched nervously, hoping that the tired dogs wouldn't start squabbling.

Large, gentle Martha ignored the tension. She blinked at the long wooden platform with its broken buildings. "I can smell the Pack," she murmured quietly.

Lucky sniffed the air. She was right—the scent of Alpha and the others was growing stronger. "Come on," he barked, his tail wagging. They started again toward the wooden platform. The looping tracks curved into the air, creaking in the icy breeze.

"Are you sure it's safe?" Moon eyed the worn platform with its damaged buildings.

She's been a Wild Dog all her life. She won't want to be anywhere near long-paws and their towns and cities, thought Lucky. Surely the same was true of Alpha, yet the half wolf's scent led him closer to the wooden platform. As they drew closer, Lucky could see that the platform balanced above the water on long wooden legs. The waves of the Endless Lake lashed against these, swirling and breaking in angry explosions of mist.

Moon was watching too. She stopped in her tracks, one forepaw raised. "We're not going onto it, are we, Lucky? I can't even smell the Pack anymore. Alpha won't have gone there. He wouldn't want anything to do with longpaws and their strange camps. Don't you remember how keen he was to leave that long-paw settlement?"

Lucky lowered his muzzle and sniffed the sand at his paws, trying to ignore the smell of salt that clung to everything. Moon was right. Alpha's scent had vanished on the air. It didn't make sense. Unless . . .

He raised his head. "They must have moved away from the waterfront, downwind. That's why we can't smell them." He turned away from the Endless Lake and started climbing up a sandbank. Moon and the others followed.

Sure enough, in the low-lying land beyond the sandbank, sheltered from the freezing wind that sliced over the water, the smell of Alpha and the Pack returned.

"This way!" barked Lucky, hurrying over the sand, eager to keep moving while he had a good grasp of the scent. Moon and Bella caught up with him, bounding at his side. He heard the thump of Martha's large paws on the ground. Glancing over his shoulder, he saw that Storm had fallen behind.

"Storm, what's wrong?" He trod back over the sand as the other dogs paused, exchanging looks.

The little Fierce Dog shook her head. "It's nothing. . . ."

"Come on!" Lucky leaned over and licked her small, floppy ears. "Something's troubling you."

The pup sighed and sat on the sand. "I didn't want to say anything. It's only that the river rabbit was quite small, and we ate it a while ago. . . ."

Bella, Martha, and Moon crept back toward Storm and Lucky. They all looked concerned.

"You're hungry?" said Lucky.

Storm sank onto her belly, her head resting on the sand. She gazed up at him guiltily. "I'm sorry."

"We're all hungry," said Bella. "This is tough terrain. It's exhausting to walk on the sand, the wind is freezing cold, and there's barely any cover."

Lucky acknowledged this with a dip of his head. His stomach churned at the thought of a river rabbit or a bite of that huge, peppery animal with the bushy tail and velvety coat.

"There are lots of those big white birds around, but they're over the water," Moon pointed out. "We could never catch them. Even if they came to land, there's no cover here—they'd see us coming and fly away."

"Well, that settles it," declared Bella. "We should explore the old longpaw camp—we might be able to find something there."

Lucky looked back toward the Endless Lake. The water was hidden behind the low sand hill, but he could see the looping tracks with the broken loudcages. "I'm not sure that's a good idea," he murmured. *What if it's nothing like the city? It could be dangerous. The platform might have been damaged in the Big Growl.* His neck hairs prickled as he remembered the water swirling beneath the platform and smashing against the wooden legs in bursts of white mist. Even now he could hear the thunder of surf.

Moon's eyes grew wide. "It's a terrible idea! We have to catch up with the Pack. If we head back to the waterfront we might lose them altogether! Nose and Squirm are all alone." Lucky's heart ached as he noticed that she had used their pup names, though they had adult names now and were old enough to survive without a Mother-Dog. "They're not used to being without me and Fiery," Moon added. Her voice croaked on her mate's name, and her body seemed to droop from sadness or fatigue.

Storm seemed to accept Moon's reasoning. She rolled onto her paws and shook off the sand.

Bella turned on her impatiently. "You're just going to accept that? Moon isn't Alpha, you know!"

Lucky cringed at his litter-sister's lack of tact. Moon was still grieving for Fiery and surrounded by dogs she hadn't known long—of course she was keen to return to her pups and the Wild Pack. And it wasn't a good idea to snap at Storm. Lucky watched the young Fierce Dog, who was looking reproachfully at Bella. *She's trying so hard to fit in . . . to be a Pack Dog. She needs to learn to control her temper.* His litter-sister should be more careful not to antagonize her.

Martha took a protective step toward Storm. Moon and Bella exchanged low growls.

The icy wind whipped over the sand hill, scattering grains like fragments of clear-stone. Lucky stood frozen to the spot as it clung to his fur. He didn't like the Pack's hierarchy, but for once he would have liked there to be a dog to make the decisions. *A good Alpha,* he thought. *One every dog trusts to do the right thing.*

Ahead there were dunes of yellow sand, expanding as far as the eye could see. Lucky's belly churned with hunger. What could they possibly find to eat on the sand dunes? His ears flicked back. He heard the rumble and crash of the Endless Lake as it rolled without pause. If they headed toward it, to the deserted longpaw camp, there was a chance of a meal.

But if they lost the Wild Pack's scent, they might never find it again.

CHAPTER FOUR

Moon and Bella had fallen silent, snarling at each other, their paws planted to the sandy ground. Storm watched with her tail around her flank. Lucky hesitated, not sure what to do.

It was large, gentle Martha who finally stepped forward. "Storm's right: We're all hungry. It's the hunger and cold that makes us snap at each other."

Lucky nodded. The difficult conditions were making the dogs ill-tempered.

"We'll feel better if we eat something," Martha went on. "There may be food at the longpaw camp. I think we'll be okay if we're careful not to lose the Pack's scent. We don't know how far ahead they are—we might walk all sunup and not reach them. Then we'll be more cold, tired, and hungry than ever."

Moon's face softened and she sniffed the air. She lowered her muzzle respectfully. "What you say makes sense. As long as we keep the Pack's scent, and we're quick, I don't mind trying to find food."

Storm's tail started wagging and she panted cheerfully.

Lucky stood up. "Let's do that. We'll investigate the longpaw camp—but if we don't find something to eat by the time the Sun-Dog reaches the top of his journey, we'd better start moving on."

All the dogs agreed.

Lucky cocked his head. *Maybe we don't need an Alpha after all. . . .* Martha had made no effort to impose her will, but her deep, reasonable voice carried natural authority.

Storm was already on the move, bounding back over the sand in the direction of the Endless Lake, her tail lashing the salty air. Martha bounded after her, and the others followed the path of their paw prints.

The dogs climbed the swells of grainy earth, scampering down hills in showers of yellow sand.

The platform jutted over the land before the sand grew damp, reaching high above the Endless Lake. The floor was built of wooden planks. A colorful arch decorated the entrance to the platform. The arch was edged by clear-stone balls. Some blinked amber, a couple flickered, and several were cracked and dark. The dogs passed under the arch and looked around, their bodies low to the ground.

The camp was totally abandoned, as Lucky had known it would be. The Big Growl must have driven the longpaws away from here, just as it had scared them from the city. Yet everywhere were signs that longpaws had been there: the seats they had rested on, the spoil-boxes where they'd put the things they no longer wanted. Farther up the platform, the great looping tracks leaped into the sky.

Martha whined softly and Lucky licked her shoulder. He hadn't been a Leashed Dog, but the desolation still struck him. *What a sad, lonely place.* There must have been lots of longpaws here, just as there had been in the city. Where had they all gone? He shook his ears. It was better not to think about it.

Lucky made straight for the spoil-boxes, remembering the ones in the city where he'd sometimes found a meal. He hopped onto his hindpaws and leaned over one, nosing about in the darkness. There was no trace of anything edible. Rats had probably finished it off long ago. Lucky buried his muzzle deeper in the box, just in case. For a moment darkness and quiet surrounded him. Dimly a memory played at the edges of his mind. He was a pup. He'd somehow become trapped in a hole beneath the earth and the air was running out. With a surge of panic, Lucky wrenched his head from the spoil-box.

The other dogs were creeping along the boards. Wooden buildings rose on both sides of them. Lucky couldn't work out what purpose the buildings used to serve. They didn't look like the Food House in the city. He remembered large buildings where longpaws went to hunt, or to find soft-hides and other things to put in their dens. They didn't look like houses, either. They were small and open at the front, fringed with tattered bits of cloth. The cloth looked like it might once have been colorful, but now sand coated everything.

Storm had stopped in front of one of the wooden buildings. The wall had split and she was craning her neck through the gap. "Look at that!"

Lucky crept up behind her and followed her gaze. A row of yellow ducks balanced on mounts along the back of the building. They weren't real—they seemed to be made of a hard, shiny material. Lucky frowned, wondering what they were there for. With a growl, he spotted a loudstick dangling from the wall by a string. Were longpaws supposed to strike the model ducks with the loudstick? What was the point? It wasn't as though they could eat them.

Lucky knew there were no longpaws around to fire the

loudstick, but he didn't like being near it. He licked Storm's ears and urged her away. "They're not real."

"I wish they were," she whimpered.

Lucky cocked his head. "We'll find something soon." Secretly he was starting to doubt there was anything here. *I hope we haven't made a mistake. . . .*

They started after Bella, who had walked farther along the platform. Storm hurried ahead but Lucky paused, catching sight of swirling waves. He lowered his head for a closer look. The water was far beneath him, and his heart gave a lurch of fear when he thought of what would happen if one of the planks gave way.

He caught up with Bella, who was sniffing around one of the small wooden buildings. This one had large, open gaps on all four sides and a ledge running along the front on the same level as the top of Lucky's head. From where he was standing, it seemed to be full of strange debris that looked like general longpaw trash. Bella pounced onto the ledge to get a better look.

Her tail began to wag. "It's full of toys!"

Martha bounded over to Bella. At her height, she could easily peer over the ledge without any effort.

"Frisbees, hoops, and balls!" barked Bella.

"And soft toys that look like animals," added Martha.

Lucky hopped onto his hind legs, his forepaws balancing against the ledge. Dusty blue balls were suspended from the ceiling of the building, with silvery hoops and fluffy toy squirrels.

Bella sprang down onto the floor of the building. She inspected a large, soft toy that had rolled on its side. It looked a bit like a giantfur, except that it wasn't scary at all. There were no sharp claws at the end of its furry paws, and instead of teeth its mouth curled up like a happy longpaw.

Bella tapped the toy giantfur with a forepaw. "The young longpaws like these. They sleep with them at night."

Lucky watched her carefully as she sniffed the toy and briefly nuzzled it with her head. Martha panted with excitement. She thumped a huge black paw on the ledge with a whine. Lucky stiffened, remembering his early encounters with the Leashed Dogs. All they'd wanted was to find their longpaws. They had each hung on to an object that reminded them of their old lives and insisted on carrying them into the wild, though the items were a burden. It had taken so long to persuade the Leashed Dogs to leave those objects—Mickey had kept hold of his, even after they'd joined the Wild Pack. Lucky remembered with a pang of sadness how the Farm Dog had finally discarded his longpaw's glove at the entrance to his old home.

What if seeing these things makes Bella and Martha yearn for their long-paws again?

Bella raised her head, catching Martha's eye. "Why are these things here?"

Martha cocked her head. "I don't know. . . . Maybe it's where the longpaws got our stuff."

"But what is it *for*?" Bella shoved the toy away with her muzzle. "I'd much rather curl up at night with a warm Packmate than with a lifeless rag."

Lucky relaxed, pleased that his litter-sister felt that way. She and the other Leashed Dogs had come far since he'd first found them in the city. He turned his head back toward land and sniffed the air. The odor of the Pack had vanished on the cold wind. He knew they would have to move inland and behind some shelter to catch it again.

"Let's keep moving," he warned. "We need to find food and get away from this odd place." He turned toward the building on the far side of the platform, but Martha growled softly. Her ears twitched and her head shot around.

Not the longpaw objects again! But no, Martha was looking the opposite way, along the wooden platform.

"Splashing!"

Moon and Storm had heard her and stalked toward the toy building.

Lucky craned his neck and listened, but all he could hear was the raging surf of the Endless Lake. He didn't like to think about it thrashing about beneath their paws. "I can't hear anything."

"Neither can I," admitted Bella.

"Trust me," Martha murmured, lowering her head to the wooden planks. She started to follow a trail that only she could detect.

Lucky and Bella paused, exchanging glances, but Moon followed Martha's lead without hesitation. She turned back to the littermates, wide-eyed. "The River-Dog talks to Martha," she reminded them. "We should respect that and see where she leads her."

Bella nodded and started to follow, with Storm by her side. Lucky followed too, wondering at how Moon seemed keener than ever to put faith in the Spirit Dogs since Fiery's death. *But they didn't save him,* thought Lucky sadly, remembering how the great fighter had been transformed by the longpaws' poison. He had been as weak and feeble as a day-old pup when Terror's Pack had attacked.

Martha led the dogs past two more wooden buildings. Lucky

was beginning to feel uneasy. *I don't think we should go near the looping tracks—they don't look safe.* He eyed them warily. One of the small loudcages was hanging upside down and looked ready to crash to earth at any moment. He was relieved when Martha paused at a stone structure.

It was larger than the wooden buildings along the platform. Cracks ran along its side, as thin and winding as spiders' webs. Martha lowered herself so her belly almost stroked the ground, and crept along the side of the building.

Lucky's eyes trailed over the cracked wall. There was something a bit strange about it. Then it struck him—there were no clear-stone gaps in the wall. That was unusual. He thought long-paws *liked* to spy on the outside world.

Martha edged along the side of the wall to a large door. Walking next to her, Lucky could see it was damaged, hanging slightly at an angle. Suddenly he could hear splashing too. He watched, his fur tingling with excitement, as Martha hooked her foreleg around the door and started to tug. It seemed lodged, but Martha worked her paw along it with patient diligence until it swung open with a whine. Water burst out, gushing over the dogs' paws. The smell of water-prey was so strong, Lucky could hardly breathe!

Fish came flipping and spinning in the water that drained

from the building. Moon sprang forward, slamming her forepaws on a fish with a long orange tail, while Martha scooped up one in her mouth. Lucky, Bella, and Storm squeezed past them into the stone building.

Lucky could hardly believe his eyes. Colorful fish darted through water no higher than his belly. It gushed through the door, leaving the fish stranded on the hard floor. Some were already dead, drifting on their sides until they came to rest on the hard stone. The live ones twisted and bucked helplessly as the dogs moved in for the kill.

"I can't believe it!" yelped Storm. "It's like a wonderful dream!"

Bella's tongue hung out as she eyed a large blue-and-white fish. "How is this possible?"

Lucky gave the room a quick once-over. Clear-stone boxes ran along the walls. Most were full of fish, but a few had smashed. Lucky turned to Bella and Storm. "Those boxes must have shattered in the Big Growl. Water would have leaked out of them, trapping the fish in the room until Martha broke the door and the water escaped."

Storm chewed on a fish tail. "But how did they survive without the longpaws feeding them?"

Bella glanced up. "They probably ate one another. Killed

the smaller ones. It's what fish do."

Storm winced in revulsion. "They eat their own kind?"

Martha and Moon joined the others as they circled the helpless fish. Lucky snapped his teeth around a blue-and-yellow fish. He threw back his head and tossed it into his mouth, crunching down on its succulent flesh, the salty-sweet flavor oozing down his throat.

"Praise the River-Dog!" barked Moon.

The dogs pounced on the fish with relish, gobbling up the tender morsels until there was nothing left. Lucky's tail twitched guiltily. *Maybe the Spirit Dogs haven't abandoned us after all.*

As they licked the last shreds of fish from between their paws, Lucky offered his own silent praise to the River-Dog.

O generous Spirit Dog, you have led us to this delicious meal, and I am grateful, he told her. Bellies full of fish, the dogs set out along the wooden platform, one step closer to rejoining their Pack.

CHAPTER FIVE

The dogs clicked over the wooden planks, murmuring contentedly and smacking their lips. Lucky had grown accustomed to the sound of the surf churning beneath his paws. It didn't scare him anymore, provided he didn't stop to think about it for too long.

Storm bounded at his side. "That was *so* tasty, wasn't it?"

Lucky cocked his head. "Yes, it was."

"We were right to come here, weren't we?"

"We were." Lucky glanced back at Bella, whose self-satisfied look said *I told you so!* At least she hadn't uttered those words out loud. Moon didn't seem to notice. She was looking over her shoulder in the other direction, across the looping tracks with the miniature loudcages and the Endless Lake beyond.

As they reached the start of the platform, Lucky lowered his muzzle, peering between the wooden planks. *Where's the water? I could have sworn it came right under that arch with the blinking lights.* He

edged back a few paces, looking between each plank until he spotted the curling white froth of the surf. For a moment, he wondered
if the Endless Lake was shrinking away from the land. He gave his
head a shake: No, that was impossible.

Storm sat under the arch and scratched her ear. "Do we go
back to find the Pack now?"

"Yes, but . . ." Lucky looked toward the town, with its leaning buildings that reminded him of the city. "It might be quicker
to move through the deserted longpaw settlement, rather than
retrace our steps over the sand."

"Easier too," said Bella. "Walking on sand is killing us."

"But we said we'd go back the other way," Storm pointed out.

Martha nodded her large black head. "She's right, we did, and
we risk losing the Pack's scent if we take a different route."

Moon caught up with them. Lucky expected her to insist they
return across the sand, tracking the path that the Wild Dogs had
taken. Instead she told them, "The town makes more sense."

Martha shook her head, which made her jowls wobble. "I
thought you wanted to go back across the sand. It's where we left
the Pack's scent. You said yourself that Alpha would have avoided
the town."

Lucky's fur twitched with unease. Only a short while ago the group had been at peace. Another spat was the last thing they needed out in the freezing cold.

The Farm Dog met Martha's gaze. Her blue eyes sparkled. "Alpha would have led the Pack onto the sand to avoid the long-paw town; that's true. They'd have looped around it and tracked back to the waterfront. This means we can *gain* on them if we cut through the town. And the town will be easier on our paws than this sand." She threw a look at Storm, who had lowered herself onto the wooden boards and shut her eyes for a moment. Lucky could see that the pup was weary, despite her steely determination. Moon turned back to Martha. "The camp the longpaws built over the Endless Lake was deserted, and the town will be too. There's nothing for us to fear."

Martha nodded in understanding. "Lucky, what do you think?"

The wind rose over the Endless Lake, lifting Lucky's fur. It seemed to be growing even colder. The Sun-Dog was continuing his journey high above them, but clouds were blowing in from across the lake, smudging out his warming rays. Lucky shook his fur, trying the tactic that Moon had showed them to keep warm. He wasn't sure which choice was better, but he wanted this journey to be over. Walking through the longpaw settlement would be quicker. Even if the hard streets were cracked and damaged, they'd be easier to walk on than sand hills, as Moon had pointed out, and they probably gave more shelter from the wind.

He met Martha's eye. "Let's go through the town."

"Stick to the middle of the street." Lucky remembered the collapsing houses in the city. This town didn't look quite so damaged, but it was sensible to keep a safe distance.

The buildings here were lower and bled less dust than those in the city. Still the torn roads and shattered clear-stone were signs that the Big Growl had visited this place. Instead of dust, the sand seemed to be everywhere, coating the streets and buildings so that they looked as though they rose from the earth as giant yellow stones. Pools of salt water collected by the curbs, filthy with debris.

Green river grasses hung off buildings.

How did they get there?

Lucky shuddered at the thought that the Endless Lake was responsible for all the sand and water. Had the Big Growl shaken it so hard that it burst its banks, surging over the land? His fur rose along his neck in spikes, and he turned instinctively toward the coast. He couldn't see the Endless Lake beyond the longpaw buildings, but he could hear its relentless roar and hiss as it broke over the sand.

"That's a longpaw's paw-cover," said Bella, nodding her head toward a filthy object in the middle of the street. It was the size of a small rabbit and looked vulnerable surrounded by sand.

Storm tipped her head quizzically. "They cover their paws?"

"I don't like this place," whined Moon, her haunches low to the ground.

Bella shot her an accusing look. "You wanted to come through the longpaw settlement."

"I'm just saying!" Moon snapped back. "You dogs grew up in strange places like this—you're used to it."

"We'll pass through here as quickly as we can," Martha soothed before Bella could say anything. Lucky was grateful to the large black dog. Her patient nature bore no grudges. She had accepted that they'd go through the town without complaint. *And she found the fish. I'm glad she's here. . . .*

His thoughts were disturbed by a sharp, alarmed bark from Storm. She stood on stiff legs, her tail straight behind her and ears pointing up. "We have to turn back!" she barked. "We have to go right now!"

Bella sighed. "Not this again! We're going through the town and that's that."

Moon glared at her. "Can't you see the pup's scared?" She turned to Storm. "It's okay, don't worry. We'll be out of here soon enough, but it'll only take us longer if we turn back now."

Storm ignored them, taking a tense step forward. Her tan muzzle was raised. "Danger!" she barked. "There's danger ahead!"

Lucky knew something was very wrong. Storm wasn't a pup who barked at nothing. He stepped alongside her, lowering his head and sniffing carefully. The salty air masked everything, yet . . . Lucky's heart lurched and a tremor of fear ran through his paws. *Could that be . . . But that's impossible, isn't it? The whole reason the Pack's traveling to find a new camp is to escape them. . . .*

"Are they here?" he whispered.

"She's just nervous, jumping at her own shadow," Bella complained.

Storm's eyes widened. "I can smell Fang and the other Fierce Dogs."

This quieted Bella, whose whiskers flexed as Martha stepped protectively to Storm's side.

Moon breathed in the air. "I can't smell them, but if they're here we should go right away—there's no point rushing into danger since Storm has managed to sniff it out."

Martha gave the pup's ears a lick. "We need to keep Storm away from Blade."

Lucky could see the whites of Moon's eyes. The Farm Dog's tail twitched nervously. "The four of us can't protect her from the whole Fierce Dog Pack."

Storm shrugged Martha away. "I don't need protecting," she muttered. She was staring along the street, her hackles rising. "Maybe we shouldn't turn back. I'm sick of running away all the time."

"The pup has a point," said Bella. "In a way."

Moon turned to her in surprise. "You're not suggesting that we challenge the Fierce Dog Pack? We wouldn't stand a chance!"

"No . . . But we could follow their scent."

Lucky cocked his head. What did his litter-sister have in mind?

Bella drew closer to the others, talking in hushed tones. "It's possible the Fierce Dogs passed through here recently on their travels, but I think it's more likely that they've settled in the town. They're a type of Leashed Dog, after all—it's probably natural for them to drift toward longpaw camps, even though the longpaws left long ago."

Lucky nodded. This made sense to him.

"I think we should follow the scent," Bella went on. "We should find out as much as we can about where they're based and what they're doing."

Bella's suggestion was met with silence. Lucky's brow furrowed. *Follow the Fierce Dogs . . . Is that wise?*

"Don't look so worried, litter-brother." She nudged him with her muzzle. "I don't mean to have a confrontation with them. Just to get close enough to work out what they're up to."

"Yes, we should follow them," Storm piped up. "It isn't just about me—we have a duty to protect the other dogs in our Pack. Won't Alpha be angry if he finds out we had a chance of finding out Blade's plans and we just ran away?"

Lucky sighed, following her gaze along the quiet street. The pup had a point. "As long as we keep out of sight."

Martha nodded, but Moon's ears twitched and her eyes flashed nervously.

"I don't like it. I don't want to be in this creepy longpaw settlement, and I don't want to go anywhere near Fierce Dogs. But I want to give Beetle and Thorn the best chance of never having to meet those horrible dogs in battle. So, yes—we'll follow them."

She's using their adult names now. Lucky took this as a good sign.

Maybe Moon was beginning to come to terms with losing her mate. "Moon, I'm sorry we weren't able to save Fiery," he whined.

Moon nodded in acknowledgment. "At least we tried. Thank you. . . ."

Martha gave Moon a lick on the nose and the Farm Dog nudged her gratefully.

Lucky and Storm took the lead, with Bella and Moon behind them and Martha bringing up the rear. Soon they could all smell the Fierce Dogs on the salt air.

Bella trailed her snout across the edge of the street. She sniffed a broken loudcage warily. "This has been marked."

Lucky was at a metal spoil-box that had fallen on its side. He turned back to her. "Here too. I think you were right—they're marking the edges of their territory. They must have a camp close by."

A volley of deep barks cut through windswept air.

"A patrol!" hissed Lucky. He leaped sideways over a mound of sand and river grass, ducking for cover behind a pile of damp rope and netting that stank of rotten fish. He could smell the Fierce Dogs coming closer and the fear scent rising off his companions. The Fierce Dogs would smell them too!

Lucky shut his eyes. *I know the land of trees is far away, but I hope you can hear me. . . . Forest-Dog, please let me know how to keep us safe.* The answer came to him immediately. He remembered how Mickey had taught him to roll in mulch of the forest to disguise his scent. Maybe they could use the same trick with sand.

Lucky's eyes flicked open. "Copy what I do!" he urged. There was no time to explain. He demonstrated, dropping against the sand and rolling until his coat was sticky with salt and river grass. Moon, Martha, and Bella copied him with looks of confusion. Only Storm seemed to understand Lucky's intention. *Does she remember the night in the forest when we hid from the coyotes?* Lucky wondered. *She was very young then, her eyes not long open.*

Once the dogs had all rolled in the salty sand, Lucky gestured that they should resume their positions behind the damp rope. He caught Bella starting to lick herself clean and he stopped her with a stern look. The dogs pressed against one another in a salty muddle just as two Fierce Dogs rounded onto the street.

With any luck, they won't smell us now. . . .

Lucky held his breath as the Fierce Dogs strutted past the damp rope. He stole a glance at them. Their jaws were set, their muscles rippled beneath their black-and-tan coats, and their eyes glared straight ahead of them. They passed the Wild Dogs without even a sniff.

Bella rose, shaking her fur. "Well, you're a clever one, aren't you, Yap?"

Lucky batted her with his paw. "Just a trick Mickey taught me. Come on." He hurried along the street in the opposite direction from the Fierce Dogs. He hoped they wouldn't check this part of their territory again until much later, by which time he and the others would be long gone.

The dogs tracked the marks that the Fierce Dogs had left along the border of their territory, ever watchful. They darted between the crumbling buildings, catching their breath behind a loudcage scorched orange with decay. The Fierce Dog scent grew steadily stronger. Fear coursed down Lucky's back—they weren't far from the camp now.

Clouds were rolling in over the Endless Lake. Great white birds glided under them, swooping over the deserted town. One dived toward the dogs with a piercing shriek. Storm sprang into the air and Lucky saw her swallow a yap of surprise just in time.

The dogs reached a building with wide stone steps and faded images of longpaws plastered over the walls. There might have been a door once, but it had probably come away during the Big Growl. The odor of Fierce Dogs escaped from the opening and Lucky could make out the sharp, earthy scent of their Alpha,

Blade. He noticed that there were no clear-stone lookouts. His stomach clenched. It must be dark in there. Shrinking against the wall of the building, he addressed the others.

"I want a closer look. But it's not sensible for all of us to walk into Blade's den. I think you should hide behind the loudcages. I won't be long."

"Can I come?" whispered Storm.

Lucky licked her on the nose. "That's not a good idea."

"You least of all," agreed Martha, nudging Storm back with her snout.

Storm nodded and followed Martha behind a row of dead loudcages, Moon walking close to them.

Bella hung back. "Be careful, Lucky." She licked his nose before turning to join the others.

Lucky crept up the stone steps and ducked into the building. He found himself standing on an expanse of scarlet soft-hides. Parallel sets of steps led up on either side of him, each meeting on the same floor with a series of doorways cloaked in red pelts. Lucky slunk up to one of these and peeled it back with his fore-paw, seeing a damaged wooden door hanging at an angle. The space beyond it was dark and cavernous.

It took Lucky's eyes a moment to adjust to the dim light. The room was even larger than he had imagined. Elaborate gold flourishes covered the ceiling, with images of winged young longpaws painted in tarnished white. The floor was covered in identical red-pelted seats. They faced forward in neat rows toward a raised platform. Looking closer, Lucky noticed that some of the seats had been mauled. Tooth marks punctured the corners of the fabric, and clumps of yellow fuzz hung out. His heart thumped as he noticed movement on the platform and made out the contours of pointed ears.

Blade was sprawled across a nest of debris that seemed to have been built from longpaw materials: shredded bedding, layers of red floor covering, and stuffing torn out of the sitting places. Two of her deputies were guarding either end of the platform. Lucky could make out their tall, muscular outlines.

So Bella was right. The Fierce Dogs have made their camp here. That's a good thing—it means they haven't caught up with the Wild Pack. Lucky had started to back out of the huge room when he heard barking. He spun around, his heart hammering against his ribs. It was coming from outside!

Lucky darted down the stairs and burst out of the entrance to the building in time to see Storm and Martha snarling at three Fierce Dogs. Two of them were almost as tall as Martha, but one was not much more than a pup. Despite his size, he growled at Storm and Martha, his jagged ears flattened and his lips peeled back. Jaws as sharp as broken clear-stone gnashed the air.

Lucky's breath snagged in his throat. He recognized this Fierce Dog. . . . It was Storm's litter-brother, the pup he'd known as Grunt.

The one they now called Fang.

CHAPTER SIX

"*Run, Martha, Bella, all of you!*" barked Storm. "I'll handle these dogs!"

Lucky froze on the stone stairs that led outside the building. A thickset black-and-tan Fierce Dog turned to growl at him, spit hanging off her teeth. Fang and the other Fierce Dog took a step toward Storm.

Lucky tensed. He knew Storm was strong, but she wouldn't be able to defend herself against two adult Fierce Dogs, as well as her own litter-brother. *I should never have agreed to track them,* thought Lucky with a stab of guilt. *We should have left the town as soon as Storm warned us they were here.*

"We're not leaving you!" growled Martha, planting herself at Storm's side.

"Martha's right!" barked Bella as she and Moon stepped out from behind a damaged loudcage. They snarled at the Fierce Dogs, their heads low and hackles raised.

Fang threw back his square head and let out a volley of high-pitched barks. In a moment, Blade and the others would be here too. Lucky remembered with a tremor of horror how many dogs were in their Pack. He and his friends would be completely overwhelmed.

O Forest-Dog, whose cunning has rescued me so many times—what can I do to outwit the Fierce Dogs?

The answer came to him at once. Lucky the Lone Dog knew how to escape scrapes; Lucky the Pack Dog would need to use his cunning.

He cleared his throat. "Hey, rat face!" he barked at the Fierce Dog who had turned to snarl at him. "Who do you think you're looking at, stinky?"

The other adult Fierce Dog whipped around, forgetting Storm. "What did you say, filthy mongrel?"

"I said, who do you think you're looking at, stinky!"

"How dare you!" snarled the Fierce Dog.

"Get him!" howled Fang.

The three Fierce Dogs charged after Lucky, who sprang off the stone stairs and tore along the sandy street at a sprint. He made for the pile of rope and netting where the dogs had hidden from the patrol. Skidding on sand, he almost slammed into a wall before righting himself, speeding up again as he turned onto the next street.

As the Fierce Dogs rounded onto the street he was waiting for them. They froze a rabbit-chase away, their dark eyes gleaming with menace.

"Stop right there, mongrel!" barked the female Fierce Dog. "When we catch you we're going to rip your ears off!"

Lucky turned up his muzzle, doing his best to appear cool and calm, though his flanks were heaving and he fought to still his breath.

"Catch me?" he mocked. "You couldn't catch a limping squirrel!"

"Insolent mutt! You'll pay for that!" The Fierce Dog sprang after Lucky, a deputy by her side. Lucky spun around, breaking along the street. A moment before he reached the rope and netting he veered sharply to the side. He heard the wild scrambling of the Fierce Dogs' claws and their howls of fury as they slammed into the rope.

Lucky looked up to see Moon, Martha, Bella, and Storm waiting for him at the end of the street.

Bella panted appreciatively. "Nice work."

Lucky risked a glance at the Fierce Dogs. Their paws flailed wildly as they fought against the knots of netting. It wouldn't take long for them to free themselves.

He started toward his Packmates but faltered. A shadow fell over the sandy street just ahead of him.

Fang. The young Fierce Dog growled as he blocked Lucky's path. "More of your pathetic tricks? You don't change, City Dog!" He snapped at Lucky's flank. Lucky sprang back, thinking fast. *He's more vulnerable without the other two, but he's strong and the others will soon catch up. We have to get out of here.*

Lucky pounced at Fang, thrusting him backward with all his strength. The pup tumbled on a heap of damp river grass. As Fang scrambled to his paws, Lucky made a break for it, joining his Packmates at the end of the street.

"Hurry!" he barked, leading Storm, Martha, Bella, and Moon down a side street.

Fang charged after them, barking a call that was answered by others.

"They're coming for us!" howled Moon, crazed with terror. The Wild Dogs slid and stumbled along the sandy streets, dodging to avoid mounds of river grass and fallen debris.

We need a plan, thought Lucky. *Somewhere to hide. And I think I know just the place.*

But first they had to shake off Fang. "Head for the wooden platform over the Endless Lake," he urged the others.

They bounded toward the edges of the town, ducking under the arch with the blinking lights onto the platform that jutted over the Endless Lake. Martha led the way over the wooden boards, passing the first set of small houses. The great dog set down a forepaw and the air split with the sound of cracking wood. She sprang backward in a midair leap, yanking her paw away just as a plank of the platform collapsed and plummeted into the Endless Lake. It crashed onto the water in a fountain of white froth.

There was a gaping hole where the plank had been. Lucky looked around desperately. *There's nowhere to run!*

Fang reached the arch, his jaws gnashing and his stout body braced. Storm turned to face him, barking. "What do you want with us?"

"You know what you have to do!" Fang replied. "You have to come back to the Pack with me. See sense—you don't belong with these mongrels!"

Lucky watched the young littermates, his head pulsing with tension. Fang was outnumbered, but would not be for long. The frenzied barks of the Fierce Dog Pack were cutting through the air. They weren't far away—how long would it take them to arrive?

"Come on, sister, what are you waiting for?" Fang pushed his chest out and bared his teeth, but Lucky realized that, despite everything, he would not hurt Storm. A pleading note entered Fang's voice. "It's better if you come of your own will. Blade won't forgive you if you struggle."

Storm locked eyes with him. "And I won't forgive *you* if you lay a claw on my Packmates. If any dog touches Martha, Lucky, or the others I will personally see to it that the fur is ripped from their faces and their eyes become food for the waterbirds. They will not be buried or accepted by the Earth-Dog; they will be left to rot. Mark my words, Fang: I will fight until there isn't a Fierce Dog left standing—even if that includes me."

Lucky shivered. Storm's words echoed with her brave resolve, yet the violent threat made his hairs stand on end. He had no doubt that she meant it.

Fang's jaw worked, but he didn't speak. He threw a look over his shoulder, then turned back to his litter-sister. The angry barks of his Packmates were close now and Lucky heard Blade's voice rising over them.

"Find the pup," she howled. "Bring her to me—and the pelt of the yellow dog!"

Lucky swallowed a whine, wishing that Fang would hurry and come to a decision.

At last the young Fierce Dog snapped out of his thoughts. He addressed his litter-sister, ignoring the others. "Hide!" he snarled. "I'll put them off. But I hope you realize it's because I haven't given up on you. You belong with your *real* family."

Storm dipped her head, her expression softer. "Thank you."

The Fierce Dogs were almost at the edge of the town. "This way!" barked Lucky. Backing up a few paces and refusing to think of the deep drop beneath, he leaped off the broken board at a running jump. Moon and Bella glided over without difficulty and Martha followed, thumping down on the board at the far side of the gap. Storm had shorter legs than the others, but she threw herself over without hesitation. Her hind legs hit the edge of the next wooden board, wobbling over the drop for a moment, but she quickly recovered her balance and followed her friends along the platform. Lucky silently thanked the Spirit Dogs that none of the smaller Pack members had joined them. He doubted that Sunshine or Whine would have made it across.

Lucky hurried in front of the small buildings that lined the wooden platform. "In here!" he barked, pouncing onto the ledge of the building full of hoops and balls. Moon, Bella, and Storm followed him onto the ledge and sprang inside. Martha was less graceful, hooking a rear paw onto the ledge and lifting herself over. She tumbled onto a mound of soft toys with a thump. The dogs shuffled down until they were buried beneath toys. Lucky held his breath, ears pricked.

"Where are the half breeds?" Blade's voice was louder now— she must have reached the arch at the entrance to the wooden platform.

"Not here," Fang barked back. "I saw them running across the sand toward the river."

Blade's voice boomed. "Toward the river! Idiot pup, why didn't you catch them?"

Fang gave a sharp yelp. Lucky winced—Blade must have nipped him hard.

"I'm sorry, Blade!" whined the young Fierce Dog.

"You're sorry?" snarled Blade.

A series of barks rose over the air. The whole Pack must have been there. Lucky tried not to imagine the Fierce Dogs surrounding Fang and bearing down on him. He told himself the young dog had chosen his own fate, but he couldn't help feeling a pang of pity.

"They were too far away," whimpered Fang. "I won't let them escape again."

"You'd better not!" growled another voice. Lucky recognized it as the brown Fierce Dog Mace, Blade's Beta.

Huddled next to Lucky, Storm made the smallest of whines. "Fang will be okay," Lucky whispered, though he didn't really know if this was true.

"Come on," snarled Blade. "He's not even worth it. We should have left the useless pup to rot with the half breeds. He can forget about eating tonight; let a bit of hunger teach him some fighting spirit!" The Fierce Dogs barked their agreement, their voices fading as they leaped off the platform and retreated into the town.

Lucky sighed with relief. They had escaped Blade this time. But there would be a price—he knew the Fierce Dogs would see to that.

CHAPTER SEVEN

Lucky and his companions kept perfectly still as the barks of the Fierce Dogs faded on the salty air, until all they could hear was the roar of the Endless Lake as it churned beneath them restlessly.

Bella raised her head above a fluffy toy shaped like a rabbit. "That was close," she panted. "At least we learned something useful."

"More than one thing," Lucky agreed. "Now we know where the Fierce Dogs have made their camp and where they patrol." He looked at Storm, who had risen to her paws and was shaking her sleek brown coat. "We also know that Fang's loyalty is to his litter-sister, not to Blade. Maybe there's still hope for him."

Storm cocked her head, panting, her tail giving a wag.

Moon scratched her neck with a hind leg and straightened up. "We should never have come here!"

Lucky sighed. "Well, let's get as far away from the Fierce Dogs as possible. We need to retrace the Wild Pack's scent." The others agreed, following Moon as she pounced on the ledge and down onto the wooden floor.

Storm gazed up at the sky with a frown.

Lucky licked her ears. "What's wrong?"

She turned to him. "It's already getting dark. Wasn't it only a short while ago that the Sun-Dog was at the top of the sky? Why do you think he's in such a hurry today?"

Her comments surprised him. *Doesn't she know about seasons?* He had to remind himself that despite her courage and resilience, which were qualities of a more experienced dog, Storm was still very young. She had never lived through the changes of weather, so she didn't know that the days grew shorter.

"When the air gets cold, the Sun-Dog doesn't like to be out for very long," he explained. "He prefers to rest and stay warm, so he spends less time in the sky. That time is known as Ice Wind. When the air grows warmer and plants spring into bloom, he is happier. We call that Tree Flower. After Tree Flower, the Sun-Dog stays out much longer; the days are hot and seem to last forever—that's Long Light."

Storm was wide-eyed. "What comes after Long Light?"

Lucky licked her nose. "After Long Light it's Red Leaf. Then the trees lose their fur and the days grow short and cold, and it's Ice Wind again."

They looped around the edge of the town onto the sand hills, ducking beneath the wind until they could trace the Wild Pack's scent once more.

"We should stick to the sand," said Moon. "It's tough going, but the Fierce Dogs are unlikely to follow us here, and at least we have the Pack's scent."

No dog argued. They scaled the hills, scrabbling at bursts of long grass to stop themselves from sliding down. Lucky threw a look over his shoulder. The town lay below them to one side, the river to the other, and straight behind them the wooden platform hung over the Endless Lake.

Lucky located the scent of the Wild Pack. He could clearly distinguish the dogs now. Alpha, Spring, Sweet . . . A tremor of excitement ran along his back. *It's so slow over this terrain, and it's growing dark. There must be an easier way.* He forged ahead, his eyes scanning the stretches of sand. They rested on an outcrop of white boulders. He bounded toward them, tail lashing. A shaft of rock rose from the boulders like a bridge over the sand.

"Up here!" he barked. It was easier to get a proper footing on the rock, but it veered so sharply that his paws ached as he climbed. The dogs clambered up one after another, panting heavily. Lucky watched Storm for signs of strain. The pup had to take running bounds up the incline to keep pace with the others. Her jaw was clenched with concentration, but she didn't complain.

Lucky and Bella were the first to reach the top of the rock-shaft. Moon and Martha followed, with Storm bringing up the rear. The dogs gazed back over the town, catching their breath. It seemed quite small now—nothing like the city that Lucky, Bella, and Martha had once known.

Lucky squinted at the distant street. "It's so dark down there."

"Because the Sun-Dog is going to sleep," said Storm.

"Yes, but it wasn't like that in the city," said Bella. "Not before the Big Growl."

The little Fierce Dog tilted her head, looking from Bella to the town beneath them. "The Sun-Dog didn't sleep in the city?"

Bella licked a forepaw. "He did, but there was always light. The longpaws set little fires."

Moon's fangs were visible as she looked around. "Dangerous creatures."

Martha sounded defensive. "The fires were quite safe. Not really fires, just balls of light that gave off no heat."

"But why?" asked Storm.

Bella's ears twitched. "I guess they don't like the dark."

Lucky was still listening, but he had noticed that the rockshaft swerved up so it overhung the Endless Lake. *It's a cliff . . .*

He trod the narrow path to the top and caught his breath. The Sun-Dog was sinking into the water, his amber tail touching the surface so the giant ripples were silvery. Lucky scanned the shimmering water. Its near bank ran from the flat, sandy riverbank to wind around the town and continue its journey as far as the eye could see. As for its far bank . . .

Bella had joined him at the top of the rockshaft. "That's impossible." The others had heard her and were climbing up behind them, taking in the same strange sight.

Lucky nodded slowly. The silvery-tipped water rolled endlessly to the edges of his vision, where the Sun-Dog dipped beneath the sky.

There is no far bank.

"It really is endless," sighed Storm.

Martha joined them, panting heavily. "And it's moved."

"Moved?" Bella frowned.

"When we were down on the bank, the water came up to the edges of the town and under the wooden platform. Look at it now."

Lucky squinted. The water-dog was right! The waves had

retreated along the bank, leaving many dog-lengths of dark, damp sand.

Moon shivered and looked at the town. "At least we're clear of the Fierce Dogs. We need to track around to the waterfront again. I can smell our Pack. It's as I guessed—they must have followed along the same path by the river, swerved away from the lake over the sand hills when they saw the town, and headed down to the water again once they were clear of it."

Lucky watched her, impressed. He sniffed the air. The Wild Pack's scent was below them, drifting from the waterfront beyond the longpaw settlement.

The dogs started the careful descent along mounds of rock and sand, looping around the town. When Lucky looked back he could just see the jagged outline of its broken buildings. The Fierce Dogs were safely behind them, hidden among that dark jumble of streets.

Lucky and Bella had a new spring in their steps as the Wild Pack's scent grew stronger. Moon's tail was wagging as she slid down the slippery sand hills. "I can smell Beetle and Thorn!" she barked. "This way!"

The others hurried after her, zigzagging toward the bank of the Endless Lake. Lucky paused, watching as Martha and Storm hurried past him. The light had faded fast. The Sun-Dog's amber pelt had merged into the water so that only his silvery whiskers still played on the surface. The Endless Lake was farther away now, as Martha had pointed out, but it still roared and hissed as it lashed the sloping bank. The water never slept.

Lucky wished he could be as strong as the waves. His paws ached with fatigue and his eyelids were heavy. How would Storm be feeling? "It's practically no-sun," he barked over the churning water. "We won't catch up with them tonight."

"We will," Moon barked back. She ran toward the craggy rocks, her tail thrashing. "Just a little farther!" She hurried around them, nose to the ground, the others close behind her.

With a last great bound the dogs emerged around the rocks onto the deep, sandy bank. The water was scarcely visible against the horizon. The Moon-Dog watched from high in the sky, almost full, but her light was faint on the sand.

"Lucky's right," barked Bella. "We should find some shelter where we can rest until sun-up. We'll catch up with them then." She padded along the damp sand, where another white shaft of rock jutted out. "It looks like there's a cave here. It'll be drier and warmer in there."

Moon looked across the sand, her tail drooping. "I guess it's too dark to keep going in this unfamiliar place. We can start again at first light." She padded toward the cave after Bella.

Martha and Lucky followed, but Storm paused, her dark eyes shining. "Are you sure we should go in there?" she whined. "There could be anything inside that cave. Maybe we're safer out on the sand? We could try to find some shelter beneath those bushes."

Bella turned on her impatiently. "Stop being such a pup! We're all cold and tired; we could freeze out here. Haven't you learned anything about surviving in the wild?"

"Leave her alone!" growled Martha, whose dark outline in the fading light looked more like a moving boulder than a dog. "Storm has a point! We don't know what's in there; it could be dangerous. Don't giantfurs live in caves?"

Lucky's breath tightened as he remembered the terrifying beast he had encountered while tracking the Fierce Dog pups with Alpha through the forest. Did giantfurs really live in caves? He frowned, approaching the yawning gap of the rock mouth. He couldn't picture a giantfur living here, so far from the woods.

Storm pressed against Martha's flank, shivering against the wind. Lucky stepped around them and took a tentative sniff inside the cave. It didn't look much bigger than one of those buildings on the wooden platform near the town. The ground was grainy against his paws. *Great, more sand. . . .* He'd hoped for something warmer, some driftwood or foliage.

He walked a slow circle around the cave. One side was raised on higher ground that backed against some rocks and dips. Lucky nosed at these, finding bits of damp debris that smelled of the Endless Lake. His snout tingled with the odor of salt and river grass.

Lucky withdrew from the cave. The other dogs were gathered at the entrance, bickering.

"What do you know about giantfurs?" Bella was saying. "You were a Leashed Dog. There aren't any giantfurs in the city."

"You were a Leashed Dog too," Martha pointed out. "So you're no expert either. Storm actually *saw* a giantfur."

"So what? That doesn't mean she knows everything there is to know about them!" Bella tapped her paw on the sand. "There's nothing in the cave."

"It's safe," Lucky confirmed, hoping this would bring an end to the argument. "It isn't ideal, but at least it's empty, dry, and sheltered from the wind."

"Told you!" snapped Bella, turning sharply and marching into the cave. The others followed in silence, each claiming a separate corner except for Martha and Storm, who stuck together.

Lucky eased himself up onto the raised part of the cave, which was farthest from the entrance. He lowered his head to the ground. He knew that they were a good distance from the shore of the Endless Lake, but its ceaseless roar disturbed him. He covered his ears with his paws, trying to block out the sound. It drowned out the snuffles and snores of the other dogs. Too late Lucky remembered the Great Howl. Maybe it would have made them feel less alone. . . .

As he shut his eyes, Lucky felt Bella settle down alongside him and he began to relax. A little later, Moon approached and snuggled up against Lucky's other side. Martha and Storm crept closer until the dogs were all together. Lucky felt the warmth and comfort of their bodies. He remembered his first night after the Big Growl, when he'd huddled against Sweet beneath a bush and awoken to a world that had changed forever.

The wind whipped Lucky's fur and he shivered, crouching low to the ground. The Moon-Dog had vanished, leaving only a scattering of stars to cast their shallow light. He squinted into the darkness. As his eyes adjusted, he realized he was perching on a blade of black rock, a tiny stone island surrounded by water. He took a tentative step over the rock and faltered. The water wasn't moving—it was frozen to ice. As Lucky lowered his head, he could see white patterns across its surface like spiders' webs. Ahead, the sky of no-sun was as thick and dark as a storm cloud, yet craning his head Lucky could just make out a circle of amber light. Was it the Sun-Dog rising, or something else?

He took a step forward, placing his forepaw on the ice. The freezing cold was sharper than a blast of fire and Lucky whipped away his paw with a howl of pain. He licked it, gazing into the distance. He could still see a light, though now it looked farther away. . . . Somehow he knew he had to reach it, but he didn't think he'd make it over the long stretches of ice. He backed over the black rock, wondering what to do. He was alone, trapped on the island—and the Ice Wind was coming.

He heard hissing and spun around. The ice was clawing its way over the edge of the island. Its touch turned the rock a shiny white, like clear-stone. Lucky's breath caught in his throat. He threw a frantic look over his shoulder. The ice was creeping onto the land from all sides, fizzing and murmuring with its cool, white tongue, freezing the land beneath its ghostly pelt.

Lucky cried out. "Bella! Sweet!"

No dog answered his calls.

The ice was close now, whispering and crackling at his paws. Lucky watched in horror as it climbed up his legs, searing him with its deathly touch, turning his fur brittle and white as frost. He tried to pull away, but his legs were frozen. He tried to cry out again, but his jaw was locked with cold.

Far in the distance, the amber light flickered and died. Now there was only chill and darkness. And then, in the darkness, the furious howls of fighting dogs.

Lucky's eyes snapped open. It took him a moment to remember he was in a cave not far from the Endless Lake. He could hear it roaring and lashing the shore, not frozen as in his dream. It sounded closer than it had before they had gone to sleep.

The cave was darker than before, as though the Moon-Dog really had vanished. Lucky trembled with cold. The other dogs were still curled around him, but it didn't seem to help anymore. He rose to his paws, careful not to wake his companions.

I'll shake out my fur, as Moon taught us to. Maybe that will do the trick.

He started toward the mouth of the cave, crunching over the sandy ground. Something cold and wet stung his paw pads, and he sprang back in alarm. *Water!* The Endless Lake crashed and hissed, not dog-lengths away along the sand, but just outside. Its waves tumbled into the cave, blocking the exit.

Lucky was so shocked he could hardly speak. Then he found his voice. "Wake up!" he whined. "The lake has moved! We're trapped!"

CHAPTER EIGHT

In an instant the dogs were awake.

"What happened?" barked Bella, springing toward the mouth of the cave. She jumped back as the water lapped over her paws. "Where is it coming from?"

"It's the Endless Lake!" Lucky howled. "It's broken its banks."

A new burst of water gushed through the entrance, bubbling and thrashing. The raised part of the cave quickly became an island. The dogs huddled together, their fear-scent mingling with the salty air.

Moon's eyes flashed in the darkness. "It's rising so quickly!"

"I'll take a look." Martha bounded down toward the entrance of the cave and plunged into the water. Her head dipped beneath the surface but bobbed up again as she struggled against the current, trying to swim out onto the bank. With a powerful shake she dived down, disappearing from sight. Lucky and Bella exchanged glances, waiting for the brave water-dog to emerge. Storm whined with fear. A moment later the water split and Martha's head burst out.

She struggled onto the island of sand. Her body trembled and she shook out her fur. "It's freezing," she whined. "And we'd have to fight the current to get out. It's like pushing against a wall of water. I've never known anything like it. I might be able to make it, but I don't think the rest of you could."

This was too much for Moon, who howled in terror. "We're trapped! We're trapped!" She turned circles on the spot. She banged into Storm, who leaped into the air with a growl. Panic clawed at Lucky's belly, his heart racing and his fur standing on end. *It's so cold, so dark!*

"We'll drown!" yapped Storm. "We'll freeze and drown!" She spun around and smacked into Bella, who snapped at her flank.

If we lose control now we could hurt one another, Lucky realized with a start. *I have to calm down. We all have to if we want to get out of here!*

The water was swirling around them, silvery in the weak light. It slapped the edges of the sand island.

"Earth-Dog, save us!" cried Moon. "Help us escape this terrible place!"

"Why ask her?" snapped Bella. "She hasn't been so kind to

dogs lately. Didn't you see what she did to the town? It's nothing compared to the city I used to know. The Earth-Dog *caused* the Big Growl; she took everything—this is all her fault!"

Lucky flinched. In his heart, he suspected that his litter-sister was right—that the Earth-Dog was more intent on causing harm than being their friend. But how could that be true? He remembered something his Mother-Dog had once said to him: "Earth-Dog takes us when we die. Until then, she protects us and gives us strength. She watches over us night and day—when you need her, she will help you." Hadn't the Earth-Dog watched over him when he'd fallen down the animal hole as a pup? What if Bella was wrong? Maybe the Big Growl *wasn't* the Earth-Dog's fault.

Lucky turned his back on the water. He could hear it tumbling through the mouth of the cave and he did his best to block out the terrifying sound, sniffing along the rocks. He tried to concentrate, despite the whines and yaps of the others. His whiskers flexed and the fur tingled along his muzzle. He could feel the faintest breeze. *An airway!*

But would it be large enough for the dogs to escape?

He glanced back to see Moon glaring at Storm. "Don't blame Storm; it wasn't her fault!"

"Then who should we blame?" barked Moon. "If it wasn't for the Fierce Dogs we'd be with the Pack by now! But no, we had to follow them; we had to worry about their latest plans because they want to reclaim their pup. And now we're trapped!"

Storm didn't try to defend herself. Instead she threw back her head and whined pathetically, just as the water splashed over the sand island where the dogs were huddling. It hissed icily over Lucky's paws.

"There may still be a way out!" Lucky barked.

This quieted the bickering dogs.

"You need to listen to me carefully," Lucky urged them. "I think there's a hole farther inside the cave, behind these rocks. We may be able to dig our way out."

Bella's eyes were silvery like the water. "What if it's like a rabbit warren, all wrong turns and dead ends?"

The same thought had occurred to Lucky. He watched the water swell up behind her. With another surge it rushed over their paws again. It wouldn't take long before the sand island was submerged. "We have to try."

"But the water's rising fast!" barked Bella. "The path will be narrow; we'd have to take it one dog at a time. Even if you find a way out, we'll lose you!"

The icy water tugged at Lucky's paws and he fought against panic. "We'll have to stick together."

Moon's ears pricked up. "I know a way! Each dog should take the tail of the dog in front. Don't pull or tug, just hold it gently in your mouth. We'll move in a line and, that way, we won't lose any dog."

"Good idea!" barked Lucky.

"I'll go last," said Martha. "My fur's the thickest, so it doesn't matter if I get wet—and I can hold my breath the longest."

Lucky was touched. He guessed that Martha's instinct was to flee the icy water as quickly as she could, just like the rest of them. But she was a real Pack Dog, always thinking of the others. "You're so brave," he told her. "We're lucky to have you with us." He turned toward the rocks, feeling Bella's jaws close carefully around the middle of his tail.

He called back to the others. "Has every dog got someone to lead them?"

"Every dog but you," Bella muttered, her voice muffled by Lucky's tail.

"I have Earth-Dog," Lucky replied. "She'll show us the way out."

Standing behind Bella, Moon whined hopefully at this. Lucky's litter-sister was silent. He knew she would be less ready to believe that the Spirit Dog was on their side.

"The sand is melting away!" whined Martha. "The island is sinking!"

"Up here, quickly, onto the rocks!" Lucky barked back. He scrambled over the rocks along the wall of the cave, beneath a sharp tooth of stone and up a steep passageway. Darkness enfolded him. The fresh breeze grew stronger and Lucky tracked it blindly. He felt Bella's weight at his tail and heard the scramble of her paws as she followed him, and the footfalls of the other dogs as they crunched over the sand.

The water couldn't reach them now, but Lucky could hear it swishing about in the cave beneath them, still rising. He tried to focus on the gentle breeze, which came and went amid the smell of salt and the fear-scent of the other dogs.

He faltered. In the darkness, he could just make out a fork in the tunnel.

"Hurry!" whined Moon. "It's getting wet back here!"

Please, Earth-Dog, show me which way to go.

"Lucky!" Moon growled more urgently, prompting Lucky to make a decision. On impulse, he sprang toward the passage on the right. He thought he'd sensed fresh air there, but he couldn't be sure. He heard the others scurry after him.

The ground beneath them turned from sand to slippery stones and Lucky skidded, kicking up a shower of rocks. One smacked him hard on the forepaw and he yelped. The paw twinged when he flexed it and he could smell his own blood.

"Are you injured?" whined Bella as he paused to lick the wound.

"Is he all right?" Storm whimpered, her voice echoing along the narrow passageway.

Lucky tried setting his paw down. It seemed able to take his weight, provided he was careful. "I'm fine," he replied. "Is every dog still here?"

"Yes!" yelped Bella, releasing his tail for a moment.

"Yes!" whined Moon and Storm.

"Me too!" murmured Martha. "The water's rising. . . ."

"Then we need to hurry." Lucky pressed forward, hobbling a little. The water ran over his paws, rising quickly along the dark passage. It would be worse for Storm and Martha at the rear.

Lucky picked up his pace. Doing his best not to skid on the wet stones, he shuffled along the passageway, sniffing for fresh air. Soon the water swished around his legs, climbing to his belly. The passage bent at a sharp angle, the way barred by a mound of jagged rocks. Lucky carefully climbed over, feeling Bella's grip tighten on his tail. A moment later she was on the other side and holding on to him more gently.

Lucky sniffed deeply. There it was again! The smell of fresh air. Lucky half bounded, half swam through the icy water.

"Help!" barked Martha. "Stop!"

Lucky's heart lurched. *If Martha is barking, that means she doesn't have Storm's tail in her mouth—and that means . . . oh no!*

"Where's Storm?" he yelped.

The water-dog's voice was desperate. "Her tail slipped out of my mouth!"

"She's not holding on to me," whined Moon. "I don't know where she's gone, and the water is high—can she even swim?"

"All of you, stay put!" ordered Lucky. Martha started barking. "Quiet!" he snapped. The dogs froze. Disguising his panic, Lucky called out to the pup. "Storm? Storm, are you there?"

For a moment, he could only hear the swish of the rising water and his panting companions. Then a small voice called out.

"I'm here! I'm okay! I slipped and fell under the water but I'm fine now."

Lucky's heart swelled with relief. He heard Martha and Moon help the pup to her paws and waited until they were all in a row once more, holding on to one another's tails. He sniffed, trying to reach beyond the stinging salt to catch the fresh air he had detected earlier. *What if the way out is below us? We'll all drown.*

"There you go," soothed Moon. "Just take small steps; it's safer that way."

"That's true," agreed Martha.

Lucky was touched by how well the dogs worked together. It gave him a rush of hope. He raised his muzzle and sniffed deeply. There it was: that sweet hint of fresh air—he'd caught it only for a moment, but it was enough.

"Follow me!" he barked, mounting the passageway. It climbed sharply, a black path between stone walls.

They kept going until the path split again.

"Which way now?" panted Bella.

Lucky pricked up his ears. He could hear the Endless Lake below them, swishing through the flooded cave, but they seemed to have climbed beyond its reach. He couldn't gauge their distance from the sounds.

"Earth-Dog, show me the way," Lucky muttered aloud, longing for guidance.

The others had grown very quiet. He could sense them waiting for an answer. Lucky waited too. There was no reassuring light to guide him to one of the pathways, no warmth or smell. *I will have to make a decision by myself,* thought Lucky, his whiskers twitching. He didn't want to scare the others—to make them feel alone, without the protection of the Spirit Dogs. *Keeping us all together and calm is more important than the truth.*

He cleared his throat. "I can feel something!" he lied. "The Earth-Dog is telling me . . . we must climb this way!" He turned toward the left passageway and started climbing, doing his best to ignore his throbbing forepaw. The others reacted with cheerful barks, staying close behind him.

"The Earth-Dog is guiding us," murmured Moon. "We're going to be all right!"

Even Bella seemed more at ease as she licked Lucky's tail before closing her jaws around it once more.

The passageway cut even more sharply through the rocks. *We must be inside the cliff,* thought Lucky, wondering where it would take them. He did not dare to think about the possibility that he was leading the other dogs to a dead end, or a gap too narrow to squeeze through. His flank brushed against stone. Were the walls getting closer? His heart was thumping hard in his chest and the pain in his paw was getting worse. He paused to lick it and felt dizzy. Had he just heard—? No, it couldn't have been a dog. . . . Then he caught it again, distant but quite clear: a rich, pure voice beyond the rock wall.

"Quiet!" he hissed, sounding sharper than he'd intended. The others fell silent.

Lucky craned his ears. A dog was barking not far away. Although her words were muffled by the rock, he knew who it was—it was the voice his mind always drifted to, the voice he had longed to hear again. "Sweet!" he breathed. At first he thought she was calling him, but then he realized that she couldn't know he was there. . . . *Not yet.*

He charged up the passageway, his tail slipping out of Bella's grasp. He no longer felt the pain in his paw as he found his way over the rocky ground. His breath came noisily; his pulse thumped in his ears. He ran until the hard stone pebbles gave way to grainy earth.

Suddenly he could make out the faint outline of his paws. The tunnel grew narrower, ending in a wall of earth. A prick of light had broken through and Lucky launched at it, digging furiously. He kicked up dirt that Bella and Moon helped to push down the tunnel. All the time he pictured Sweet's slender face, her velvety ears, and her large brown eyes. With a last, frantic scramble the earth crumbled before him, collapsing in a tangle of soil and sand.

Piercing sunshine broke through the darkness.

CHAPTER NINE

Lucky burst out of the tunnel in a cloud of sand and soil. He rolled onto a patch of grass, taking in great gulps of cool, clean air. Bella pranced past him and Storm shot out behind her, running in excited zigzags.

"We're out! We're free!" barked Storm. "Lucky, you found the way!"

"The Earth-Dog spoke through him!" panted Moon, collapsing in a beam of sunshine.

Martha lay down next to her with a sigh. Her thick coat was covered in dirt, and she licked her forepaws a couple of times before giving up and stretching them out in the sun. "I never thought fresh air could taste this good."

Bella shook her fur vigorously. "Even the cold wind is welcome. *Any wind* is a relief." Lucky watched as she padded back to the collapsed entrance of the tunnel, sniffing the debris. "I think this was a fox den once; there's something of their sharp scent in the soil."

Lucky met her eye. He remembered how his litter-sister had struck a deal with foxes and used them to attack the Wild Pack. But it seemed *so long ago* now that Leashed and Wild Dogs were divided. If the scent of foxes reminded Bella of that dark time, she didn't show it.

He stretched his forelegs and drew himself up, taking a good look around. They had emerged at the top of a cliff. He edged closer to the drop with a shudder. It lurched down to a cluster of gray rocks. The Endless Lake spun and crashed against them in plumes of white mist.

He backed away from the drop and looked over the grass. It sloped gently into a valley out of reach of the lashing wind. Some low trees grew down there, the first Lucky had seen since the dogs had reached the Endless Lake. Something glinted green between their trunks. Lucky licked his lips, guessing it was a freshwater pond.

It looks sheltered and comfortable, an excellent camp for the Pack. And where there are trees, there are squirrels. . . . There must be other prey around too.

His fur tingled as he took in the odors of the Wild Dogs.

They were so close that he had no trouble distinguishing them on the air: Alpha, Snap, Bruno, Sunshine, Sweet . . . Then he heard the murmur of her voice again.

"The Pack is in the valley!" he yelped. "Let's go!"

He took off down the slope at a run, delighting in the freedom as his paws sped over the grass. He dived between the trees, straight into the middle of the Pack. There she was, licking an elegant paw. He started to bark a greeting when a great weight thumped down on him and his muzzle hit the earth.

"Stop right there! Who are you?" snarled a gruff old voice.

Lucky knew that thick, heavy scent. "Bruno, it's me!"

"Lucky?" The old dog pulled back. "It really is you!" He licked his brown muzzle sheepishly. "I'm sorry, I didn't recognize your smell. . . ."

Lucky sniffed his own paw. Dirt, mud, and salt water caked his fur, mingling with the sharp whiff of fox. *No wonder Bruno didn't know it was me.*

"You're back!" yipped a shrill voice. A small dog sprang forward with an excited hop and threw her forepaws on the ground in front of Lucky like a pup. Her filthy gray pelt, once soft and white, hung around her head in long twists. Beneath it he could see she was painfully thin.

"Sunshine?" he asked uncertainly. *She's changed so much....*

Mickey stepped beside her. "Lucky! Is that really you?" The Farm Dog touched noses, his black-and-white tail thrashing. His eyes sparkled, but Lucky could see the sharp outline of his bones beneath fur. Little Daisy sprang after him with Snap and Spring. Lucky was submerged beneath their happy licks. They fell back as Sweet trod lightly between them and lowered her narrow head.

She nuzzled Lucky's face. "It's good to see you.... I thought... maybe something had happened to you."

Their eyes met and Lucky's breath snagged in his throat. She was still beautiful, though her lithe body was more bone than muscle and there were circles beneath her dark eyes. *She's so thin,* thought Lucky. *They all are....* He held Sweet's gaze, his fur tingling. Then Sweet seemed to remember her status as Beta and stepped back, sitting by the trunk of a low tree and watching as the Pack clambered about Lucky excitedly.

Mickey's ears pricked up. "Martha too!" Lucky and the other dogs looked around as the great black dog stepped out from between the trees. She looked more herself now, having shaken the dirt from her thick coat.

Storm, Moon, and Bella were close behind her. They greeted the Pack with excited yaps.

"Mother!" Thorn and Beetle tumbled toward Moon, burying their faces against her chest as she gathered them close and licked their ears. Their tails wagged so energetically that their whole rumps swung back and forth.

"My sweet pups, you've grown so much!"

Beetle pushed out his chest. "We have?"

Thorn pulled away from her Mother-Dog, looking toward the trees. "Where's Father?"

Beetle lowered his head and looked around as the other dogs fell silent. They sniffed the air, their tails stiffening. Lucky swallowed a whine, his ears dropping sadly as he watched the young dogs.

"Yes, where *is* Fiery?"

The wolfish voice made Lucky jump. Alpha stalked between the Pack. He stared down his long muzzle at Moon. His musky odor fanned out around him.

Moon's posture slackened. She lowered her head with a small whine, seemingly unable to speak in front of her pups and the gathered dogs. She looked as if she was beseeching some other dog to tell them.

None of the rescue party stepped forward. Lucky's heart sank as he looked at Alpha and the other dogs, who waited expectantly.

He sucked in his breath. *I'll have to tell them. . . .*

"Fiery has joined the Earth-Dog," he said quietly to a series of whimpers. "We found him caged by the cruel yellow-furred longpaws. They'd trapped other creatures too. We saw a coyote, some foxes, and a sharpclaw. There were rabbits too. And all the creatures were sick."

Sweet's jaw was set. "Why were they sick?"

Lucky shook his ears. "I don't know. Fiery thought that the longpaws had been making them drink the shiny, green river-water, the type that made Bruno so unwell." The old hunt-dog whined at the memory and Lucky frowned, trying to figure out what the longpaws had been up to. "Maybe the longpaws were trying to see if it was safe to drink. But it can't have been, because even Fiery, who had once been so strong . . ." Lucky's voice faltered and he closed his eyes, picturing the fierce, powerful warrior as he had once been—before the longpaws had caught him. He didn't want to think about the feeble dog that he had become in the end. Lucky opened his eyes and went on. "We freed Fiery and the others, but it was too late. He was hurt on the inside; you could see it in his eyes. He died on the way back." Sadness prickled Lucky's whiskers and he fell silent, unable to go on.

Thorn threw back her muzzle and howled in grief. Her

litter-brother, Beetle, flopped on the ground, his head on his paws and his eyes staring into the distance. "Why would the longpaws do that?" he whined to no dog in particular.

Alpha shook his head slowly. "It is a great shame to lose a dog as worthy and loyal as Fiery. He was a true Pack Dog to the last and he will be missed." Snap and Spring whined, lowering their heads, and Daisy gazed at her paws. Lucky's whiskers twitched. There was something about Alpha's voice that didn't ring true—a false note of grief that sounded insincere. Lucky searched the dog-wolf's face. The cold yellow eyes showed no emotion. *He can't be as sad as he's pretending to be. If Fiery had made it back he'd have challenged Alpha for leadership of the Pack.*

Alpha caught Lucky staring. One pointed ear rolled back, his bushy gray tail stiffening.

"There's more news," said Lucky hastily.

The half wolf sat and started washing his forepaw, abandoning any appearance of grief. "Go on."

Lucky suppressed a twinge of anger. *So much for caring about Fiery.*

Bella met Lucky's eye briefly. He guessed she was thinking the same thing. Still, the Pack was all watching now, and there was no point expecting Alpha to feel anything more than relief that Fiery was dead. He cleared his parched throat. "After we freed Fiery and the other creatures, we ran into Terror's Pack."

Sunshine yipped, her dark eyes shining.

Snap raised her muzzle. "What happened?" Her hackles rose beneath her wiry fur.

Lucky wondered how much the Pack needed to know. Terror was dead now; they weren't a threat anymore. "There was a fight and Terror died. He was crazy and vicious; he made his Pack fight us. We had no choice but to defend ourselves."

Moon shuddered and whined quietly. "Terror had one of his strange attacks."

Alpha dropped his forepaw. His ears swiveled forward. "When was this?"

Lucky started pacing between the dogs. "Before we reached the Endless Lake. But there's nothing to worry about now, not with Terror gone." Lucky forced away the memory of Storm standing over the mad dog's bleeding body. "He made his Pack fight. Without him, they're no danger to us."

Spring stepped forward, shaking her long black ears. "What happened to Twitch? He's in that Pack, isn't he? Is he okay?" Her dark eyes widened and her tail gave a cautious wag.

Lucky paused to face her. "He's strong and healthy," Lucky assured her.

"He helped us when Terror attacked," agreed Moon. "He fought alongside us."

Spring's tail started to wag. Then she looked from Moon to Lucky, Bella, Martha, and Storm. "But he didn't come back with you?"

Bella shook her head. "He stayed with his new Pack." She paused, a knowing look on her face. "He's their Alpha now."

Several of the dogs yipped at this and Spring's eyes widened in amazement. "He's their *Alpha?*"

Dart, the lean brown-and-white hunt-dog, licked her black nose. "But how . . ." She met Spring's eye and pulled away guiltily. "He was so badly injured when he left the Pack. We all thought . . . I'm glad he made it, really glad, but the *Alpha?*"

"He's a remarkable dog," said Lucky. "And he proved something to me. There are different forms of strength. You don't need to be just like everyone else to succeed in this world."

"My litter-brother, an Alpha!" yapped Spring in disbelief.

Lucky nodded his golden head. "They all respect him, Spring. He'll make a great Alpha. He's a good fighter and he's fair and loyal. We wouldn't have made it without him."

The Pack started barking in praise of Twitch. Lucky's ears pricked. He thought he'd caught a low growl. Glancing around, he spotted Alpha's lip twitch, revealing one long fang. *The others may not notice, but I can see through the dog-wolf. I don't trust him. . . .*

"I'm sorry I wasn't more welcoming when Twitch found us in the town," whined Spring, her black-and-tan tail falling low. "I should have been proud of him. I am now. I hope he's happy in his new Pack, and I hope I'll see him again one day."

Dart the hunt-dog trod over to Spring, licking her friend's nose. "You will," she murmured.

"Twitch, leading a Pack," yelped Snap, her short tail wagging. "Just think of that!"

"Enough of this pointless yapping about the three-legged dog!" snapped Alpha, flashing his deadly fangs. "Who cares about that motley Pack of misfits?" This quieted Snap and the other dogs. Only Thorn ignored him. The pup's tortured howl had subsided into a plaintive whimper as Moon licked her ears and tried to console her. Now that the Pack was silent, it hung on the cool air. Lucky could scarcely bear to hear that pitiful sound.

If the dog-wolf was moved by Thorn's cries, he didn't show it. He ignored the young dog, staring down his snout at Lucky. "Was there anything else?"

Lucky had no choice but to speak over Thorn. "You must have seen the longpaw town back along the waterfront."

"We saw it and avoided it," Alpha replied, confirming Moon's suspicions that the Pack had looped around rather than go anywhere near a longpaw settlement.

Lucky nodded. "We wanted to catch up with the rest of the Pack. To make up time, we cut through the town. And we discovered something—the location of the Fierce Dogs' new camp."

Ripples of anxiety ran through the Pack—Lucky could smell the fear-scent on the air. Alpha's yellow eyes grew rounder and his hackles rose. "They're in the town? I knew I was right to avoid it!"

"They've built a camp there, in a large building at the center."

Whine, the stumpy little snub-nosed dog, shook his wrinkled face. "This is a disaster! The Fierce Dogs are close!"

Dart barked in fear.

Lucky saw Spring tense, hackles rising. "On the contrary," he soothed, "it's good news. At least we know where they are, and that they're settled. They weren't tracking the Pack. We shouldn't go near the town, that's all."

"Why would we?" sniffed Alpha.

"I wouldn't go near that town if you paid me in chew toys!" yipped Sunshine. Her dark eyes still sparkled.

Lucky nudged her with his muzzle. "We won't make you go there."

Sunshine's tail thumped furiously. "Well, that's okay, then."

Alpha stretched his long legs, rising to his paws. "If there's nothing else . . ." He started to strut away.

Lucky turned to Storm, cocking his head reassuringly. "There is one last thing. The puppy you knew as Lick has come of age! Her teeth have grown through and she's been of great help to us, loyal and committed, as useful as any adult dog."

Storm sat up proudly, her tongue lolling from her beige muzzle.

Alpha froze in his tracks and his head snapped around.

Lucky went on. "We performed the Naming Ceremony a few days ago and she chose the name Storm."

The Pack barked in surprise, looking from Lucky to the little Fierce Dog.

Good-natured Snap was the first to step forward, her tail wagging. "Congratulations, Storm."

Taking her cue, Spring followed. "Welcome to the Pack, Storm."

"Welcome, Storm," echoed Mickey and Bruno.

Alpha's furious howl cut over them. "Stop that immediately!" The Pack fell back and Storm cringed, her small ears flat against her head. The half wolf's eyes fixed on Lucky, then shot to his companions on the rescue expedition: Bella, Martha, and Moon.

It was only Storm he ignored, as though the pup herself was of no relevance. Anger swelled in Lucky's chest.

Alpha glared. "How dare you perform a Naming Ceremony without my permission?"

Moon carefully averted her eyes. "You weren't there, Alpha. It felt right. Storm had fought hard to protect us from Terror. She was loyal and brave, and it was her time. She deserved it."

"The *right thing to do?*" mocked Alpha. "Who are you to speak on these practices, Farm Dog?" He flashed his teeth at Moon and she fell back. Beetle and Thorn watched with their tails around their flanks, the girl-pup finally silent.

Lucky's lip twitched and he swallowed a snarl. *All those big words about Fiery, but where's Alpha's compassion now?* It hadn't taken long for the half dog to show his true colors.

Alpha gave his fur a haughty shake. "The ceremony means nothing without my authorization! It has not been done *properly*, and it doesn't count a whisker." Finally he eyed Storm, but with so much scorn that the little Fierce Dog cowered. Even as he looked at her, he addressed the others. "Nothing has changed. This pup remains just what she is—a wild and uneducated Fierce Dog pup. You will all continue to call her Lick, if you call her anything at all."

"Alpha, be reasonable," Martha began, coming to Storm's side.

"Or you will have *me* to answer to," the dog-wolf growled.

Martha lowered her head sadly and licked the top of Storm's head. The young Fierce Dog looked crushed and she slumped down onto her belly. There was a murmur from one or two of the other dogs, but no one else challenged Alpha's decision.

Lucky sat very still. Anger coursed through his fur and his throat felt hot. Storm's choice of name had left him feeling uneasy, but it was her right to choose it. *There's no point saying anything. Alpha will just use it as an excuse to kick Storm out of the Pack, which is what he's wanted to do since the beginning.* Still, he wished some dog would challenge Alpha. He looked around the dogs, wondering who might take Fiery's place to fight for the leadership of the Pack. His eyes rested on Sweet, who had been watching in silence.

She may have been thinner than before, but her sinewy body still looked strong, her eyes bright and alert. *Could she be persuaded to abandon her place as Beta?* Lucky wondered. If she made a bid for the leadership, the wolf-dog would be forced to accept the challenge. Then Sweet and Alpha would do battle. *Could she win a fight against Alpha?*

Alpha turned, then sloped back between the trees. The meeting was over.

The air was thick with tension. Sunshine skipped up to Lucky and his companions. "It's so good to see you all!" she panted. Lucky looked down at her cheerful face, his mood lifting instantly. There was a twig hanging off her fur just under her muzzle, but she didn't seem to notice. She was obviously still the Pack's Omega, but the role suited her. "Follow me. I'll show you our new pond, where you can drink and wash the dirt and sand from your coats."

Lucky yipped gratefully as Sunshine led the way. But when he turned to look back, he saw that Alpha had paused between the trees. His broad silhouette was in shadow, but Lucky imagined the dog-wolf watching them through narrowed eyes. A ripple of unease ran down Lucky's back. *Alpha's up to something,* he thought. *And I'm not sure I'm going to like it.*

CHAPTER TEN

Lucky waded into the pond, sighing with relief as the sand and muck drifted off his fur. He didn't even mind the aching cold. He watched as Martha and Storm splashed about, and was grateful to the kind water-dog for cheering up the young Fierce Dog. He added his thanks to the River-Dog. *Thank you for your soothing waters,* he told her.

Bella paddled over to him, nudging his shoulder with a forepaw. "I'm proud of you, litter-brother."

"You are?" Lucky's tail did its best to wag under the shallow water.

"The way you led us out of the cave was amazing. A wrong turn and we might have drowned down there. You acted so decisively . . . and enlisting the help of Earth-Dog like that!"

Lucky nipped her on the nose. "Stop teasing me!"

"I'm not teasing." Bella nipped him back. "Well, not entirely."

He leaned closer to her. "To be honest, I didn't know where I was going. All that talk of Earth-Dog was really to make the rest of you feel better. No one led me; it was just a lucky guess."

"I know," murmured Bella. "But at the time, even I was comforted by your words. Earth-Dog or not, you're in touch with your dog-spirit."

Lucky watched Moon from the corner of his eye. She was climbing out of the pond, being greeted by Beetle and Thorn. "You don't think I was wrong to pretend?"

"No, you did the right thing. And Earth-Dog did protect us, in the end. I'm sure she'll forgive you for lying about that!"

Sweet was waiting for Lucky at the bank of the pond. Dewdrops clung to the long grass so it sparkled with light, and air smelled crisp and clean. Lucky padded toward Sweet, a crackle of excitement running through his whiskers.

"It's good to have you back," she murmured.

Lucky nodded. "It's good to be back. It seems like a fine camp."

"Perhaps . . ." Sweet glanced back at the trees, toward the Endless Lake. "I want to talk to you some more about the Fierce Dogs—where they're based and where they patrol. But we can do that later. For now, you should rest. You must be exhausted." Her brown-eyed gaze was gentle.

Lucky shook out his wet fur and lay down in a sunny patch of grass, sheltered from the wind by overhanging trees. He closed his eyes with a sigh, picturing the swift-dog's thoughtful face.

Maybe Ice Wind won't be so bad here after all.

There was a noise and his eyes snapped open. Martha was approaching, Storm trotting happily at her side. They sat down on the grass next to Lucky and the three dogs watched the Pack go about its business. Daisy, Dart, and Spring were on patrol while Bruno, Mickey, and Snap formed a hunting party. The hunt-dogs greeted Lucky and the others as they passed.

Mickey's tail was wagging. "I'm still so happy you're back, Lucky. You too, Martha and . . . erm . . . Storm." He spoke *Storm* quietly, with a furtive look over his shoulder.

"Yes, it's great to have you here," agreed Snap. "Storm, you've really grown." Unlike Mickey, her use of the Fierce Dog's adult name was bold and unapologetic. Storm's tail wagged and her tongue lolled, clearly thrilled.

Lucky was thoughtful. *They're defying Alpha. Is his hold on the Pack loosening?*

When the hunt-dogs and patrol party had left, Storm turned to Lucky and Martha.

"They like my name. They think I should use it!" she yipped.

Martha looked thoughtful. "Alpha said the ceremony wasn't done right."

"But Snap's a real Wild Dog, and she didn't care about that," Storm pointed out. "Maybe it doesn't matter. What does Alpha really know about Naming Ceremonies? He's not even a proper dog!"

Lucky's belly felt tight and he glanced around. What if she was overheard? Talk like that was enough to see Storm thrown out of the Pack. "Be careful, little one," he urged quietly. "You don't want to get on the wrong side of Alpha."

"I'm already on his wrong side," growled Storm. "Maybe *he* doesn't want to get on *mine*."

By the time the Pack gathered in the clearing between the trees the Sun-Dog was sinking. Lucky licked his chops, looking forward to his share of the prey.

As the hunt-dogs took their positions in the Pack order, Lucky noticed that none of them looked very happy. Bruno's ears had rolled back, and standing next to Lucky, Mickey's head was bowed and his tail sagged. Then Lucky understood why. The store of prey brought out by Sunshine was meager, just a couple of mice and a skinny pigeon. Lucky could see the hungry faces of his Packmates as their eyes fixed on the prey. They would all be thinking the same thing. *That's scarcely a mouthful each. . . .*

"Is this it?" he whispered to Mickey.

The Farm Dog was glum. "That's all we could find today. It's Ice Wind—food is becoming scarce."

Sunshine scrambled to position beside Whine as Alpha strutted toward the prey, sniffed it briefly, and wolfed down the mice. *Both of them.*

Lucky looked on in disgust. The dog-wolf had left almost nothing for the rest of the Pack. The scrawny pigeon wouldn't go far. He watched as each dog took the small portion that was their due. Alpha presided, looking coolly down his wolfish snout before turning away to lick his paws.

By the time the pigeon reached Sunshine, there was almost nothing left. The Omega chewed on her scraps, sucking the spindly bones.

Lucky drifted to her side. "Has it been like this every day?"

"Not every day . . ." Sunshine scooped up a bone and crunched it down with a wince. "But it's getting worse. It's Ice Wind, you know. There isn't much prey about."

Lucky frowned. Now he was close to Sunshine, he could see that under her thatch of graying fur she was painfully thin. "But it should be shared more fairly."

"It's the way of the Pack," she sighed. "It has to be like this."
Her eyes flicked to Alpha, who was still washing his paws and
looking out over the valley. She continued, voice lowered, "But
sometimes . . . sometimes I wish I was back in my longpaw's house,
with two big bowls of food every day, and a warm bed too." She
shook her fur. "No, that's silly. I'm a Pack Dog now." She spoke
with a forced cheerfulness. "I just hope you catch lots of delicious
prey tomorrow!"

The Moon-Dog rose over the sky, round and full.

Alpha rose. "We thank the Earth-Dog for her generous
bounty."

Generous? thought Lucky, but he knew better than to say anything. He was as silent as the other dogs as Alpha introduced the
Great Howl.

As Lucky's voice rose with his Packmates, he felt his bitter-
ness toward Alpha drain away. Spirit Dogs danced before his eyes,
those brave, cunning dogs who understood all things, and were
connected to the earth, the sky, and the water. Lucky howled in
thanks to Forest-Dog, who always watched over him, even in the
places where trees feared to grow. He thanked the Sky-Dogs for
the air that had carried the Pack's scent to the rescue party and

allowed them to return to their friends. Finally he thanked Earth-Dog, who had delivered them from the cave. He asked her to take care of Fiery's spirit.

Please look after that brave, noble dog.

Lucky's belly tingled with hunger and his head felt light. He lowered himself onto the ground, his limbs trembling. For a moment, all he saw was a dazzling white light. Then he glimpsed Fiery racing over the valley beyond the trees. When Fiery's image faded, the world around Lucky grew cold. As he looked about he could no longer see the Pack or the circle of trees. Snow sprawled over the land, painting it silver in the light of the Moon-Dog. Surprised, Lucky scrambled to his paws and backed away, his pads crunching on the freezing ground. An icy wind clawed at the fur along his back and he turned to see a frosty plain. A frozen river snaked through it, its surface shimmering with white light. The furs bristled on Lucky's muzzle. Growling, he saw a dark smudge swelling along the edge of the frozen river and caught the metallic scent of blood.

His stomach heaved. Blood ran over the river and sank into the snow. Lucky's ears pricked. Paws were thundering over the plain, coming closer. In the distance he saw dogs. They charged over the snow, howling and snarling, their glossy coats streaked with blood. Fierce Dogs!

A yelp came from behind him, and Lucky turned to see Bella, Sweet, and Storm. They were pounding over the snow, making for the Fierce Dogs, their lips pulled back and fangs bared. Mickey and Martha were close behind them, followed by Bruno, Snap, and Daisy. Where was the rest of the Pack? Where was Alpha?

The Fierce Dogs sprinted past Lucky as though he was invisible, and rushed up to his Packmates. They fell into a line, square heads dropped as they snarled, their lips bubbling with spit. The Wild Dogs backed into one another, outnumbered.

"They've surrounded us!" barked Bella. "There are too many of them!"

Moon threw herself in front of her terrified pups. "We have to run!"

Bruno's breath heaved and the old dog trembled. "We'll never make it!"

Two wild-eyed attack-dogs sprang at Storm, throwing her to the ground. Lucky's heart hammered as he ran to her aid. He heard a crazed whirring overhead and his eyes shot up. The air was spinning! A furious wind twisted down from the clouds, churning up the snow-covered earth. It slapped Lucky back and sent him tumbling.

"Bella! Storm!" he barked, but the wind swallowed his voice.

I can't get past it! I can't help them!

Every time Lucky tried to run to his Packmates, the swirling white wind threw him back. Squinting against it, Lucky watched in horror as the dogs barked and sprang at one another, their fangs gnashing wildly. Sunshine cried out and Daisy whimpered with fear. He saw Mickey round back before launching himself at Mace. The attack-dog gripped him by the neck and threw him against the snow.

Mickey's white paws flailed and he threw back his head with a piercing howl.

Lucky was sick with fear. He ran at the twisting wind and fell back in despair. Then his eyes fell on Sweet. She was fighting Blade, her teeth bared. Sweet was slimmer than the muscular Fierce Dog Alpha, but she was faster on her paws. The two dogs wrestled, snapping at the air, before Sweet leaped back. Blade launched herself at the swift-dog with open fangs and Sweet ducked, jabbing at the Fierce Dog's flank with her teeth before twisting out of reach. Lucky watched, overwhelmed. Sweet was so determined, so brave . . . Then he spotted Dagger, the lighter-furred Fierce Dog. He was creeping up behind Sweet, edging around a mound of snow.

She can't fight both of them. I have to help her!

Lucky lunged forward with all his might, but the spinning white cloud batted him back, tossing him into the air as though he were as light as a leaf. For a moment the world was a haze of white before Lucky dropped down onto his back with a thud. A twinge shot through his limbs and the air was knocked out of his chest. His eyes clenched shut as he fought to regain his breath.

The Storm of Dogs . . . It's coming . . . It's almost here!

He opened his eyes. At first he saw only the swirling white cloud overhead. Then a dark shape loomed into view—a pitch-black dog, as large as a loudcage, her eyes as white as snow and as cold as ice. Her stare pierced through Lucky and he shook with terror, but he couldn't look away. The black dog's huge fangs spread wide and she howled so loudly that Lucky thought the sky was ripping open. The metallic smell of blood returned, but it was closer now. His own blood.

"Lucky? Is that you?"

He could just hear Sweet's voice beyond the screeching howl but he couldn't see her. The black dog was expanding—her great shoulders blocked out the sky. Her tail swept away the swirling white wind until there was only darkness.

CHAPTER ELEVEN

Lucky could hear a mumble of voices overhead. *The Sky-Dogs...* Had they hushed the great dog with the piercing white eyes?

He blinked, confused. *No, not the Sky-Dogs.* It was his own Pack, crowding around him, whispering and yapping.

"Passed out..."

"Slumped on his side..."

"Must be sick..."

Lucky clamped his eyes shut. His head was screaming like a couple of sharpclaws were fighting in there. Foul chunks rose in his throat and he swallowed them down with a grimace.

When he opened his eyes again, Alpha was looming over him. The half wolf's head was lowered and slightly cocked.

Lucky watched him woozily. *Pull yourself together. It was just a bad dream.* But why had he fallen asleep in the middle of the Great Howl?

Alpha's yellow eyes were narrowed. Lucky's instinct told him to flatten his tail around his flank. He blinked, taking in the surprised looks of his Packmates. Daisy exchanged glances with Mickey as Whine's eyes bulged in his squashed face. Lucky lapped his nose with his tongue. *How long was I out? Did I yelp in my sleep?* His fur tingled with shame.

Sweet stepped past Alpha and lowered her head, nuzzling Lucky's neck. "You should take a moment to get yourself together."

The smell of her fur relaxed him, and the fighting sharpclaws in his mind grew still. Lucky nodded, rolling onto his paws. For a moment his head was foggy, but the dizziness passed and he trod slowly between his Packmates, careful to avoid Alpha's yellow gaze without lowering his own. No dog spoke as he left the camp and walked through the long grass, winding between the trees toward the pond.

Down by the water there was only the sound of wind rustling the leaves. Lucky paused at the edge, catching his reflection in the moonlight. His ears hung low; his face looked gaunt. His eyes swam in front of him, two dark hollows.

This is just what Alpha wants. . . . I look like a fool in front of the whole Pack. What sort of dog sees visions—ones so powerful that they frighten him to sleep? Why did it happen? Was it hunger, or exhaustion?

He turned to the grass bank, where he flopped on his belly. He rested his muzzle on his forepaws, taking deep, calming breaths.

He heard the soft pad of paws over grass and looked up to see Sweet. Her body was a slim silhouette in the moonlight. On impulse Lucky straightened up. He couldn't let her see him so feeble and confused. His head felt light and he sank down again.

"Are you okay?" she asked softly. "What happened, Lucky?"

Her voice was so gentle and full of kindness that he yearned to confide in her. Lucky cast his eyes around into the thickening darkness. They were alone. "I had visions tonight."

Sweet dipped her head in acknowledgment. "It isn't the first time, but you've never reacted like that."

Lucky swallowed. He had always been honest with her—even more so than with his own litter-sister. "It was different this time. More intense. Almost *real* . . ."

Sweet sat in front of him with a worried tilt of the head. "Like a nightmare."

"Worse than a nightmare. More like a bad memory—a memory of something that hasn't happened yet."

The swift-dog shook her head and her tail tapped the grass. "A memory? Of something that hasn't happened? That isn't possible, Lucky." She lay down beside him with a sigh. Lucky shut his eyes a moment, enjoying the warmth of her body against his flank. He still remembered her in the Trap House, so frightened and skittish. Here she was strong, and it was his turn to be weak. He longed to reach out to her, to lick her nose, but he held back, ashamed.

"I guess I'm not doing that well," he confessed, mumbling into the grass. "I used to be independent. When you met me, I was a Lone Dog. I never wanted to be a Pack Dog."

"I know that, Lucky."

He met her gaze in the silvery light of Moon-Dog. "But something changed. I guess I'm *glad* to be in a Pack. I didn't expect that...."

"That's natural," Sweet assured him.

"Maybe. But it's strange, at least for the Lone Dog in me. I don't know who I am anymore. It's awful to think that I might not have survived the Big Growl on my own, without a Pack. I took so much pride in relying on my own wits, but that's gone now. Since the Big Growl, I have needed others. That's when the world changed and my visions began. I've been glad of it—the Pack—glad to be part of it. But it's caused me heartache too. I've found myself in situations where I don't know what to do, like in the Dog-Garden. Mickey and I couldn't leave Storm and her littermates. But taking them with us has caused so many problems."

"The world changed for all of us," Sweet soothed. "We wouldn't have survived without one another. I couldn't have even escaped the Trap House without you."

Lucky's whiskers tingled with gratitude.

"It's all so uncertain," he whined. He caught himself, and his tail slumped with shame. "It scares me."

Sweet's nose quivered with each breath. *Why am I telling her this? I should try to look calm and brave.*

He lowered his voice, holding her gaze. "Sweet, Fiery was going to challenge Alpha before he was caught by the yellow long-paws. They would have fought for leadership. Fiery would have made a good leader. He wasn't afraid to put himself forward, to take risks. And the Pack liked him. . . . He was fair."

Sweet's tongue lapped at her nose and she blinked nervously. "We shouldn't be talking like this," she whispered.

Lucky lowered his voice. "But it's true," he went on. "Alpha is a strong leader, but he sets dogs up against one another. It's cruel the way that dogs are ranked, with the Omega and others at the bottom of the heap having so little to eat. Sunshine is practically starving. We're supposed to be a Pack, to look out for one another."

Sweet sighed. "I know how you feel about it, but that's just the way things are. That's how it works in a wild Pack, and it wouldn't have changed under Fiery. Every dog has a role; it's how we all feel secure."

Lucky's eyes widened. "But, Sweet, it doesn't have to be like that. And do you really think that the lower-ranking dogs feel secure? They're anxious not to upset any dog, and they're always hungry. I'm worried about Sunshine. She's so thin. Even high-ranking dogs need to watch their backs in case they upset Alpha. If every dog has a role, shouldn't every dog be rewarded? Why not share things more equally?" Lucky's headache had faded and he felt more himself, more alive, than he had in ages. His fur rippled in the cool air and his whiskers tingled with excitement. "You would make every dog count . . . if you challenged Alpha."

Sweet gasped. She glanced warily into the darkness surrounding them. "*Me?*"

"You could do it, Sweet. You're strong. You could beat Alpha, but more importantly, you could lead the Pack. The dogs trust you."

Sweet stayed silent but Lucky caught the silhouette of her tail as it thumped the ground. Her eyes twinkled in the moonlight. Then she rested her head against his neck and closed her eyes.

Lucky's heart gave a leap of happiness as he breathed in her sweet, warm scent.

After a moment, the swift-dog rose to her paws with a stretch. "We should get back to the others. Are you okay now?"

Lucky stood, feeling better. They paused, side by side, gazing at their reflections in the moonlit pond. This time, Lucky had no impulse to look away.

He trod after Sweet as she made her way through the long grass. As they reached the trees, he threw a last, lingering look at the pond. Light glanced over the surface. Turning back to Sweet, he caught a shadow shifting between the trees. He thought he saw a pair of long ears and the hint of a gray pelt. Was Alpha there? Had he been watching? *Even if he saw us, he couldn't have caught what we'd been saying. We were so quiet.* But as Lucky followed Sweet back to the camp, he wondered about Alpha's wolfish hearing. The fur rose along the back of Lucky's neck. Didn't the half wolf hear more than other dogs?

When Lucky awoke the next sunup, he couldn't remember his dreams. He was thankful not to have experienced more visions in the night. He stretched in the bright sun of Ice Wind and rolled onto his paws. Most of the Pack had already risen. He could see

Martha with Mickey, Bella, and Storm. Snap was setting out on a hunt with Bruno. Moon was washing Beetle's and Thorn's ears as they tried to protest.

Lucky's glance trailed over the clearing between the trees till he spotted Sweet. His tail gave a thump of pleasure. Then he noticed Dart and Spring, who were facing the swift-dog, their muzzles tense.

He padded toward them. He caught the end of Spring's words.

" . . . like Lucky said, they're only in the town. They could get here in a couple of days, maybe less. . . ."

Sweet looked resolute. "We can defend ourselves."

"But how?" whined Dart. "The camp is so open. Blade and her Pack could take us by surprise. The wind charges back and forth like a mad dog. Can we trust that we'll smell or hear them coming?" The hunt-dog's ears were low, and her eyes seized on Lucky as he approached. She turned to address him. "Isn't that right? The Fierce Dogs could come here!" Her voice rose sharply, drawing the attention of her Packmates, who padded closer. Lucky spotted Alpha sloping between two trees. The dog-wolf paused, his head low and watchful.

Dart grew more emphatic. "You remember Blade, don't you? She could rip a dog's head off with her teeth!"

The Pack started barking fretfully.

"Quiet!" howled Alpha.

The dogs jumped, turning to look at the half dog. He strode between them, his tail stiff behind him. Lucky licked his nose uneasily as Alpha raised his wolfish muzzle. "It is a leader's job to think and say the things that other dogs fear to." His yellow eyes darted between the dogs as they each looked down, unwilling to meet his gaze. "Dart and Spring are right to be worried."

There was a murmur of fear from the Pack. Moon stepped back, gathering Beetle and Thorn close to her.

The dog-wolf continued. "I have given the situation some thought. Right now, we are vulnerable. Not because we are open to attack. Not because of the camp. Not because of the wind. *Because of Lick.*"

Lucky's lip curled back and a growl caught in his throat. He caught Sweet's eye. She shot him a warning look. The swift-dog was right. *If I challenge Alpha now, in front of the whole Pack, it'll just make matters worse.*

Storm broke from her Packmates before any dog could stop her.

"My name isn't Lick anymore!" she snarled. "No other dog seems to have a problem with that!"

Mickey threw Snap a guilty look as Alpha's yellow eyes

narrowed. The dog-wolf turned not to Storm, but to the other dogs. In contrast to the young Fierce Dog, his voice was silky. "See how aggressive she gets, and how quickly?" He strutted past, towering over her. "A dangerous temperament, and trouble will doubtless follow. The Fierce Dogs wouldn't even know about us if it weren't for her. They say that *Lick* belongs with them, and they aren't going to stop until they bring her back to her Pack." Alpha sat, staring down his wolfish snout. "With this Fierce Dog walking among us, we will never be safe. How long do you want to keep looking over your tails?" He turned to Dart and Spring. "Wouldn't it be nice to live without fear?" His cool eyes fell on Moon, who licked Beetle's ear with a whine.

Lucky felt like he'd swallowed a mouthful of sand. His throat was dry and scratchy. He had to speak. If he didn't, Storm might— and if that happened, things would get worse.

"If you're so sure an attack will come, the best thing to do is to make sure the Pack is protected." Lucky looked over the dogs to the green valley and the cliff face beyond. "This is a good camp, but it could be better—the first thing we need is to feed ourselves so we have strength. After that, we can post Patrol Dogs at the edge of the cliff at all times, to keep watch over the beach and the passage through the cave. We should post another patrol by the

SURVIVORS: THE ENDLESS LAKE

bank of the pond to guard against enemies coming from behind."

"That's a good idea," agreed Bella, who had been listening in silence.

"We have plenty of dogs." Snap nodded. "It wouldn't be hard to set up the patrols." Lucky felt proud of his Packmates—immediately they were forming strategies.

Alpha turned angrily on them. "Have you all forgotten who your Alpha is?" he snarled. He sprang around, slamming his forepaws against Lucky, who tumbled to the ground with a gasp. "I won't have this City Dog making our defensive plans!" Alpha snarled. "What can he know about anything? And it doesn't count for a thing. It's another lie. He knows you're in danger, but he doesn't care; he'll do anything for his little beast, his own trained Fierce Dog!"

Storm lowered her head, growling.

Lucky bristled and threw Alpha off him. He didn't fight back—that would have been suicide. Instead he climbed to his paws and shook his fur.

Alpha glared around the Pack. "You should prepare yourself. Today you are all going hunting!"

"Even Patrol Dogs?" asked Dart in a small voice.

Alpha slammed one wolfish paw onto the grass. "*Every dog!*

That means Patrol Dogs, pups . . . even Omega." He stalked off angrily, shoving between Mickey and Martha.

Sunshine stared after him, tilting her head nervously. "I haven't hunted since it was just the Leashed Pack," she murmured.

Lucky hurried to Storm's side. The young dog's flanks were heaving. He nuzzled her neck, doing his best to comfort her. Rage leaped off her fur.

"Don't listen to Alpha; you're not going anywhere."

"Alpha!" she snarled, gnashing her teeth. "He'd better stop picking on me! I'm not some silly milk-pup—I'm old enough to challenge him. I don't want to be Alpha, but I'd love to sink my teeth into that gray fur. I'd rip out his throat so he could never insult me again!"

Lucky shrank back, his fur on end. So much fury. Storm was right: She wasn't a little pup anymore. If Alpha kept provoking her, it would lead to a fight.

A fight that would end in bloodshed.

Alpha's doing this on purpose, he thought. *He's dividing the dogs by picking on Storm. And a Pack divided can't win any fight.*

CHAPTER TWELVE

Clouds were gathering over the cliffs as the dogs set out on the hunt. Alpha took the lead and Lucky dropped back, watching Sweet and Snap as they strode after the wolf-dog. His belly rumbled with hunger. The other dogs must have been feeling it too, but Bella made a good show of cheerfulness as she trotted up to Lucky and nudged him with her muzzle.

He let her pass—he could see the dogs at the rear of the Pack were struggling and he wanted to keep an eye on them. Whine was already panting heavily, scrabbling along on his stumpy legs. Sunshine had the added disadvantage of her long, disheveled coat, which swept up dirt and twigs. Lucky fell into step alongside her, giving her soft ears a lick.

The dogs wound their way over the far side of the territory, where the grass grew patchy and the trees vanished. The earth beneath their paws turned yellow and grainy, thinning into sand.

It stopped abruptly at a new outcrop of rocks and white cliffs. The Pack avoided the cliffs, skirting around them and down toward the wide bank of the Endless Lake.

Sunshine tripped over the sand. "It's so hard to walk on this!" she whined to Lucky. "I feel like I'm sinking."

A short distance ahead, Spring inspected a forepaw. "Me too."

Pausing next to the floppy-eared dog, Dart ran her eyes up the white cliffs. "Up there, on the rocks, it's hard on the paws. But at least it's easier to walk."

Lucky plodded behind them in silence. *They're moving so slowly, and making so much noise. We'll never catch any prey this way. . . .*

Bella must have overheard as she turned back, her tail wagging cheerfully. "You'll get used to it. Soon you'll love running over it."

"How can a dog *run* on this crumbly yellow earth?" Dart growled. "It's impossible; you'd just fall over. I don't know how we're supposed to catch prey here."

Lucky suspected that she'd struggle to catch prey anyway, being a Patrol Dog and not used to hunting, but he thought better of saying so.

"It's easy!" barked Bella, her tail lashing the air. She trotted forward, drawing up her legs and taking prancing strides over the sand—something between walking and jumping. Lucky gave an amused whine at the sight, but the dogs all stopped to look, cocking their heads.

Dart's ears pricked up and she rose up tall, imitating Bella's jaunty steps. Spring tried it too. Soon Mickey, Daisy, and even old Bruno were doing their best to copy Bella's movements over the sand. Lucky could feel his spirits lifting. They all looked a bit crazy prancing about like that, but he was impressed that they were giving it a try. Even Storm did her best to take light, hopping steps, her ears flying and flopping.

"Stop this at once!" Alpha had turned and was glaring at the dogs, who tumbled down onto the sand. The half wolf shook his gray fur. "This is no way to be carrying on." His cool yellow eyes rested on Storm as he continued. "Dogs *walk*; they don't leap about like that!"

The Pack fell into line behind Alpha, abandoning Bella's prancing technique. They waded over the soft ground as it sank uncomfortably underfoot. The Endless Lake rolled over the damp bank and peeled off the sand, fanning plumes of white froth. Its sharp, salty stench rose on the air. It was so strong that Lucky thought he could actually *taste* the salt in his mouth.

He looked doubtfully at the dog-wolf, wondering how they were expected to feed the Pack in this environment. *How are we supposed to sense prey under all this salt?*

The frosty wind was rising, and clouds were weaving together in a heavy veil, growing darker. Their damp pelt blocked out the light of the Sun-Dog. Was it about to rain? Lucky paused, his nostrils pulsing. He tried to detect water overhead, but could smell nothing through the salty wind rising off the Endless Lake.

Sweet was ahead of him, at Alpha's side, but still within earshot. "The Sky-Dogs are grouping. We need cover," she told the dog-wolf.

She was right. Standing several dog-lengths behind, Lucky squinted at the long, sandy bank and the jumble of rocks at the base of the cliffs. They would need to find shelter when the rain came. He had scarcely had time to think this when a droplet of icy water splashed on his snout.

Ahead of Lucky, Alpha nodded at Sweet. "We'll wait under that rock until it passes," he grunted. The half wolf made for a low-hanging white rock just as the clouds shook out their heavy pelts. The Pack hurried after him, jostling beneath the shelter that was only just large enough to cover them all. Lucky squeezed in between Storm, Mickey, and Martha. He did a quick head count, running his eyes over the dogs beneath the rock. The Pack were all there, but they weren't all comfortable. Crouching at the edge of the shelter, Sunshine's hindquarters looked like they were growing wet.

"Get a bit closer," whined Lucky. "Let Sunshine have more room."

The dogs started pressing together. Lucky could feel Mickey shivering alongside him.

At the deepest point of the shelter, farthest from the rain, Alpha snapped back. "You don't give orders, City Dog! The Omega is fine where she is."

Sunshine cringed and she dipped her head.

Lucky's lip twitched, but he controlled his temper. *Poor Sunshine—this has nothing to do with her. Alpha just wants to get at me.*

But the little Omega didn't answer back, sinking down onto her paws with a sigh. Water tumbled down from the sky and she gazed up at it with her dark, shiny eyes.

Lucky couldn't bear to look at her. His gaze drifted to the bank of the Endless Lake. The rain fell in gray sheets, running into the sand and melding into the white-topped waves.

This isn't right. Sunshine is a Pack Dog, just like the rest of us. She shouldn't be treated like this. As Lucky looked away, his eyes met Sweet's. He thought he saw some sadness there, some doubt. *She doesn't agree with this either. Alpha's a bully; he's not being fair. It doesn't have to be like this!*

There was another way; Lucky felt sure of it. Maybe Sweet was beginning to see it at last.

When the rain finally began to peter out, it felt to Lucky as though a whole day had passed. His tummy churned with hunger and he raised his muzzle, peering over the other dogs. He was surprised to see the Sun-Dog staring back at him from between the clouds.

The dogs rolled onto their paws, stepping out from under the rock to stretch. The air was cool and fresh, a little less salty than before the rain.

Alpha trod between the Pack, his whiskers twitching as he sniffed the damp air. "We should turn back now and try again tomorrow."

Moon's blue eyes were wide. "Now?" she barked anxiously. "Without a single piece of prey?" She glanced at Beetle and Thorn, who were play fighting by her side. "But we're all hungry."

Daisy was nibbling at her white-and-tan fur. Her ears pricked up. "It's true!" she yipped. She took a deep breath and stepped forward, addressing Alpha. "I know it's not my place to speak . . . but . . . it's okay for *some* members of the Pack, who have a steady diet and all the best pickings. Other dogs are going hungry. . . . Whine and Sunshine are getting weak, and the rest of us will too if we don't find something to eat soon."

Whine gave a little whimper. Lucky found he felt sorry for the wrinkly-faced dog, even though he'd been so nasty when Lucky was Omega. Whine was different from how he had been in the forest and the old camp. The rolls of fur hung more loosely and his coat was dirty and drab. His eyes oozed liquid and his nose looked runny. He didn't seem to care about anything as he hung back from the others, tapping the wet sand with a forepaw.

Alpha's lip curled back and he took a step toward Daisy, towering over the little terrier. "It's the Alpha's *job* to stay strong," he snapped. "For the sake of the Pack!"

Daisy flinched but her paws stayed planted to the ground. A murmur of sympathy rose from the Pack.

"The dogs are hungry," said Martha gently. "We need to find more food."

Bella nodded her golden head. "And if we can't feed ourselves, we won't be able to defend the camp. We *saw* the Fierce Dogs in the town. They're close—they could reach us within a day. If we don't get stronger we can't stay in this area!"

There were whines and yaps from the Pack, and Alpha spun around, his eyes flashing. He dropped his head and took a threatening step toward Bella, who backed away. "I'm well aware of that," he snarled. "And we might have found some food and gotten out of here if you knew what you were doing. Half of you couldn't catch your own tails, and all your yapping would scare a rabbit at a hundred paces." He prowled between the dogs, his wolfish tail rising before he stopped with a decisive thud of his forepaw. "I will send our best hunters to the cliffs to find food. The rest of you should head back to the camp." He blinked up at the sky, which was growing clearer. "For all your whines and complaints, don't you realize it's the rain that kept the prey hidden? Now that it's passed, the prey-creatures will start to come out."

Lucky's tail stiffened irritably. *He's making excuses for his own mistake in bringing us to this barren place. And he isn't dealing with Bella's point. The Fierce Dogs are far too close. . . .*

Alpha dropped his head and his eyes narrowed. "Lucky will go with Snap and Mickey. They are to bring back prey for the Pack to eat—and a white rabbit. The rest of us will relax, and get our strength back. We have a long journey ahead of us."

Lucky gave a curious whine. "Why do you want the rabbit?" He knew the answer. . . . It was for Storm. *He won't accept that she's already named,* he thought with a wrinkle of annoyance. Well, at least this would make things official. He gave Storm an encouraging nod. *And it sounds like he's preparing the Pack to leave the camp.* At least the wolf-dog seemed to be taking their worries seriously.

"Something came to me in a dream last night," Alpha replied with a wicked glint in his yellow eyes. "A way to make sure the Pack needn't worry about Lick in the future."

Storm cringed at this use of her pup name as Alpha continued. "We should have a *real* Naming Ceremony, conducted by the Pack's *Alpha*. That is the right way to do things."

"But I already have a name," Storm protested.

Alpha snorted, turning back to the cliffs and starting along the path to the camp.

Storm's haunches rose and her lips curled back. Lucky hurried to her side, recalling for a moment the image of whirring snow and fighting dogs from his vision at the Great Howl. His fur rose on end and his heart quickened in his chest. If she spoke out now, it would lead to trouble.

"This could actually be a good thing," Lucky whispered.

"How is it good?" Storm snarled, glaring at Alpha's back.

"It's good if it means he accepts you and stops giving you a hard time. The whole Pack will take part in your Naming Ceremony, and it'll all be official. In a way, it's the right thing to do."

"I guess so," she grunted, her eyes firmly fixed on the dog-wolf. "But I don't trust him. Nothing he does is *right*. And one of these days, some dog will teach him a lesson." Drool bubbled at her lips and she ran a pink tongue over her teeth.

"Lucky, are you coming?" asked Mickey, wagging his black-and-white tail.

Lucky followed the Farm Dog and Snap as they set out on their hunting expedition. But he couldn't shake the memory of Storm's bubbling lips, or the fury he'd heard in her voice.

Lucky's foreleg was throbbing again as he pounded up the rocky incline behind Snap and Mickey. His paws slipped on the wet ground and it was an effort to keep upright. He stayed away from the cliff face, doing his best not to think about the steep descent down to the sand and the Endless Lake that crashed and churned relentlessly. He was relieved when Snap and Mickey ducked behind a large rock.

The three dogs crouched in silence, their muzzles trembling and their ears pricked. Lucky concentrated on picking out the scents of prey from the damp, salty wind. *Alpha's right: There are creatures emerging from their hiding places.* Lucky detected warmth and a prickle of sweet, oily skin. It was far away, though. Too far to chase.

Snap shifted from paw to paw. "I doubt there'll be any rabbits up here—there's nowhere for them to burrow."

Lucky thought this was probably true. He wondered if Alpha's talk of a ceremony for Storm was dishonest, a way to mislead the young dog and toy with others in the Pack. *I wouldn't put it past the crafty half wolf.*

Snap's head shot up, her nose twitching with excitement. She must have picked up a scent! Lucky sniffed. *An animal, not far away!*

"Slowly," urged Mickey.

Snap nodded. Lucky felt a surge of relief. The tan-and-white mongrel was usually quick to chase—he had expected her to leap out from behind the rock in pursuit of the prey. Down on the ground, if a dog missed its prey in the scramble to hunt it down, it didn't matter—they might end up scurrying past and roll on the ground to right themselves, but it wouldn't be dangerous. Up here they risked charging into a sheer stone wall, or worse, falling off the edge of the cliff.

The prey-scent was drawing closer. The three dogs hung by the rock so they couldn't be seen. Lucky's belly growled with hunger and he licked his lips.

Snap took the lead, creeping around the rock. She turned to Lucky and Mickey with a look that said, *Wait for the signal.* She paused, one forepaw raised, before barking, "Now!" and charging around the rock. Mickey sprang over the center of the rock and Lucky looped around the other side just in time to see Snap slam her forepaws onto a large white bird. It squawked and thrashed, one huge wing flapping while the other jerked more feebly.

The wing must be broken. That's why it didn't fly away. . . .

Mickey fell on the bird, holding it down with his forepaws as Snap closed her teeth around its neck. With a firm shake, the bird was dead.

Lucky sniffed it appreciatively. It was a plump creature, large enough for every dog to have at least a mouthful to eat. He licked his chops, lowering his muzzle, when a flutter of white fur caught his eye.

A rabbit!

Lucky froze. No, there was brown fur too. . . . That wouldn't do for the Moon Pelt. It would certainly do for a meal, though. Lucky charged between the rock crags as the creature zigzagged fearfully. For an instant it seemed to have disappeared. Lucky froze, sniffing the air. *It's close; I can sense it. . . .* He took a cautious step forward and spotted the rabbit by the edge of large rock, twitching. As he moved to pounce he saw a silhouette farther up the cliff, the dark figure of a muscular dog with pointed ears. As

Lucky landed on the squealing rabbit, he looked again but the figure had vanished.

A tremor of fear clutched his chest. *Are the Fierce Dogs tracking us?* He wondered if he should tell his Packmates, but decided against it. *I'm not sure what I saw... and it will only panic them. It sounds like Alpha is preparing to leave the camp. We'll be away from the Fierce Dogs soon.*

The Sun-Dog was drifting low in the sky when Lucky, Mickey, and Snap arrived back at the camp. Alpha threw a disapproving look at the mottled brown-and-white creature as Lucky dropped it at his paws.

"It was the only rabbit the mountain offered," he explained, his throat dry. His limbs ached and he longed to lie down and rest.

"Its belly is white," barked Sweet encouragingly, padding up to Alpha's side.

Alpha's yellow eyes rested on the limp body of the rabbit. He tapped it with a forepaw. "Yes. Maybe it will do—for a Fierce Dog."

Lucky flinched. Several of the dogs were approaching, with Bella and Bruno already in earshot. It was lucky that Storm was too far away, as Alpha's words would have upset her.

Mickey had managed to catch a mountain rat, and together with the white bird there was plenty to go around. The Pack scarfed down the prey with satisfied crunches and slurps. Mickey tore the prey into pieces before stepping back and letting Alpha select the juiciest morsels. Then Sweet took her share and offered the rest to each dog along the hierarchy in turn.

Beetle sighed. "That bird is delicious!"

"New favorite food!" Thorn agreed.

Lucky struggled to share their enthusiasm, thinking of the pointy-eared dog he thought he'd spotted on the jagged cliffs. He tried to reassure himself that he had just imagined it, but another possibility nagged at him. *The Fierce Dogs know we are here.*

A sharp wind rose over the valley. The Sun-Dog bounded into the warmth of his camp beyond the horizon, trailing his burnished tail. Alpha strutted to the center of the Pack, casting a cool eye over Beetle and Thorn.

"Tasty it may be, but it won't fill us up for long."

The young dogs fell silent, the Pack growing watchful. Alpha's voice rose on the cool air. "And if this is the best that the hunters could do, despite shelter and fresh water, there is no use staying in this camp." He scowled at Lucky, Mickey, and Snap.

Lucky's muscles tensed with anger and his hackles rose instinctively, though he did his best to coax them down. *How dare he blame us for not finding more food? I didn't see him out there on the cliff. He was probably snoozing all afternoon.*

The dog-wolf sat, stretching out one hind leg. "We know the Fierce Dogs are in the town. We leave at sunup."

There were whimpers from the Wild Pack.

"Again?" asked Daisy in a small voice.

Whine licked his snub nose and little Sunshine whined.

"Anyone who wants to stay is welcome to wait here for the Fierce Dogs!" snapped Alpha.

Despite his irritation, Lucky agreed with the half wolf. *The Fierce Dogs are too close. We're in danger.*

As the last fizzle of the Sun-Dog's light evaporated on the horizon, the dogs waited for Storm's Naming Ceremony. The young Fierce Dog's tail lashed and she pawed the grass, gazing up at the darkening sky. Lucky watched too. When the Moon-Dog appeared, Lucky's tail sank dejectedly—half of her face was in shadow. She hadn't been full on the night of Storm's previous ceremony, but it hadn't mattered. Tonight was different. *Doesn't Alpha want to do it "properly"?* He looked to the dog-wolf, expecting him to say they would wait. He was surprised when Alpha rose to his paws and addressed Snap and Mickey.

"Bring the rabbit to me."

The hunters scooped up the rabbit as the Pack gathered closer.

Storm's tail stopped wagging and her face grew serious. She licked her chops nervously.

"Hold it down," ordered Alpha.

Snap and Mickey pinned down the creature's head and hind paws. Alpha stepped over it and plunged his fangs into its throat. He skinned the rabbit with a single jerk of his gray head.

These are such lean times, thought Lucky. *I wonder if I could get Sweet to ask him to save the rabbit for the Pack. It seems such a waste not to eat it.* He knew Alpha would never accept the idea if it came from him.

The half wolf sniffed the furless body. "Take it to my den," he growled at Snap. She dutifully gripped the body in her jaws and made for the camp.

Lucky's fur prickled with anger. *He's keeping it for himself!*

Alpha held up the brown-and-white pelt to the low light of the half moon. There was no slab of rock in the grass clearing. Instead he dropped it on a patch of grainy earth. It fell, slightly crumpled, dusted with sand. A clod of soil hung off a patch of white fur.

This isn't right! thought Lucky, remembering the quiet enchantment of Beetle and Thorn's Naming Ceremony. The Moon-Dog had shined brightly and the white rabbit fur had glowed under her light.

Alpha didn't seem to care. He nodded curtly at Storm. "On the rabbit skin, Lick."

Lucky tensed. He watched the young Fierce Dog anxiously, hoping that she wouldn't rise to Alpha's jibes or the taunting gleam in his yellow eyes. He was proud of the dignified way in which she walked toward the skin. She stepped onto it carefully. The rabbit had been skinny, not like the plump ones they'd caught near the forest, and Storm was now so large that her hindquarters covered the whole thing.

"Look at the Moon-Dog and choose your name," growled Alpha, barely sparing her a glance.

Storm gave a confused whine. "But . . . but I already chose my name."

"We haven't got all night!" he snapped impatiently.

Lucky cringed. There was nothing special about this ceremony. It couldn't have been more different from that magical night when Beetle and Thorn had chosen their adult names.

He could see that the young Fierce Dog was trying her best not to show her distress. She licked her lips and looked at the Moon-Dog, whose thin light was partially covered by a bank of ghostly clouds.

When she spoke, her voice was clear and calm. "I choose the name Storm."

Anger flashed across Alpha's face and he slammed down a forepaw. "You can't have that name!" he snarled. "You chose it during a *false* Naming Ceremony. That name is lost to you forever."

Lucky rose to his paws, clenching his teeth against a growl. The half wolf had gone too far this time. *He wants to talk about false Naming Ceremonies? Here, while the Moon-Dog is half-asleep, with the pelt of a brown-and-white rabbit he means to keep for himself, and without a rock for the pup to sit on!*

The dogs exchanged worried looks. Martha made a move toward Storm but was stopped in her tracks by a warning glance from Bella.

Alpha's tail shot out behind him. "Choose a name now, or I will choose one for you!"

Storm swallowed. Lucky could see how hard she was working to stay calm, and his heart swelled with pride. "I choose Storm."

Alpha snorted. He started pacing a slow circle around the seated Fierce Dog. "Very well," he snarled in amusement. Storm bristled as he slipped behind her, but kept her position on the rabbit pelt. When he looped around to face her, his teeth were bared in vindictive triumph. "By the Moon-Dog, as you have foregone the opportunity to choose your own name, *I* will name you, as is my right and duty as the Alpha of this Pack. This name will be yours for the rest of your life, and others must use it when addressing you." At last, he met the Fierce Dog's eyes. "From now on, you will be known as Savage."

CHAPTER THIRTEEN

As the Sun-Dog rose over the valley, the Pack started down to the waterfront. Alpha took the lead, his webbed paws thumping down on the sand and his tail billowing in the wind. Sweet trotted awkwardly at his side. The usually graceful swift-dog struggled to keep her balance on the sinking earth.

Lucky trailed behind them with the rest of the Pack. He yawned, gazing over the Endless Lake. A low mist clung to the water, bleeding into the white-capped drifts. The bank followed the path of the waves as far as the eye could see. The white cliffs hung over the bank, sharp and imposing.

What if it's like this around the next set of cliffs? What if the bank and the water go on forever?

Lucky's thoughts were interrupted by Beetle's excited yapping.

"A bird! Like yesterday!"

"Let's get it!" howled Thorn.

The young dogs eyed the waterbirds that circled overhead. They barked and pounced up toward the sky, gnashing their teeth.

"I'll have you, bird!" Thorn snarled, leaping into the air, only to topple back onto the sand.

Alpha's head snapped around. "Foolish pups! Can't you see that the birds are well out of reach? Keep up, all of you. We can hunt when we reach the next camp."

Beetle winced and Thorn dropped her muzzle dejectedly. Moon hurried to their sides.

Lucky hated to agree with the dog-wolf, but he was right: The dogs would never reach one of those birds. They'd only caught one yesterday because it was injured.

If only he'd send a proper hunting party inland, away from the Endless Lake, where everything's so salty that the grasses and trees can't grow. There's got to be prey to be found somewhere, even in Ice Wind. Lucky resolved to speak about it with Sweet the next time they stopped. Maybe she could convince Alpha to lead the Pack away from the shore of the Endless Lake, beyond the rocks and cliffs. She was the only dog who had a chance of getting through to him. Alpha would listen to Sweet.

Lucky's lip twitched and his back curved, as though preparing to fight. Sweet was Alpha's Beta; he respected her—she had won that privilege in a challenge. Lucky watched the lean swift-dog. She and Alpha were ahead of the others, talking in hushed tones. Lucky's muzzle crinkled. For the first time he admitted to himself that he was uneasy with their relationship. It wasn't unusual for an Alpha and Beta to become mates. . . . He knew that. The thought made his belly crackle with anger and he snorted irritably. *If only Alpha would disappear!*

The dog-wolf spun around. For a horrible moment, Lucky was sure that he'd somehow read his thoughts. Then he realized that Alpha was looking past him, at Storm.

"Keep up, Savage!" he barked, before returning to Sweet.

Storm recoiled as though struck. Lucky hung back. Forgetting his own troubles, he waited for the young dog to catch up.

He gave her an affectionate lick. "We all know that 'ceremony' wasn't a real one," he whispered. "It doesn't count, whatever Alpha says. And he's the only one who uses that . . . *fake* name. He should use your *real* name."

Storm nodded but her dark eyes were downcast.

Lucky licked her ear. "It won't stick because *you're* not savage by nature." He uttered the words with so much conviction, he felt sure, just then, that they were true.

* * *

As the day drew on, the mist thickened over the water. The waves of the Endless Lake lapped closer, climbing over the sand so that the dogs had to creep closer to the rocks. The cliffs had petered out. Beyond the rocks, there were swells of yellow sand and still no sign of greenery or prey.

Lucky plodded at Storm's side in silence. The Pack walked listlessly, working hard to progress over the sand.

A sharp yap made Lucky jump.

It was Daisy. "Look!" Her short tail wagged furiously.

Mickey joined her. "A house!"

Lucky gazed across the mist. He could just make out the contour of a building. If it was a house, it was a tall one, shaped like the trunk of a large tree. It must have been striped red and white, but only the red stripes showed against the mist. Lucky squinted. *It can't be, can it . . . ?* The house seemed to be floating on the Endless Lake. At the very top, the walls seemed to be made of clear-stone.

All the dogs stopped in their tracks. Lucky frowned. *Why is a longpaw house out here, over the lake, so far from a settlement? Don't longpaws usually group together?*

"We need to go there!" barked Daisy, hopping on the spot, prancing forward, and turning to the Pack.

Mickey pawed the ground excitedly. "She's right! There could be longpaws in that house. They might have *food!*"

This was enough to get Sunshine going. "We should see!" she yipped in her shrill voice.

Bella met Lucky's eye, her tail low. She must have been thinking the same thing. *After all this time, are the former Leashed Dogs going to go back to being helpless and dependent on longpaws, like they were before the Big Growl?*

His stomach growled as he remembered what Sunshine had said about her two bowls of food a day. Was it hunger that had awakened this behavior? Lucky was worried about how Alpha would react. What would Sweet think? Would she try to stop them?

Sunshine didn't wait to find out. The little white dog bounded toward the longpaw house with a rush of energy. Her froth of white tail lashed the air as her short paws scrambled over the sand. Lucky had never seen her run so fast. Her pale coat soon vanished in the swirling mist.

It was too much for Mickey and Daisy, who burst after her.

Alpha's face darkened. "Get back here immediately!"

They didn't listen—they sped across the bank of the Endless Lake, making for the red-and-white house as fast as their paws could carry them.

The half wolf fixed Lucky with a stern glare. "I doubt they'll find their precious longpaws in that strange building. I don't care about the Omega—that little white rat we can do without—but the Pack can't afford to lose Mickey or Daisy. Not when it's clear we're short of *competent* hunters." His gaze lingered on Lucky meaningfully. "Get them back, Street Dog! Immediately!"

Lucky flinched, not because of Alpha's insults—he was used to the dog-wolf putting him down. It was the thought of poor Sunshine, who tried so hard to fit in and contribute to the Pack. *Alpha probably doesn't even know her name. To him, she's just Omega.* At least the half wolf was keen to keep the Pack together.

With a nod, Lucky spun around and started after the three former Leashed Dogs.

He heard determined barking behind him. Bella was coming too, and so was Storm. Lucky glanced back to see the rest of the Pack following and felt his tail wag with pride. They were in this together.

The mist curled around the striped house and sprawled over the sand. Lucky could no longer see his friends on the horizon, not even the black patches of Mickey's coat. "Sunshine!" he barked. "Daisy! Mickey! Be careful—you don't know what's out there!"

He scrambled to a halt, spotting some paw marks. He was

surprised to find that they ended at a hardstone road, which seemed to lead over the Endless Lake directly to the house. He caught the excited barking of Daisy and Mickey up ahead.

"This way!" he told Bella and Storm. They hurried along the lake road, overtaking little Sunshine, who had run out of energy. "Stay with the others!" barked Lucky.

Sunshine nodded, panting heavily, her eyes dark circles against the mist.

Lucky and Bella ran on, Storm just behind them. The water of the Endless Lake crashed against the edge of the road, showering them with white foam. It churned and bucked angrily, threatening to rise over the hardstone and pull them into its grip.

Bella froze in her tracks, her eyes wild. "Mickey and Daisy have woken up the lake!" she whined.

Water frothed over Lucky's paws and he fought the fear that was clutching at his belly. He knew he needed to keep the other dogs calm and remembered how it had worked in the tunnels. "It must be the Lake-Dog. . . ."

"The Lake-Dog?" echoed Bella. She clung to the lake road, her haunches trembling.

Lucky nodded. "Remember how the River-Dog is always running? Sometimes she's fast, sometimes she slows down, but she never stops. . . . The Lake-Dog can only run in circles. Remember how we used to dash about, Bella, when we were milk-pups and the longpaws kept us inside? We had so much energy and nowhere to go. . . . Maybe that's what happens to the Lake-Dog. She's just playing a little rough because she's got nowhere to run."

Bella's trembling subsided and she turned to Lucky with a grateful nudge. "That makes sense."

Lucky turned back to Storm, worrying that the young dog would be terrified. She was sniffing the water that hissed over her paws. Lucky noticed with surprise that she didn't seem frightened at all.

Other Pack members appeared behind her, silhouettes in the mist, stopping short of the lake road. Sweet stood panting next to Spring, just ahead of Alpha and Moon. The dogs stopped, their ears flat, watching the foam break over the road.

The others aren't coming, Lucky realized. It would be down to the three of them to get Mickey and Daisy back.

They stalked along the lake road, proceeding more slowly. At the end of the lake road they reached a narrow path, which looped around the house. This close up it was enormous, towering over them in red and white. Mist rolled over the Endless Lake in banks, curling thickly around the trunk of the building.

Why did the longpaws build this place out in the middle of the lake? Lucky couldn't see any other houses nearby. He peered up at the house and saw a dark clear-stone lookout at the top. It didn't make sense.

The three dogs trod through the mist, calling out to their friends. Lucky noticed that the path around the house was surrounded by a jumble of huge rocks. Waves dashed against them, exploding in billows of froth.

Bella flinched as she took them in, her tail curling around her flank. "Mickey? Daisy? Come back; it's dangerous here."

"Bella?" The Farm Dog stepped out of the mist, shaking his silky fur. Daisy padded behind, looking sheepish.

"We barked," said Mickey. "We scratched our paws on the door.... Why won't the longpaws come out?"

Lucky approached his Leashed friend, giving him an affectionate lick. "Just because there's a house here doesn't mean there are longpaws. You remember that from your Leashed Dog days, don't you?" He cocked his head at the large house. This close he saw it was round, without corners, like a tree trunk—but unlike a tree it was perfectly smooth. The red-and-white stripes were large, each a dog-length in width. It was a strange sort of house. "I don't think a longpaw would live here.... Even before the Big Growl, they must have had some other use for this place. Longpaws like to be near one another and the house is so . . ." He struggled to find the word.

"Lonely . . ." whined Mickey, his tail slumping dejectedly. "You're right; we were stupid to come here. We shouldn't have run off. Alpha must be furious. . . ."

Daisy wasn't as quick to accept this. "Were we? If even Lucky can't explain what this house is for, how can he know for sure that there aren't any longpaws in there with nice food? We've come this far; we should at least try to get inside and take a look." Her wiry tail wagged hopefully.

"For heaven's sake!" snapped Bella. "There aren't any long-paws here. And even if there were, why would you think they were friendly, after everything we've been through? Have you forgot-ten about Fiery already?"

Daisy whined and her eyes fell. "The yellow longpaws are dif-ferent," she murmured.

Bella puffed out her chest, as though about to continue, but a volley of barks interrupted her.

Lucky's ears pricked up and his head whipped around. He could hear the Wild Pack racing down the lake road, barking in alarm. Why were they coming?

Sweet was the first to appear, her slim outline cast against the misty road. Alpha sprang after her and the other dogs piled in, their eyes wild. They backed into one another, shunting one another in their eagerness to get away from the lake road and the violent waters beyond it.

"What's going on?" barked Lucky. He caught his breath. The fear-scent wafting from his Packmates was almost enough to drive him crazy. He squinted at the road, trying to make out the bank of the Endless Lake. The mist had drawn in again. For a moment the world was buried beneath its soft white pelt. When it lifted, Lucky saw figures slinking over the lake road. They walked in rows, their dark eyes flashing. Their sleek, muscular bodies were stark against the sky.

The Fierce Dogs had arrived.

CHAPTER FOURTEEN

The Wild Pack whined and barked as they backed into one another, jostling to get away from the Fierce Dogs. Thickset Bruno turned abruptly, almost knocking Lucky off his paws. The fear-scent was dizzying. Blood thumped at Lucky's temples and his instincts whined in his ears, telling him to run. But where? The only path away from the house was blocked by the Fierce Dogs. The Endless Lake encircled them, thrashing against the rocks. Lucky doubted even Martha would survive it.

"What are we going to do, Alpha?" barked Bruno. He shook his thick fur, the color of wet sand.

The half wolf didn't answer. He stood frozen to the hardstone ground, staring at the Endless Lake, perhaps wondering, as Lucky had, if he could swim to freedom.

"The water! It's crazy with anger!" whined Daisy. She raised her forepaw over a huge puddle that was spreading over the lake road.

Lucky's ears flicked back. She was right: It was getting worse—rising, just as it had in the cave! His stomach lurched with horror when he thought of how quickly they'd been trapped. How high would the water come? Would it flood over the hardstone road? They couldn't run to land—the Fierce Dogs were on the move again, slinking closer in formation. Where could they go?

The house!

Alpha was still frozen to the spot. It was up to Lucky. "We need to get in the house!" he barked. "There must be a way!"

A clear command was just what the Pack needed. They stopped shunting one another, instead turning to the striped building and scouting frantically along its base. Moon was sniffing and shuffling while little Daisy threw her paws on the wall, looking for a way in.

"There is no way out of this, Street Mutt!" rumbled Blade, rising to her full height on the lake road and glaring at Lucky and the Wild Pack.

Lucky recognized the dogs who flanked her on either side—Mace and Dagger, Blade's deputies, their fur glossier than ever in the damp air. He thought he could make out a smaller dog near the rear of the Pack. *Fang . . . At least he's not up front with Blade, and Storm doesn't have to face him. . . .* Suddenly the Fierce Dogs sprang forward, barking furiously.

"Quickly!" cried Lucky, sprinting around the far side of the striped building. Storm ran alongside him but she shot angry looks over her shoulder.

She wants to fight. . . . He knew that fleeing was against her instincts, but there was no way she could take on so many of her former Packmates.

"Come on, Storm!" he urged.

She snorted but said nothing.

"The door's here!" barked Mickey up ahead. "But it doesn't open!"

Several of the dogs had formed a semicircle around the wooden door. Lucky ran at it, rearing onto his hind legs and slamming his paws against the damp wood. It creaked but held firm. *Maybe if we try it at the same time . . .*

Blade's voice rose from the lake road, growing closer. "Where's that Street Mutt and his mongrel band of rats?"

The Wild Dogs yapped and collided, frenzied with panic. Lucky was lost amid the writhing fur. His paws splashed against the water as the Endless Lake crashed over the rocks. He squeezed himself out of the tussle and looked around urgently. *Where is Alpha? Why isn't he doing anything?* Lucky remembered how the dog-wolf had lost his nerve beneath the black cloud as the Pack had run for the forest. It was happening again!

Storm growled over the panicked yelps. "Lucky, get that door open. I'll hold them!" She started shunting dogs aside with her powerful head, muscling her way to the lake road, where Blade's Pack was marching in formation. Like Storm, they didn't seem to care about the water that leaped over the road.

Lucky could hardly breathe. "No!" he howled, throwing back his muzzle. "Storm, you'll be killed!"

The young Fierce Dog ignored him, squaring up to her old Pack. They were only a few dog-lengths away now, and they towered over her, their muzzles lowered and their haunches raised.

Blade's voice was calm and silky smooth. "Living among these mongrels has ruined you. It's time you were taught a lesson about a Fierce Dog's true nature."

Storm's paws stayed rooted to the hardstone ground. "I don't need any lessons from *you*," she spat. "I know my true nature, and it is nothing like yours." Her lips curled over her sharp white teeth, up over her shiny pink gums. "I will *never* be like you!" she rasped.

Lucky could hardly believe his eyes. Storm was so angry, so self-assured. He saw no sign of fear, weakness, or doubt as she pressed back onto her hindquarters, preparing to pounce. Blade lifted her muzzle and two Fierce Dogs darted at Storm, blocking her path to their Alpha. They snapped at her head and neck, forcing her back along the lake road toward the house.

Storm wasn't going to be stopped so easily. She swiped at the first attack-dog's muzzle, knocking him sideways with a powerful blow and spinning around to sink her fangs into the other's neck fur until the Fierce Dog whined in pain. The first attack-dog regained his balance but held back, suddenly less confident. He threw a glance back at Blade, who glared, lip twitching.

Lucky turned to Bella and Sweet. "We have to find a way into the house! Inside we'll have the advantage—they won't have so many angles of attack. Do everything you can to get that door open!" He searched for Alpha among the tussle of dogs but couldn't make out his wolfish face. "We should go and help her! Bruno, Spring, you too!" Lucky charged forward, trying to look braver than he felt. He threw himself at the nearest Fierce Dog. He knew better than to exchange bites with an attack-dog—he wouldn't last long that way—but if he could drive their Pack toward the edge of the lake path he might awaken their fear of the turbulent waters.

He didn't know much about the Lake-Dog. He wasn't sure she even existed. But he said a few words to her, just in case.

Fearsome Lake-Dog who controls these great waters, please protect us and lead us to safety.

Blade's jibes cut through his thoughts. "Get the Street Mutt and his stinking pet rats!"

Lucky closed his eyes a moment and silently added, *Lake-Dog, we are your friends—please keep us safe. Take a bad dog instead.*

His tail gave a guilty twitch. Was it right to wish destruction on your enemies? Maybe he should have stopped at protecting his friends. Lucky didn't have time to dwell on this thought—the Fierce Dogs were marching toward him. He made as though to spring at Mace. The Fierce Dog reared up, flashing his fangs. As he pounced, Lucky rolled out of reach and slid through a pool of salt water, kicking it into the Fierce Dog's eyes. Mace stumbled back, forcing the front line of his Pack to the far side of the lake road, toward the crashing waves.

"Be careful!" snarled one of the attack-dogs, shoving another Fierce Dog who had fallen against her.

"How dare you talk to me like that!" he snarled.

The mist swirled around them, confusing Lucky's senses. He felt a surge of hope when he spotted Spring and Bruno. They bolted along the near side of the road, slamming their forepaws against the salt pools so they sprayed over the Fierce Dogs. Lucky bounded after them, yapping and twisting, helping to drive the Pack toward the water. Chaos broke out on the lake road as Fierce Dogs leaped back, smacked into one another, and snarled through the mist.

"Stop this immediately!" thundered Blade. "Fierce Dogs, hold your positions! We will *not* be cowed by these mongrels!"

"But, Alpha, we're going to fall into the water!" whined one of the attack-dogs through the mist.

"I don't care if you all drown as long as you're fighting when you go! I will personally slay anyone who runs!" Blade's voice quivered with rage.

The Fierce Dogs stiffened at their Alpha's threats, snapping back to attention. Some made for Lucky, Bruno, and Spring, their teeth gnashing, as others broke toward the rest of the Wild Pack.

Lucky spun around, searching for Storm. He spotted her a few dog-lengths from Blade. The young Fierce Dog stood motionless, staring at her.

A piercing howl cut through the mist. "Savage!"

Lucky could just see Alpha at the far edge of the lake road. His forepaws hung over the hardstone, his hind legs sinking from view beneath a burst of white foam. Lucky's fur stood on end. *He must have backed away from the Fierce Dogs without seeing how close he was to the lake!*

Alpha needed help. Most of the Pack was hidden from view behind the house. Lucky could just hear yelps and whines as they worked to force open the door. He looked about him. Bruno and Spring were busy dodging the attack-dogs. Lucky tried to make a break for it, but Dagger blocked his path. He shot a look over the Fierce Dog's shoulder. Storm was close enough to reach the dog-wolf, but the young dog stayed planted to the ground, ignoring his howls.

"Savage! Savage, help me!" he called, using the name he had chosen for her. The dog-wolf's claws raked the hardstone as he struggled to maintain his grip. He threw a wild look over his shoulder. A great wave was charging over the lake, tumbling toward him. Pressed down on the road, the great dog looked broken—a pathetic tangle of gray fur and pleading eyes. "Savage, please!"

Storm's cool gaze rested on Alpha only for a moment. Then she turned back to Blade, her haunches rising.

"Get the Alpha!" snarled Blade.

Mace bounded toward the dog-wolf, baring his teeth.

"Alpha, I'm coming!" barked Lucky, dodging Dagger and

making for the far edge of the road.

The half wolf didn't seem to hear him. His huge yellow eyes flitted from Blade to Mace. He cringed away from the Fierce Dog deputy, slipping farther off the lake road as the giant wave arrived. It smashed down over the hardstone in a blast of foam.

"Help!" howled Alpha.

The air was a blur and Lucky rubbed his eyes with his forepaws, unable to see beyond his nose. The water drew back with a sigh, gliding toward the heart of the Endless Lake. Lucky trod as quickly as he dared to the edge of the lake road, low on his sodden paws.

Alpha's dark head reared over the froth-streaked ripples.

"Hang on!" barked Lucky.

It was no good. The dog-wolf had already drifted from the edge of the road into open water, out of anyone's reach. Lucky watched in horror as Alpha threw back his head and tried to howl. His voice came out as a strangled gurgle as he sank in a crest of froth.

CHAPTER FIFTEEN

Lucky's jaw slackened with shock. He gazed into the swirling lake, waiting for the half dog to break through the waves and scramble ashore. For a moment he forgot the Fierce Dogs behind him, and the salt water that slapped over the edge of the lake road, drenching his coat. Reeling, he remembered his words for the Lake-Dog: *We are your friends—please keep us safe. Take a bad dog instead.* . . . His thoughts slipped away from him and his head felt light. *I didn't mean Alpha!*

Frenzied barking brought Lucky back to the present. His head snapped around to the center of the misty lake road, where the Fierce Dogs were charging at Bruno and Spring. Spring, true to her name, was doing a great job dodging their lunges. Bruno looked like he was struggling. The gruff old dog growled and gnashed his teeth, but he couldn't move as quickly as Spring, and the Fierce Dogs were closing in on him. Storm was stalking toward Blade, perfectly calm, ignoring the chaos that surrounded her.

"Storm!" barked Lucky. "Bruno! Spring! We need to return to the longpaw house!" *If the Pack has got the door open . . .*

Bruno and Spring didn't need to be told twice. They spun on their heels, making for the striped house.

Storm paused, seeming unwilling to retreat.

"Now!" snapped Lucky, still bewildered by the memory of Alpha sinking into the Endless Lake. He couldn't shake it from his mind. *Stop it!* he told himself. *If the Fierce Dogs catch up with us we'll all end up in the water!* He barked as loudly as he could, his voice cracking. "Storm! *Now!*"

Storm turned with a reluctant growl and ran to Lucky's side. He kept pace with her along the lake road, unwilling to let her drop behind. When she started to turn back to Blade, he nudged her on with his head. "Come on!" he whined.

They slipped over the slick stone. The Fierce Dogs thundered after them, barking. Lucky's forepaw throbbed where he'd hurt it in the cave and his mouth was so dry he felt as though he could hardly breathe. The salty air seemed to suck the moisture from him, despite the water that heaved all around.

The four Wild Dogs scampered along the back of the longpaw house just in time to see Bella and Sweet burst through the wooden door. Lucky shot a look over his shoulder. The Fierce

Dogs were still some dog-lengths away, farther up the lake road. His heart swelled with hope. They might survive this yet!

A huge wave broke against the rocks, crashing over the lake road.

"Fierce Dogs, fall back! Off the lake road!" barked Blade, her voice scarcely audible above the surging water. "This isn't over, City Rat!"

Lucky couldn't worry about the Fierce Dogs right now. With a shudder, he pushed away an image of them lining up on the sand, waiting for the lake water to grow calmer. Alpha had drowned— and the rest of the Pack didn't know it yet. Some dog had to lead them to safety. He had to be brave.

The side of the longpaw house nearest the rocks took the worst of the blow as the huge wave flooded the hardstone. Lucky braced himself as water crashed over him. At first he thought he'd be okay, but the water burst over again and threw him onto his side, sending his legs flying. He opened his mouth to howl but it filled with salt water. He choked with terror. *I can't breathe!* He scrambled to his paws, coughing and spluttering as the water surged back over the rocks.

He heard a panicked whine and saw Sunshine spinning in a pool of water, veering toward the rocks. Martha seized the white dog in her jaws and tugged her to safety. Sweet and Bella lost their footing and slid dangerously near the edge of the path, fighting their way back toward the longpaw house.

Lucky spat out the last of the salt water, shooting an anxious look at the rocks. His stomach clenched. The mist shifted and Lucky saw a giant wave tumble over the Endless Lake, even larger than the last. It was still far in the distance but moving fast, sucking other waves into its path, channeling straight for the longpaw house. They'd all be washed away!

"Sunshine, get inside!" he barked, his voice hoarse.

Sunshine had struggled to her paws. She shot through the open door to the house. Martha, Sweet, and Bella were just behind her.

Lucky paused at the entrance of the striped house. "All of you, get inside—*hurry*!"

Mickey and Daisy obeyed immediately, skidding over the water pools and dashing into the building. Snap, Dart ,and Bruno were right behind them, and Whine scampered as quickly as he could on his stumpy legs.

Lucky licked his lips, unable to get rid of the vile salt taste in his mouth, trying to think if there was anyone he'd missed. Were they all inside now? He ran through the dogs in the Pack: *Sweet, Snap, Bruno, Mickey . . .*

Sweet's elegant face emerged from the doorway. "Where's Alpha?"

Lucky winced, picturing the gray head sinking under the water.

She seemed to understand, lowering her head with a whine.

An anguished howl rose over the sound of the buffeting waves. "My pups!" cried Moon. "Where are my pups?"

Lucky's eyes widened. "They aren't inside?"

Moon shook her white-and-black head.

Lucky turned a panicked circle. "Has anyone seen Spring?"

"The Lake-Dog has taken them!" barked Bella, staring out at the three dark shapes moving in the foaming water by the rocks.

Martha must have overheard. She charged out of the longpaw house with a determined bark and made for the rocks.

"Martha, no!" yelped Sweet.

The water-dog took no heed. She bounded over the rocks, launching herself into the Endless Lake.

Lucky and Sweet ran to the edge of the lake road, where water crashed over the rocks in bursts of spray. Beetle and Thorn bobbed on the surface, their forepaws scrabbling against the frothing water. Martha swam toward them furiously.

Thorn yipped in terror as her litter-brother's head disappeared under a wave.

Moon started scaling the rocks at the end of the lake road.

"No!" barked Sweet. "You can't help them if you drown!"

The Farm Dog hesitated, terror and uncertainty flashing across her ice-blue eyes.

Martha pushed forward with frantic beats of her webbed paws. She plunged her head under the water as Lucky held his breath. A moment later her dark head reappeared, Beetle's scruff clasped in her jaws. She scooped Thorn close with one webbed forepaw and started back toward the rocks.

Lucky, Sweet, and Moon watched as the great water-dog struggled against the pummeling waves. Her eyes were determined as her legs pumped tirelessly. Lucky's belly tightened as the giant wave tumbled closer. *Will the River-Dog protect Martha out here?* he wondered. *The Lake-Dog and River-Dog must be littermates.* That had to be good news. Tension shot through his limbs as he thought of Fang and Storm. Not all littermates were friends. . . .

He pressed his paws up against the rocks, marveling at Martha's resilience. She shunted the pups closer.

"Be careful, Lucky!" whined Sweet as he climbed over the rocks. His paws slipped and he almost cut himself on the rocks' sharp edges, but he managed to keep his position by hunching. Martha bobbed up just beneath him and he craned down as low as he dared. With another wave, the water-dog and the pups were yanked back again, but Martha furrowed her brow and pushed forward until her free forepaw was hooked over a rock.

Lucky ducked his head and waited for the next wave to raise the pups closer. As soon as it did he seized Beetle's neck fur and hauled the sodden pup over the rocks where his desperate Mother-Dog was waiting.

"Lucky!" yelped Martha.

He turned back to the water's edge. Thorn was bravely scrabbling at the rocks, but she wasn't able to scale them. Martha gave her a firm shove and Lucky scooped her up with his teeth.

Sweet helped Moon carry the exhausted young dogs into the house.

Lucky searched for the giant wave in the tumbling mist. There it was, rising above the other waves and charging toward the rocks. It seemed to be picking up speed.

"Martha, you need to get out of there!" barked Lucky.

The huge black dog still floated on the water, panting heavily. She looked too exhausted to climb up the rocks. But instead of trying, she started to turn back to the Endless Lake. Lucky followed her gaze to a mound of black, tan, and white fur.

"Spring needs help!" barked Martha. "I think I can reach her!"

Lucky hovered over the rocks, watching the long-haired dog drift on the current, farther and farther from land. One of her long ears bobbed on the surface. The other curved over her eye, as though in sleep.

Lucky gave an anguished howl. "It's too late! There's nothing you can do—nothing anyone can do. Spring belongs to Earth-Dog now."

"No!" whined Martha, shaking her huge black head. "I won't leave her to be carried away by Lake-Dog. I can't abandon her." She floundered, looking back at Spring's body, not sure what to do.

Lucky's eyes fixed on the giant wave hurtling toward them. "Martha, please come back!" He cocked his head, his ears half-raised. "If you go out there you'll die too. The Pack needs you!"

Martha turned back to him. She hooked her paws onto the rocks, gasping with effort as she dragged herself over them. "Spring is all alone in the water," she whimpered in sorrow. "Lake-Dog took her and now Earth-Dog will never find her. Her dog-spirit will be trapped here—she won't rejoin her ancestors and return to the earth. She'll stay out in the freezing cold forever."

Lucky pressed his muzzle close to Martha's ear. "Earth-Dog

always takes dogs when it's their time," he whined softly. "She will find Spring."

Martha met his eye with a grateful nod. He followed as she trod wearily to the longpaw house. A winding staircase led up from the entrance. Lucky gave a sniff—the rest of the Pack must have gone upstairs. He hoped they would be safe up there.

Lucky heard a roar of water as the giant wave charged over the rocks. "Quickly!" he yelped. He and Martha scampered along the winding stairway as water splashed through the open door. Fear raced down Lucky's spine. *How high will it rise? Is it safe upstairs?*

Water chased at their paws as they bounded up the stairway, but it soon sloshed back. Lucky wasn't taking any chances—he urged Martha on until the stairs came to an end.

There was only one large, circular room at the top of the longpaw house—the one Lucky had spotted with the massive clear-stone window that ran all the way around the wall. There was a clear-stone globe at the entrance of the room, and the Pack huddled around it in fear and shock. They yelped with relief as Lucky and Martha trod inside. The water-dog flopped onto her belly with exhaustion, her breath heaving. Lucky slunk down alongside her.

"Thank goodness!" whined Sweet, rising to lick their noses.

"Where's Alpha?" asked Bruno.

Dart rose to her paws, her brown eyes wide and fretful. "Did you see Spring?"

Lucky lowered his head so it rested against the hard floor. "The Lake-Dog took them."

Silence fell among the stunned dogs. Dart backed toward the wall and curled up in a trembling ball.

"Maybe we shouldn't be here," Storm piped up.

"Would you rather be out on the lake road?" snapped Sweet.

Mickey whined, lowering his head onto his outstretched fore-legs. "I never want to be out there again. I'm so sorry we led you all to this terrible place. It isn't a normal longpaw house, and there isn't a thing to eat. I should have known, after everything that's happened."

"I wish I never saw the house!" cried Daisy. "Now we're trapped here."

"What if the Lake-Dog never stops being angry?" Moon whined. "She's already taken Alpha and Spring, she nearly took my pups . . ."

Dart whimpered and pressed herself closer to the wall.

"She'll stop soon," said Lucky with confidence he didn't feel.

"She wasn't always like this. The Endless Lake was calm before. It will be calm again."

Bella shuffled closer to Lucky. "What if the Fierce Dogs are still waiting for us?" she murmured.

Before Lucky could answer, Storm gave a sharp bark. "If they're out there, we'll deal with them! Because of Blade, we lost two of our Pack—we'll teach those monsters that blood must be taken for blood!" Her voice echoed in the stone room.

Lucky shivered and didn't reply, his head still resting on the floor. He could hear the water churning against the rocks below, the ceaseless whoosh and hiss of the waves drowning out all other sounds.

In time, the lake grew gentler and Lucky could make out the anxious whimpers of his Packmates. Then he heard another noise—an angry growl, low in a dog's chest . . . the sound of a young Fierce Dog as she dreamed of revenge.

CHAPTER SIXTEEN

Lucky awoke with a violent shiver. Gray light drifted through the clear-stone, bringing no warmth. It was sunup, but the Sun-Dog himself was scarcely visible beyond the clouds.

It was bitterly cold in the longpaw house. At least they were out of the wind and rain. Sweet was already awake, washing herself. Bruno was scratching his ear with a hindpaw and grumbling under his breath.

With a start, Lucky remembered Spring floating on the Endless Lake, her black, tan, and white fur riding into the waves. His throat tightened and he whimpered. His thoughts drifted to Alpha's last moments, howling for help at the edge of the lake road. Calling for Savage. And Storm, squaring up to Blade, indifferent to Alpha's pleas.

Lucky sighed, wishing there was a way of burying memories. For a moment, he pictured himself digging a deep hole and offering them to Earth-Dog. *No, she wouldn't want them.*

He stretched, throwing his forepaws in front of him. His limbs were so stiff with cold, he thought he could hear them creaking beneath his skin. His coat, which had been soaking wet from the waves that had broken over the lake road, now cracked with a layer of frost. He remembered what Moon had advised, and climbed to his paws, shaking out his fur. The hunger in his belly had passed from a gnawing ache to something vague and dull, and his limbs felt heavy.

A deep, mournful howl broke through the air, making Lucky jump.

All the dogs were awake now, blinking at one another in confusion.

"What is it?" Sweet barked.

Lucky frowned. The howl pulsed through the wall, reminding him of the honking growls that loudcages made in the city, back when the longpaws used to live there. "I think it's coming from the building. . . ."

Bella shook her ears. "A house that howls!"

Lucky gazed at his litter-sister. He hadn't known that buildings could talk. They weren't *alive*—were they? He thought of the dead clear-stone globe in the room with them. It was like the globes that lit up longpaw streets at night, but huge and lightless. Had the house seen Spring and Alpha carried away by the Lake-Dog?

"It sounds sad," murmured Beetle, pressing himself closer to Moon.

In the weak morning light, Moon's eyes looked gray. Her ears drooped and her tail was limp behind her. She opened her mouth and started to whine, her voice mingling with the howl of the building. Beetle and Thorn joined in, their high voices rising in sorrow. Soon the rest of the Pack was howling with the longpaw house, calling to Moon-Dog and Sun-Dog, though neither were visible in the murky sky.

Lucky shut his eyes and threw back his head. *O Spirit Dogs, who watch over all things, please lead our dead Packmates to safety. Let their dog-spirits find peace with Earth-Dog.*

When he opened his eyes, he saw waterbirds through the clear-stone. They turned loops in the sky and Lucky's heart ached, wondering if he'd ever feel free like them—like he used to a long time ago, as a Lone Dog before the Big Growl. He lowered his gaze. His Packmates all looked weary and disheveled, their coats straggly. They would be hungry too, and thirsty. Lucky swallowed, unable to rid himself of the taste of salt water. He was desperate to drink from a cool, clear spring, and the thought made him lick his chops.

"We can't stay here," he told the others. "There doesn't seem to be anything to eat."

"And the Lake-Dog is dangerous," whimpered Dart. "If she can take a dog like Alpha, none of us is safe."

Sunshine whined, shaking her knotted fur. "But leaving means crossing that horrible lake road, doesn't it?" Her haunches quivered and she took a step back, bumping into Bruno with a start. "What if the Fierce Dogs are on it, waiting for us?"

She had a point. "I could go and find out," said Lucky.

"No!" whined Sunshine. "Not alone."

"I won't be caught. It will be fine." He trod over to her and gave her nose a comforting lick.

"Can I come too?" asked Storm, rising to her paws.

"No," he said quickly. He wouldn't put it past her to challenge the whole Fierce Dog Pack. "One dog can find out just as much as two, with less risk."

Storm looked like she was about to protest, but stopped herself.

Lucky stepped down the stairway, careful not to slip on the pools of water that had collected on the hardstone. Reaching the bottom of the longpaw building, he peered outside. The mist had settled into a heavy white fog. It hardly moved as it hovered above the water. He could hear the Endless Lake shifting beneath, calmer now, just as he had predicted. The waves lapped against the rocks but did not reach over them.

He edged along the longpaw building. It continued to howl and Lucky's ears swiveled forward, trying to detect other sounds beneath its mournful call. The fog hugged the Endless Lake, but only tendrils of mist reached the lake road. Lucky slunk closer, low on his belly. There was no sign of movement.

His muscles relaxed and he let out a slow sigh. *There's no dog here.*

Lucky heard pawsteps behind him, and his nose twitched as he picked up the scent of a Fierce Dog. Heart lurching in his chest, he spun around to see Storm. He thumped the hardstone with a forepaw. "I told you not to come!"

He expected her to gnash her teeth and insist upon vengeance against her former Pack. He was surprised when she lowered her front quarters, dipping her head and gazing up at him submissively.

"I know I shouldn't have followed you, Lucky. But I was worried about you, out here alone. I'm sorry for being so angry before.

I'm just tired of all this running and hiding, but I didn't mean to challenge you." She looked beyond Lucky, where the lake road met the sand. "I thought you might need help if the Fierce Dogs spotted you." There was a hint of disappointment in her voice. She licked her chops.

Lucky nuzzled her ear in thanks. "That's okay. I understand," he murmured, though it troubled him to see how much she yearned for a confrontation with Blade.

They returned to the longpaw house, calling the rest of the Pack to join them. The dogs made a sad procession over the lake road, their heads bowed. Lucky peered beyond the rocks. He found he was grateful for the fog. If Spring's and Alpha's bodies were out there, floating on the water, at least they couldn't be seen. He hoped they weren't there, though—that Lake-Dog had shown mercy to the two unlucky dogs, at least in death, and had delivered them to land far from here. A place where the earth was soft and brown, not hard, yellow sand, and where Earth-Dog would greet them.

As the Pack trod uphill along the bank of the Endless Lake, Lucky thought about Twitch. *Spring wanted to see him again, and now she never will.* He wished there was a way to let Twitch know what had happened to his litter-sister.

They climbed the steep incline to the cliff, puffing with strain. There was no sign of the Fierce Dogs, but Lucky half expected to see them any moment, jumping out from behind a rock.

Lucky led the way, looking back at the rest of the Pack to make sure no dog had fallen behind. They made a ragged bunch. Filthy and bedraggled, Sunshine whined about the green stains that clung to her coat like slimy river grass. Bruno limped and was panting heavily. Moon kept Thorn and Beetle close, protecting them from the edge of the drop with her body and making sure they were safe on their paws. "Not too quickly, take your time," she murmured.

Sweet and Bella trod close to Lucky, pressing determinedly uphill. Martha trailed them, her head low to the ground. The exhausted water-dog scarcely seemed able to lift her paws. *She used all her energy saving Beetle and Thorn,* thought Lucky. *And she still blames herself for not rescuing Spring.*

The cliff path was barren and rocky. Icy wind leaped over the Endless Lake. At least there were pools of fresh water to be found in the dips between rocks. Lucky drank gratefully, finally ridding his tongue of the vile salty taste.

When they reached the top of the cliffs, they stopped to catch their breaths. There was a clearing where spiky grass burst out between the sand and scatterings of large, smooth rocks. From this vantage point, Lucky could see the full scale of the red-and-white-striped house. It still howled mournfully. Between pelts of fog, Lucky could spot the Endless Lake. It lapped against the rocks, much lower than it had been the day before. He remembered the dog-wolf's horrified face as he'd tumbled into the water. Had his body been broken against the rocks? Lucky lowered his head in a mark of respect. He might not have liked Alpha, but no dog deserved to die like that.

It's all because of Blade and her Pack. Why couldn't she just leave us alone? Lucky knew the answer to that: It was because of Storm. Blade believed that the young dog had been stolen from her. She would never rest while Storm was with the Wild Pack. *Alpha knew it too. He said it would end in disaster.* Lucky watched Storm from the corner of his eye. She was standing alongside some of the others, discussing hunt trails.

Sweet was giving instructions. "Mickey and Snap, I want you to follow the cliff uphill, and check around the crags for any prey-creatures. Take Storm. Everyone else should take the opportunity to rest."

Lucky watched, the back of his neck tingling with unease. Had the young Fierce Dog heard Alpha's pleas as the half wolf had begged for help at the edge of the lake road?

"Storm?" said Lucky, on instinct.

The young dog swirled around immediately, gamboling toward him with her tail thrashing. She cocked her head, her tongue lolling. "What is it, Lucky?" she asked, wide-eyed, desperate for his approval.

Lucky's voice was soft. "Catch me something tasty."

"I will!" she barked cheerfully, spinning back toward Sweet and the others and bounding back to them. There was nothing wrong with her hearing.

Lucky watched, a dead weight in his gut, as Storm left with Snap and Mickey. They padded along the edge of the cliff and disappeared from view behind a jumble of rocks.

He felt a light touch on the shoulder and turned to see Sweet.

"They may actually catch something. I saw rabbit droppings along the way." She tried to look encouraging, but there were shadows under her eyes and she shivered as she spoke. She was a skinny thing with such short, fine fur. *She must be even colder than I am,* thought Lucky.

"Come and have a rest," he said, spotting a dip between the rocks that was sheltered from the wind. He led her to the spot and Sweet lowered herself to the ground with a sigh. Lucky wrapped himself around her, pressing himself close. Her body quivered with cold.

Lucky licked her neck, trying his best to warm her up. "Remember how we were next to each other in the Trap House, the night the Big Growl arrived? I couldn't see you through the wall, but I knew you were there."

"Of course," she murmured, her eyes closing.

He watched her for a long time. The sleek fur that covered her muzzle was creamy white and still seemed fresh and clean, despite everything they'd been through. Along her back, her coat was the color of the sand on the rare occasions that the Sun-Dog shone his rays over the bank of the Endless Lake. Her scent had been so delicate and comforting when they'd been in the Trap House. It was still delicate now, rich and sweet, but he wasn't so sure it was comforting. So much had changed since the Trap House. There was a lot to the swift-dog that Lucky hadn't known then . . . fear, suspicion, but also strength.

Lucky sighed and closed his eyes too. Soon he sank into a dreamless sleep.

When Lucky opened his eyes, the Sun-Dog was lower in the sky. He looked around, confused for a moment. Then he remembered the night at the edge of the Endless Lake, and the Fierce Dogs, who couldn't have been far away. Sweet was still by his side, but she was awake, her dark eyes glittering. She looked beyond Lucky to the foggy white sky. "In my old Pack, I was just an ordinary dog, not part of the leadership. But things changed after the Big Growl. Being Alpha's Beta was an act of necessity. You do what you have to, to survive." She met his eye for a moment, then looked beyond him once more. "And I've grown to realize that being part of the Pack's leadership is important to me. You understand that, don't you, Lucky?"

Lucky wondered why Sweet was asking him that question now. She had explained all this before. Unless . . . *Is she worried about whether she'll become the new Alpha, now that the half wolf has gone?* Then another thought occurred to him. *She doesn't think that I want the responsibility, does she?*

He opened his mouth to reply, but Martha's deep bark interrupted him. "The hunters have returned!"

The dogs converged on the sandy clearing, tails thrashing in anticipation. Snap set down the last of the prey-creatures in a little mound, a triumphant gleam in her eyes. She stepped back to reveal four juicy rabbits to the yips of the Pack.

"Every dog will have something to eat today!" barked Mickey, exchanging a satisfied look with Snap and Storm. The Farm Dog's tail beat the air.

Bella ran up to the hunters, congratulating them. The other dogs joined in, barking their thanks.

Lucky felt a pang of sadness that these dogs were reduced to worrying where their next meal was coming from, surviving from day to day without knowing what to expect. He thought back wryly to the river rabbit. He'd considered that a small meal between five. He looked at the prey-creatures, running his tongue over his lips. They looked delicious, but it wouldn't be much between so many dogs.

Although it's two dogs fewer than yesterday . . .

He snapped out of his thoughts to see that all the dogs were standing by the prey-creatures in silence. Some looked to Sweet, who watched the rabbits uncertainly, her whiskers flexing. Lucky realized what was happening. *They don't know how to begin without Alpha to take the first bite.* Even Leashed Dogs like Bella and Daisy had grown so used to the ritual that they hesitated.

Sweet cleared her throat and raised her muzzle decisively. "Since we have no Alpha right now, we should all eat together and share the food equally. We can settle the question of leadership later."

The hungry dogs didn't need to be told twice. They fell upon the rabbits, crowding around in a tussle of fur until there was nothing left. As they settled onto the sandy earth to clean their paws, Moon climbed onto a large, flat rock.

"Packmates, gather closer," she urged. "So we can remember Alpha, who led us so bravely."

There were whimpers as the dogs drew toward her and settled in a circle. No keening howls, though, Lucky noticed.

Storm stared across the foggy the lake, her eyes blank. Was she remembering how the half wolf had insisted on calling her Savage? Was she thinking of Alpha's final moments on the lake road?

"We have all come so far," Moon continued. "You have all shown bravery, loyalty, and resilience."

The dogs whined in appreciation and Lucky cocked his head. Moon carried a great deal of respect in the Pack. He could understand why.

The Farm Dog's eyes were a dazzling blue once more. "We are all suffering from having lost our Packmate Spring, and our leader, Alpha."

Dart whimpered, lowering her head onto the ground.

"But is Alpha dead?" said Whine, his tongue lolling from the side of his mouth. "We don't even know that for sure!"

"Yes, we do!" Martha growled. "Lucky saw him fall off the lake road. The water down there is so rough that no dog could survive."

"Alpha had webbed paws, like you," Bruno pointed out.

Martha glanced at her own paws, with their rubbery webbing. "Not even I would have survived it for long."

Moon raised her muzzle to the sky and let out a long howl. The dogs threw back their heads and joined in. The mournful sound rose over the cliff, over the distant cry of the longpaw house on its lonely sandbank. The dogs huddled closer together. Lucky could smell their scents weaving on the air. As his own scent mingled with theirs, he felt the bond between them grow stronger.

Eventually the howl petered out. Moon jumped off the flat stone and padded toward the remains of the rabbits. She gathered some bones and a fluffy white tail.

"Let's bury these," she suggested. "As a mark of respect to Alpha and Spring, who can never be buried."

Mickey was the first to start digging, working his black-and-white paws through the frost and sand. The others joined in. They had soon dug a trench deep enough to bury the rabbit's remains. Sweet kicked dirt into the hole with her hind legs and Snap helped to pad down the earth.

Moon looked up at Lucky. "Will you speak a few words for us? You always know how to say the right thing."

Lucky was taken aback. *Since when am I better at speeches than any other dog?* But now was no time to argue. The whole Pack was looking at him, waiting for him to continue.

He stepped onto the flat stone and turned to address them. "Farewell, brave Spring. Devoted friend . . . loyal Packmate. We will miss you, now and for always."

Dart let out a terrible howl. Daisy went to comfort the huntdog, nuzzling her soft ears.

The others were still watching Lucky. His mouth opened and closed. He knew he had to say something about Alpha now, but what? He remembered the ferocious dog-wolf he'd encountered when he'd first joined the Wild Pack. Alpha hadn't been the most compassionate of leaders, but he knew he couldn't say that. Lucky's tongue lapped at his nose. *It doesn't matter what I think. The Pack needs comfort right now.*

"Farewell, Alpha," he began in a solemn voice. "Half wolf, half dog, you were born to lead. Courageous in life, heroic in death." The words felt like dust in his mouth and he had to stop his tail from stiffening, betraying his insincerity.

The dogs didn't seem to notice, yipping their agreement and dipping their heads in respect.

As Lucky stepped off the flat stone, Sweet approached and quietly thanked him. "You are a good dog. You knew that was just what the Pack needed to hear. Alpha would thank you too, if he could."

No, he wouldn't, thought Lucky. *He'd be angry with me for outliving him.*

While the rest of the Pack stayed close to the buried remains as a mark of respect, Lucky padded to the edge of the cliff. He stood alone, gazing out over the endless expanse of white fog, which covered the lake like a pelt. His memories of the dog-wolf were complicated. A tough, uncompromising leader. Sometimes he had seemed cruel, like when he had threatened to brand Lucky a traitor, and the way he had treated Storm. Other times he had been bold, and even wise.

Lucky thought he had glimpsed a softer side to Alpha once or twice. He remembered how the leader had spoken of his puphood.

It couldn't have been easy being half dog, half wolf. Always viewed with suspicion, never totally accepted.

"So long, Alpha," Lucky whispered to the wind. "May the spirits of both dogs and wolves be with you."

CHAPTER SEVENTEEN

The fog crept over the Endless Lake as white birds circled overhead. Where its white pelt parted, Lucky could see the water shifting in great rolls. He stood at the edge of the cliff, the wind blowing back his fur. Alpha's wolfish face drifted as a vision before his eyes. Only Fiery had dared to challenge him. Who could guess what would have happened if the hunter had lived? Both dogs had seemed invincible. It was hard to believe they both were gone.

An angry snarl broke over the wind and Lucky spun away from the cliff. It was Snap. Her paws were set apart, her hackles up. She was confronting Moon, who was growling at her between gritted teeth.

Lucky bounded down to them. "What's going on?" he barked.

"This little upstart is trying to deprive me of my right!" spat Moon. "Fiery was third in command after Sweet. As his partner, I am high in the ranks and am entitled to chew on that bone!" She made a move toward the mottled remains of the prey, a piece of the rabbit's thigh that hadn't been buried. Snap blocked her with a snarl.

Beetle and Thorn whimpered fretfully, standing close to their Mother-Dog. The rest of the Pack hung back nervously.

Snap took a step toward Moon, her eyes blazing. "No dog is *entitled* to wolf down the remains, just like that! There are plenty of us here; you're not better than anyone else. If anything, you're lower in the ranks than *I* am, and you don't see me stealing food!"

"How *dare* you! I am *not* stealing anything—this is my right!" Moon flung herself at Snap. Snap darted toward her. Lucky only just had time to throw his body between them.

"Stop it immediately!" He glared at Snap, then turned to Moon. His head pulsed with anger and it was all he could do to stop himself from taking a sharp bite of her rump. "What ranks? What are you talking about? Look about you! Alpha is dead and so is Fiery. We're only just managing to survive. I don't understand you, Moon. After such a lovely ritual you want to ruin it for . . . " His eyes trailed over the rabbit bones. "For a mouthful of scraps. What's wrong with you? What sort of example are you setting for your pups?"

Moon's sky-blue eyes grew so wide they were ringed by a circle of white. She cowered away from Lucky as though injured, threw back her head, and howled in grief. "I'm sorry! So much has happened; so much has changed. I don't know who I am anymore. I don't know how the Pack will manage. How will we carry on?"

Beetle and Thorn crowded around her, licking her face and whining in sympathy. Lucky sighed, guilt twisting in his belly. *I shouldn't have been so hard on her.*

Snap lowered her head, her hackles relaxing. The dogs stood about, exchanging furtive looks. Lucky noticed that Sweet held back, watching with her head slightly cocked.

Daisy stepped toward him and cleared her throat. "We shouldn't be fighting. But Moon is right, in a way. We have a problem, don't we? We don't have a leader. We won't get far without one."

Bella raised her muzzle. "That's true. We need order or we're going to run into trouble every time we eat, or need to make a decision about where to go. A Pack can't manage without an Alpha."

"But does that mean that dogs need to fight? That's the custom, isn't it?" asked Daisy, her tail dropping uneasily.

"There doesn't have to be a fight," Lucky assured her, and the little dog's tail gave a wag of relief. "When Twitch became Alpha of his Pack there was a ritual, but no aggression. All the Pack wanted him to do was lead, so a fight would have been stupid. Another dog formally challenged him but went on to submit so that Twitch was immediately Alpha."

"That sounds a bit weird," murmured Dart. Lucky turned to her thoughtfully. The chase-dog had always lived in the Wild Pack. *It's probably hard for her to imagine there's another way.*

Snap was quicker to accept what Lucky had said. The scruffy little dog shook herself. "Maybe it is a bit weird. But does that matter? Nothing is the same since the Big Growl. We just have to do the best we can."

Lucky flashed her a grateful look. He caught Sweet watching from the corner of her eye. Her slim tail gave a hopeful wag, but she lowered her gaze. The swift-dog wasn't getting involved. *She was Alpha's Beta. She has more of a claim in the hierarchy than anyone here.* He was about to ask what she thought when Bruno spoke up.

"You should be the leader, Lucky." The gruff old dog raised his dark muzzle. "You've brought us such a long way, and showed more courage than any other dog." His feathered brown tail thumped the ground.

Mickey barked his agreement. "Bruno always has the best ideas! Remember how he rescued us from Terror by getting us to climb into that longpaw dwelling? This is another great idea."

Bruno's chest puffed out with pride and he gave his nose a satisfied lick.

Mickey's large brown eyes fixed on Lucky. "Without you, the Leashed Dogs wouldn't have made it. You taught us to hunt and to work as a Pack. Since we joined the Wild Pack, things have been more stable, and a lot of that is because of you."

Bella trod toward Lucky and nuzzled his ear. "You *should* be the Alpha, litter-brother!"

Lucky gave a surprised whine and turned to the others.

"Lucky for leader!" yipped Daisy.

Storm joined in, bouncing excitedly. "Lucky for leader!"

Whines and barks rose from the Pack. Lucky's tail started wagging. *But I don't want to be Alpha,* he reminded himself. He caught Sweet's glance. Her eyes were pained. He cocked his head, keen to reassure her. *I didn't ask for this!*

Sunshine started bounding back and forth on her short legs. "Lucky for leader! Lucky for leader!"

"Be quiet!" snapped Sweet.

The little dog quailed, her small ears flat against her head.

Sweet's jealous. She wants to be Alpha; she practically said so.

He was surprised when Sweet's voice softened. "Sorry, Sunshine. But do you know how much noise you were all making? We don't want to attract the Fierce Dogs."

Sunshine shot a look over her shoulder and the other dogs grew quiet.

Sweet turned to Lucky with a gracious twist of her long neck. "You are a popular choice for leader. You have the support of the Pack. Do you wish to be Alpha?"

She showed no sign of resentment. Lucky looked from dog to dog, remembering his life in the city before the Big Growl. *I was a Lone Dog then. I'd share the odd bit of food, and tips about the best place to find it, with Old Hunter. But that's not the same as being in a Pack, with all its rules.* With a shudder, he remembered his time as Omega, when Alpha had sought to humiliate him by giving him the lowliest tasks. Whine had grinned with wicked pleasure and his friends from the Leashed Pack had guiltily averted their gazes, unable to look at Lucky. It still felt raw. *I don't want to be in charge of a system like that.*

Lucky sat up straight, an idea coming to him. "What if we don't have a leader at all? What if we don't need one?"

"Don't *need* one?" yipped Sunshine in alarm, forgetting Sweet's warning about keeping quiet. The little dog started darting in tight circles, her ears pinned back. "No leader—are you crazy? We can't survive without some dog to make our decisions! We'll starve; we'll starve to death!"

Lucky waited patiently as Sunshine ran several loops, kicking up sand with her small paws. "Starve to death!" she repeated in her shrill voice, then turned back to Lucky. Her tail hovered uncertainly. When no dog joined her protests she let out a whine and flopped on her belly. She took to nibbling at a twig, which had tangled in the fur of her flank.

Lucky licked his chops and continued. "What if we shared responsibilities?"

Bella's ears were pricked. "Shared them how? We already divide up tasks. There are hunting parties, Patrol Dogs, and the Omega helps to prepare the camp."

"I don't mean that." Lucky tried to think of a way to explain, realizing that he didn't have a word for what he was suggesting. It was nothing like usual Pack structure, with an Alpha on top, an Omega at the bottom, and plenty of hierarchy in between. He stared down at his paws, thinking. When he looked up, the dogs were all watching him, waiting for him to speak. Even Sunshine had stopped pretending to be busy. Gray clouds drifted over their heads and an icy raindrop fell on Lucky's ear.

He shook his head and took a deep breath. "What if we lived by the rule of . . . of . . ." He looked around him desperately. What was it he was trying to say? If only he could find the words! He dropped his glance to the ground. The other dogs were crowded around him, their paws close together, yet each dog managed not to jostle others out of the way. Paws . . . His head shot back up. "Four Paws! We'll call it Four Paws." There were low growls of bemusement.

"Go on," Sweet said, in an uncertain voice.

Lucky could feel excitement building in him as the plan took shape in his mind. "We need four dogs to place a paw close to one another, in a sort of circle. Just four dogs. What they say will carry a decision. Don't you see? Say we had to decide which way to travel—we'd ask four dogs to cast their vote. Where to hunt? Four dogs decide—together! No dog is in charge and every dog's opinion has a turn to be heard. If we can't get at least four paws—that is, agreement from four members of the Pack—we won't move forward with a decision."

Lucky found that he was panting, his tongue lolling out, as he waited for the other dogs' jubilant reactions. Couldn't they appreciate the sense of what he said? Why did they all have to rely on one dog's decisions? But the dogs leaned back on their haunches, some of them pretending to scratch an itch.

Lucky sighed, sitting heavily. Sometimes talking to these dogs felt like chasing a loudcage—impossible, and pointless! He tried to keep his patience, looking until he spotted a line of gravel that wound along the cliff top. "You see the route there? Shall we see where it leads?" The dogs followed his gaze to the gravel path, then turned back to Lucky. "I think we should." He planted a forepaw firmly on the ground. "I vote yes! Now I just need three other dogs to do the same thing, and we have a decision."

Most of the Pack still looked confused, but Dart nodded with understanding. She took a last look at the gravel path with a yelp. "Me too!" She placed a paw beside Lucky's. "We can't stay here till nightfall, not when the Fierce Dogs are near. I say yes, we follow the path!"

"Yes!" grunted Martha, thumping down her huge black paw. She met Lucky's eye, her bushy tail swishing. "So I'm helping to make a decision?"

"Exactly." Lucky was relieved that Dart and Martha had caught on so quickly. The other dogs were looking less confused. "We just need one more dog to lend a paw and we'll have made a decision without needing a leader. How great is that?"

A growl made his whiskers bristle. Moon stalked around Dart and Martha, her haunches low. "Alpha always made our decisions for us. He didn't need anyone else. It was easier that way."

Lucky remembered times when Alpha had failed to make

decisions—when the wolf-dog had lost his confidence. *He was ter-rified of the black cloud. He couldn't cope at all.* But it felt disrespectful to say this so soon after Alpha's death. "He isn't here anymore," Lucky pointed out instead.

"*You're* here, though," whined Sunshine, unable to contain herself. "Lucky, why can't you decide for us?"

"It would be easier," Snap agreed. "The Four Paws thing might be difficult if we are in a hurry."

Lucky peered into the darkening clouds. The Sky-Dogs were prancing overhead, releasing drops of rain. They fell more quickly now, tumbling over Lucky's coat. The Pack needed to get going. "Yes, it would be easier if I made all the decisions." Lucky met Snap's eye. "Easier for you. But do you want to be led by the nose all your life, as though you were living with longpaws, like a Leashed Dog?" He turned to give Sunshine a hard look. "Is that what you've fought and survived for—to let others boss you around? You want me to tell you what to think, what to eat, when to sleep, when to wake up? Even if it means you hardly eat at all? Even if you sleep in the draft and wake up freezing cold?"

"Dogs of rank eat well," Moon whined defensively.

"Dogs of rank should know better," snapped Lucky, los-ing his patience. The rain was pattering on his head and his pelt was damp. "You want to be someone's servant? How boring for you! But fine, I can do that if you want me to. I can make all the choices. I can decide for you, for Thorn, for Beetle, for the whole Pack—if that's what you want."

Moon's cool blue eyes darted to her pups, then rested on Martha's, Lucky's, and Dart's forepaws, still pressed close together in the dirt. The Farm Dog gave a reluctant shake. Then she stepped forward, lowering a white paw alongside Lucky's. "I think we should follow the gravel path," she murmured.

Lucky barked in delight. "We have a decision!" He sprang excitedly, butting Moon with his muzzle, his tail thrashing the air. "We follow that gravel route and see where it takes us. Hopefully to somewhere warm and dry with lots of food, where the Fierce Dogs can't find us!"

Moon barked in agreement, her tail starting to wag too. "We made our own decision!"

"You see, it feels good," he whined as he licked the soft fur at her neck.

Sunshine was cheering up. "We can make decisions for ourselves! We don't need an Alpha!" she yipped, as though the thought had only just dawned on her.

One step at a time, thought Lucky, starting toward the gravel path. *We'll get there in the end.* It wasn't just that he wanted to avoid a leadership role; he wanted the dogs to think for themselves. *That's the only thing that will save us,* he thought. *Quick wits and sharp minds.* The Fierce Dogs were bullies, but Lucky knew his dogs could be better. They could be clever.

CHAPTER EIGHTEEN

The dogs trotted over the gravel path. Lucky held back, careful not to lead them. Moon's tail wagged as she paced ahead with Beetle and Thorn at her side. Mickey gave a cheerful yip and nudged Martha's flank.

"The world is so big," said the Farm Dog. "Did you ever imagine there was all this in it, back when you were a Leashed Dog?" He looked about and Lucky saw his black-and-white snout in profile. "I never even saw much of the city back then. Since the Big Growl I've seen forests, lakes, places where the grass grows as high as your head, or where sand covers the Earth-Dog so there's no trace of her brown fur."

"I didn't imagine it," replied Martha. "How could I? My long-paws took me out of the city now and then. We would travel in their loudcage for a long time. I couldn't see where we were going because they locked me in the back."

"That sounds scary," whined Dart, who had overheard. "I'd never climb in one of those things."

"I got used to it," said Martha. "We'd end up in nice places, like a big yard with trees and a stream. They would let me run off the leash, which never happened in the city. It was worth putting up with the loudcage for that."

Padding behind them, Lucky couldn't see Dart's face, but he caught the mournful tone of her voice. "I couldn't bear to be on a leash all the time. . . ."

"Neither could I," said Martha. "Not anymore."

Lucky fell back. He felt a deep satisfaction that the dogs were getting on so well, despite their recent difficulties. Alpha was gone but they would survive, helping one another. *We don't need anyone to lead us.* He felt lighter on his paws as he followed the gentle incline of the gravel path. It led away from the cliff face, curving inland, where low shrubs offered some protection from the wind. The clouds hung over the Endless Lake and it was drier here. *We made the right decision, and we made it together.*

Lost in his thoughts, he didn't see Sunshine until he was whiskers away from her, and only just stopped himself from bumping into her. Lucky realized that the other dogs had stopped not far ahead.

"What's going on?" he asked, his ears pricked.

He could see Sweet and Bella talking up ahead. His litter-sister called over to him.

"The trail splits. We don't know which way to go."

Lucky approached her. Sure enough, the gravel path forked, with one side veering up toward the edge of the cliff while the other cut deeper inland. Lucky glanced along the cliff path with a shiver, thinking of the sharp wind and the rain that hung over the water. *We should go inland, away from all that.* He pictured Alpha's terrified face as the great dog fell into the Endless Lake, and Spring's floating body, one ear resting over her eye. He would have liked to get away from the memories too.

Bella was watching him intently. "What should we do?"

Lucky opened his mouth, then shut it again. *No. I won't tell them what to do—that would make me their Alpha.*

After a moment of silence, little Sunshine piped up. "Let's move away from here. I've had enough of that stinky river grass! And the Sky-Dogs are always raining over the Endless Lake. Maybe that's where all that water comes from. It looks better through the shrubs. Drier!"

Storm stepped in front of her, addressing the Pack. "Who cares about a bit of rain? We should turn back along the cliff toward the abandoned town."

"But the Fierce Dogs are down there!" whined Dart.

"Exactly! I, for one, am sick of running from them. They won't expect us to go back there. We could creep up on them and take them by surprise."

That's a terrible idea, thought Lucky, but he stayed quiet. *Let them come to their own decision.*

"So that's my vote," Storm continued. "We follow the cliff until we reach the town." She slammed her paw on the gravel. "I just need three more dogs. Who's with me?"

Moon howled in protest. "Back toward the Fierce Dogs? Have you lost your mind?"

Mickey's brown eyes widened. "Why would we face off with them when we don't need to?"

"Because I'm sick of running away!" Storm growled. "If they hadn't attacked, Alpha would still be alive. We should avenge him!"

Lucky could hardly stop himself from growling at her. *Storm hated Alpha. She had a chance of saving him, but ignored his cries. She can't possibly care about avenging his death. This is just an excuse to fight Blade!*

Fortunately he wasn't the only one to balk at Storm's words. Martha sat down heavily, her jowls trembling. "You're being a silly pup!" she rebuked. "You haven't given a thought to the danger we'd be in. Mickey's right: There's no reason to fight those savage attack-dogs when we don't need to."

The young dog bristled, her hackles rising and her eyes flashing. "My brother is with those *savage attack-dogs*," she snarled. "Don't you remember how he protected us from the rest of his Pack? He isn't completely lost to us! Don't you care about getting him away from Blade?"

Squash-faced Whine muttered beneath his breath. "Her litter-brother was no great loss to the Pack. Maybe Alpha was right and Storm *should* go to the Fierce Dogs—by herself." His bulging eyes roved over the dogs. "It's where she belongs." He put his small forepaw on the gravel and waited for three other dogs to agree with him.

"You disgusting rat!" howled Storm, and she lunged at Whine, her teeth bared. Lucky's breath caught in his throat. *She could rip his head off!*

Martha leaped in front of Whine, knocking Storm aside. The young Fierce Dog tumbled against a shrub in a flurry of small leaves. Whine shrank behind Sweet, his flanks quivering in terror.

Storm scrambled to her paws, shaking the leaves from her fur. She barked furiously. "How dare you, Martha? How *dare you*!"

To Lucky's amazement, she charged at the water-dog. She scrambled under Martha's belly, spun around, and sprang at her back. Her foreclaws raked Martha's shoulders.

Sunshine started yapping in fear. The rest of the Pack watched in shock as Storm snapped at Martha's ears.

The water-dog yelped, trying to shake Storm off, but the Fierce Dog locked her paws around her neck. It was hard to tell how deep Storm's nips went in Martha's thick black fur. The young dog was wild-eyed and looked angry enough to cause real harm. Martha tried again to shrug her off, but Storm just dug in deeper. Then Martha threw back her head, rising onto her hindpaws. With a massive heave of her body she bucked Storm off her back. The Fierce Dog fell to the ground, leaping onto her paws and pressing back—preparing to pounce at Martha again. Martha sprang away with a shocked growl as Storm charged, breaking through a wall of shrubs and heading straight for the edge of the cliff.

"Storm, no!" barked Lucky.

The young Fierce Dog howled with dread as she realized she was heading to the cliff face. She scrambled desperately, but she was going too fast to stop. One forepaw slid off the rocks, send-ing pebbles hurtling down toward the Endless Lake. Lucky sprang toward her, grasping her neck fur with his teeth and dragging her inland. He thrust Storm into a gorse bush and dropped his head, panting for breath. He couldn't bear to look at her.

There were anxious murmurs from the Pack, but no dog moved. Eventually the gorse bush shook and Storm climbed out. Her head was lowered and her tail slunk behind her, but her eyes still glowered as she passed Martha to sit by Lucky's side.

"By the Spirit Dogs, what were you thinking?" he snapped. "Martha is practically your Mother-Dog; she's done nothing but support and protect you from the start. How could you attack her like that?" His voice trembled with anger and his flanks quivered from the shock. He looked back over the cliff, trying not to think of what had almost happened. *Does she realize she nearly fell to her death?* The fog was creeping toward them. Lucky scanned the scrubby land, then turned back toward the cliff. Where the gravel path forked left, he could see a faded white wall up ahead—what looked like part of an abandoned longpaw building.

"Let's go over there to rest and decide what to do," he said. The dogs yapped their agreement and Lucky started treading toward the building, at the head of the Pack despite his resolve to let them lead themselves. He heard a scrabbling sound and Storm appeared alongside him, strutting in front of the line of dogs. Her nose was proudly raised and her ears were pricked.

Lucky could hardly believe it. *Why is she looking so smug?* Then he realized. *The longpaw place is in the direction she wanted to go.* Anger gathered at Lucky's belly and crept up his throat. It was all he could do not to nip her around the ears. *Foolish dog!* She hadn't listened to a word he'd said.

He took a deep breath, too angry to confront her. He was also aware of how close they had come to the edge of the cliff. A wood-and-wire fence ran along it by the stretch of scrub nearest to the longpaw building. Some of this had fallen away, revealing a steep drop down to the Endless Lake. It had probably been damaged in the Big Growl. This thought made Lucky consider the building more carefully. Was it safe? There were thin cracks running along the wall, and the clear-stone lookouts had shattered, but it seemed less damaged than the houses in the city. The door had fallen open.

"Should we go inside?" one of the dogs asked, but Lucky was already tentatively padding through the opening.

It led into a large, empty room full of seats that had fallen on their sides, and long wooden platforms on legs—the kind that longpaws ate their meals off in the Food House, back in the city. But if there had been food here once, it had gone a long time ago.

Lucky sniffed, disappointed but not surprised. Still, the worn wooden floorboards were dry under his paw pads and it was warmer inside, protected from the icy wind and driving fog.

"A soft-hide!" yipped Daisy, squeezing past him and hurrying toward a fuzzy pelt at the far end of the room. "Like the ones the longpaws had in their houses! It's so comfy and warm."

The dogs followed her, gathering on the soft-hide. Lucky sighed as his paws sank into the spongy fabric, feeling cozy and warm for the first time since leaving the old camp on the rescue mission to find Fiery. Moon started washing Beetle and Thorn as Mickey licked Martha's ear, doing his best to comfort his friend, who still looked upset from the skirmish with Storm.

Little Sunshine cleared her throat. "The cliffs are dangerous. It would be so easy for one of us to lose our footing." She lowered her eyes, avoiding Storm's hard gaze. "And it's colder by the cliff face, without anything to eat." She took a deep breath and raised her gaze. "I still think we should take the route that goes inland." She placed a dirty white paw on the soft-hide ahead of her. "What do you all think?"

Martha placed her huge webbed paw next to Sunshine's. It was almost as large as Sunshine's head. "You are absolutely right," said the water-dog, catching Storm with an icy glare. Sunshine's curled-back tail wagged eagerly, and Lucky felt a wave of affection for the little dog. *She's not used to hearing anyone agree with her,* he thought.

There was hesitation among the other dogs, who exchanged curious glances. Beetle whispered something to Thorn and the young dogs stepped forward, placing their paws down on the soft-hide.

Moon's ears flattened. "You're only pups; you can't do that." She beckoned them away, but Lucky interrupted.

"Every dog gets to make their own choice. We all have the right to be heard, every last one of us."

"The fog is horrible," yipped Thorn. "It's dangerous and really cold. We think it would be safer to go the other way, and Beetle thought he smelled rabbit."

Beetle nodded and Thorn pressed her forepaw harder on the soft-hide.

"That settles it," said Lucky. "We'll take the route that leads inland, once this fog has disappeared. We won't even be able to see the gravel path soon; it's too dangerous to be out there now. We should take the opportunity to rest."

Thorn and Beetle yipped excitedly, clearly proud that they had contributed to a decision. Sunshine also panted with satisfaction as she padded back and forth, her frothy tail jerking cheerfully.

Martha climbed to her paws with a yawn and walked toward a long piece of raised wood. "There's something up here," she murmured.

"Something we can eat?" asked Bella, trotting after her.

Martha frowned. "I'm not sure." She threw her forepaws onto the wooden ledge. It tipped under her weight and a large, clear object rolled off, bouncing onto the floor. Small white balls scattered over the ground. Martha lapped a couple up with her large pink tongue. "Mmm . . . "

The dogs pranced after the white balls, snapping them up in their teeth. Lucky sniffed one. It was sweet and nutty. He gulped it down with a grimace. *Too sweet.* He watched as the other dogs wolfed them down. Soon Snap was zipping around the room, bumping into the longpaw seats and yipping. Beetle and Thorn bounded after her and Daisy hopped on the spot.

What's wrong with them? thought Lucky. The sweet pellets had filled them with energy. *So much for resting.* He had to admit it was funny. He watched as the dogs pranced around him. Then Storm sidled up and stood hesitantly by his side. "I'm sorry for how I acted earlier. I didn't mean to lose my temper."

Lucky stiffened. "You aren't just saying that to get out of trouble, are you?"

Storm looked offended. "Of course not. I know I shouldn't have gotten angry; it was wrong of me."

Lucky nodded. "It's really Martha you should be apologizing to."

"I will," Storm assured him as they watched the large black dog bound about with the others.

Lucky turned to Storm, wondering why she was so impulsive and given to rage. *The last few days have been tough. Maybe the shock and grief have gotten to her.* He softened and his shoulders dropped. "Was there something else you wanted to talk about?"

Storm licked her chops, still watching the others at play. "I really think we should follow the cliff path back in the direction of the town. Blade has my litter-brother and she's tried to get me back, even after she killed Wiggle before my eyes. I don't know what it is that she wants, but I think it's time we found out. We're a strong Pack with capable fighters and we can't keep running forever."

"You make a good point, Storm. We don't really know what all this is about, why the Fierce Dogs are so intent on dragging you back. But confronting them would be dangerous." He lowered his voice. "Not every dog is a born fighter." *Not like us*—was that what he was saying? No, that wasn't what he meant. He eyed the thickset young Fierce Dog. *It's in her blood. But that doesn't mean that she has to be bad.*

Lucky watched the other dogs. They had stopped their crazy prancing and were finally settling down for a nap on the soft-hide. Already the Sun-Dog was bounding low in the sky. Lucky looked up through the shattered clear-stone opening. It was beginning to grow dark.

"Please, Lucky," whispered Storm.

He turned toward her eager face. "All right," he murmured. "We'll rest for the night and you and I can take a look first thing in the morning, before the others wake up. It would be good to know if we're being followed. But you have to promise that you won't do anything before checking with me first. No throwing yourself into fights! *Promise me.*"

Storm lowered her head submissively. "I promise."

"And you'll apologize to Martha tonight, before we go."

Storm raised her eyes. "You sound like a leader with all your orders!" she teased.

Lucky bared his teeth in mock aggression. "Are you going to do what I say or not?" He watched as Storm trotted over to Martha.

"I'm sorry," Storm began. "I shouldn't have lost my temper."

The water-dog sat stiffly. "No, you shouldn't have," she said gruffly.

Lucky waited to hear what Storm would say next. He felt the cold, wet touch of a dog's nose on his ear and smelled a pleasant scent. Sweet sat down next to him and his heart gave a little tremor. He could feel the heat rising from her body.

"I appreciate everything you've done for us," she said quietly. "The Four Paws idea is . . . so original."

Lucky's whisper was tingled with amusement. "Are you sure you mean that?"

The swift-dog cocked her head. "Well, let's just see how it goes. It's worth a try, and if it doesn't work, we can always choose a leader then."

Lucky tilted his head at Sweet. *She really did want to lead the dogs.*

She raised her narrow muzzle. "If one of us became leader, the other could be their second in command." She pressed her flank next to Lucky's and for a moment he felt overwhelmed by her warmth and sweet scent.

"We already know you're great at that," said Lucky with a

playful twitch of his tail. "As long as you unlearn some of those lessons Alpha taught you."

She turned to him in shock. She must have caught the amused glint in his eye, as she gave his ear a playful nibble. "You're so cruel," she murmured, "mocking me like that!" Her tongue tickled the base of Lucky's ear and he squirmed away. "You can't escape me that easily!" she play snarled, nibbling harder.

"Is that so?" barked Lucky. Secretly he liked the warmth of her breath, and the way his ear tingled beneath her teeth. He nudged her cheek with his snout. "You *wish* you could be my Beta!"

"Do not!" she growled, shunting him back. She threw down her forepaws in a play bow. "Oh, great Lucky, how can I serve you? Like this?" She pounced forward and knocked him to the ground, licking his ears. He yipped happily, giving her flank a playful nip. They gamboled about the large room, barking and playing as the others rested. Eventually they collapsed on the wooden floor, panting.

Sweet rolled onto her elegant legs and padded toward the soft-hide, where most of the dogs were already asleep. She sat, and Lucky settled alongside her. He shut his eyes, breathing in her soothing scent.

"Good night, Lucky," she whispered.

He wriggled closer and she didn't pull away. He rested his head next to hers. "Good night, Sweet." With a sigh Lucky fell into contented sleep.

CHAPTER NINETEEN

Lucky's body slumped on the snowy ground. He tried to raise his paws, but they were heavy as rocks. He heard desperate barks and saw a mass of fighting dogs. A flurry of dark pelts flew past him and fangs flashed white beneath the Moon-Dog. Dread rippled along his back and the breath snagged in his throat. Through the blizzard, he saw an attack-dog squaring up to two young chase-dogs, spit bubbling at his jaws. A Mother-Dog turned on her pup, sinking her teeth into his neck. Her face was concealed in the twisting snow, but Lucky thought she looked familiar. He tried to cry out—to beg her to stop—but the words would not leave his tongue.

Why was this happening? Lucky struggled against the weight in his limbs, stumbling onto his paws. Icy flakes spun through the air, falling to the ground, where they mingled with streams of blood.

A whirring sound overhead made him look to the sky. Was it one of the giant birds that had carried longpaws over the city? He could hear its wings beating the air. A column of light fell from its body, illuminating the fighting dogs. Lucky was horrified to see the vicious snapping of teeth, the tearing and gouging, the frenzied eyes. This was madness! He threw his head back to howl but no sound came out. Lightning flashed in the sky while thunder shuddered through Lucky's limbs. The Sky-Dogs were furious, filling the air with a white blizzard. Lucky's legs buckled beneath him and he sank once more. He could hear his own name, but he couldn't reply; his jaws seemed webbed together.

Lucky? Lucky?

"Lucky . . . ?"

He opened his eyes, feeling the warm, wet sensation of his muzzle being licked. Sweet was staring into his face. His body ached with tension and his jaw was clenched so hard that a sharp pain ran through it. *Another bad dream.* He took a deep breath and forced his body to relax. *But it felt so real.*

"Was I chasing rabbits in my sleep again?" He nuzzled up to Sweet, hoping his casual words would fool her.

She pulled away from him, still staring hard. "No, you weren't," she whispered.

Lucky's hairs prickled along the back of his neck. Had he yelped in his sleep? Had he revealed something of his black dream? He looked around, remembering that they were in the longpaw building. It was dark, lit only by the Moon-Dog, who gazed through the gap where the clear-stone had been. The other dogs were nearby, curled on the soft-hide. Lucky could hear their gentle snores. There was Storm, curled into a tight ball. *At least I didn't wake them.*

Sweet's narrow face was tense. "I saw what was happening," she murmured. "You were having a terrible dream. Your lips were moving, but you didn't make a sound, almost as though you *couldn't*. But still . . ."

Shame plunged through Lucky. He held his breath, waiting to hear what she would say. Had he revealed something about the Storm of Dogs—the terrible battle?

Sweet glanced over at the sleeping Fierce Dog at the far end of the soft-hide, then turned back to Lucky. "You mouthed the name Storm, over and over. 'Storm, Storm, Storm.' You were howling, but silently. Was your dream about her? Lucky, what's going on?"

Lucky could no longer meet her gaze. He turned, spying the first hint of light creeping through the open door. He would have to leave with Storm soon; he'd promised her they would check up on the Fierce Dogs. He started to stretch and rise to his paws. He wobbled, surprised to find that his legs were trembling.

Sweet quickly rose, blocking his way. "You're not going any-where until you tell me what your dream was about." Her tongue lapped at her nose. "Have you had it before? Was it like when you collapsed during the Great Howl? Is it always the same one?"

Lucky wanted to protest, but his resolve drained from his body. *I promised myself I'd never lie to her again.* He'd known Sweet longer than any other dog in the Pack, except for his litter-sister, Bella. Despite everything that had happened, they were still here, weren't they? He looked around at the sleeping dogs, some Wild, like Moon and Snap, some Leashed, like Mickey and Bruno. He felt a pang of warmth for these dogs, who had been through so much. If they really were in danger, Sweet should know about it. She might be able to help.

With a sigh, Lucky lowered himself back onto the soft-hide, resting his muzzle on his paws. He remembered his dream and fear washed over him. He started whimpering quietly, no longer able to keep it in.

Sweet settled beside him. "Just start at the beginning," she whispered.

Over the sound of Martha's gentle grunts, Lucky quietly told Sweet about the dreams that had started after the Big Growl. "Each one is different, in a way, but the battle is never far off. Sometimes I'm alone, surrounded by ice. Other times, like tonight, there's snow and wind, with dogs clashing all around. It's always bitterly cold, and the smell of blood is in the air."

Sweet shuddered, pressing her body next to his.

Lucky breathed. "The Storm of Dogs." It was the first time he had said the words out loud. Doing so filled him with panic. *What if that makes it real? What if the words bring my dreams to life?* He shook his head. Superstitious nonsense. He was surprised to look up and see the fear in Sweet's eyes.

"I have heard of it." The swift-dog frowned. "I can't remember when . . . maybe when I was a pup. There were tales of the Storm of Dogs, a vicious battle, where Lightning and the Spirit Dogs went to war. And now you tell me you're dreaming of this battle." She cocked her head. "What does it all mean?"

Lucky's fur stood on end. "I don't know, Sweet. But every whisker on my muzzle, every hair along my back, is telling me it's real—that danger is coming. A battle that will change our lives forever."

"With the Fierce Dogs?" she asked.

Lucky licked his lips. "It feels bigger than that. Not just a fight against dogs we don't get along with. It's a battle for the future." The smell of blood still stung his nose. "A terrible battle. There will be death."

Sweet's ears pricked in alarm. She looked over the sleeping

Pack. "Will these dogs be involved?" she whispered. "Will they be okay?"

Lucky pressed his eyes shut, trying to remember. The images from his dreams were indistinct: a shifting white sky, snapping teeth, snatches of fur . . . He whined in frustration. "I just don't know. I'm sorry."

Sweet licked his nose. "It's okay. I'm glad you told me. If it's real, if it's going to happen, I'd rather we were both prepared." She hesitated, her ears trembling. "Did you tell Storm about these dreams?"

"No," Lucky said. "She chose the name for herself, after we'd battled Terror. Almost as though she had some sense of what I'd been dreaming."

"Do you think she knows something about the battle? Should we ask her?"

Lucky looked around, his eyes trailing across Martha's heavy black frame, over Bella, Mickey, Dart, and Snap. He frowned, rising to his paws. He couldn't see Storm anywhere.

Sweet followed his gaze. "Where has she gone?"

He swallowed hard, pushing past Sweet, a little rougher than he'd intended. "Sorry," he mumbled. "I have to find her; she's really just a pup." *She must have gone without me. What if she reaches*

Blade before I can catch up with her?

Wisps of fog were floating through the doorway as Lucky hurried across the room.

"But where are you going?" whined Sweet.

He padded back to her. "I'm going to find Storm, before she does anything stupid."

Sweet's eyes darkened. "She wouldn't confront Blade, would she? Not alone?"

Lucky's ears flicked back. "Please don't tell the others. I don't want to worry them. I'll return with Storm as quickly as I can."

Sweet sighed. "All right. Go, but hurry!"

Lucky nudged her gratefully with his snout before turning and rushing toward the door. He stepped out in the cold, misty air. An arch of dawn light rose over the edge of the cliff. The Sun-Dog was waking up.

Lucky blinked through the mist. He could smell Storm's fresh scent and followed her trail down toward the abandoned town. Sure enough, it grew stronger as he crept along the cliff top. His chest felt tight and his heart beat quickly. He would have liked to run, but it wasn't safe this close to the cliff face under deep fog. He shivered as he carefully hopped down the craggy path, listening to the Endless Lake as it pounded the shore below him.

The path dropped steeply and Lucky worked hard to keep his footing. By the time he was nearing the sandy waterfront and the abandoned town, his forelegs were aching from the strain.

The fog grew thinner this close to the water. It felt as though Lucky had walked through a cloud and come out of the other side. He could see the white-capped waves lick the land, and the outskirts of the town with its jumble of sand-coated buildings. His ears pricked. He could hear barking. Creeping low, careful to stay upwind, Lucky drew toward the Fierce Dog camp.

Sniffing hard, he knew that Storm couldn't be far. A moment later he spotted her crouching behind some shrubs a few dog-lengths away. Lucky slunk closer, hurrying behind a tree. He was almost near enough to Storm to risk whispering to her when he froze, his fur on end. Just up ahead, the Fierce Dogs were in plain sight. They were performing some sort of morning exercise ritual. They stood in organized rows as one dog played with a rabbit, chasing after it and pinning it down with her paw until the creature was finally allowed to wriggle free. Then it was the next attack-dog's turn to chase and trap the rabbit. Lucky watched as the Fierce Dogs growled and yelped, amused by the terrified rabbit as it hopped in broken circles, trying to get away.

Lucky's belly tightened. *This is horrible!* Prey was hunted for food. But killing for sport, torturing an animal like that . . . It was against the laws of the Forest-Dog. It was *barbaric*—something a *sharpclaw* would do.

There was a volley of cruel barks as the rabbit stumbled to its paws, turned, and made a break for the shrubs where Storm was hiding. Lucky gasped in terror as two Fierce Dogs sprang to their paws, pounding after it. He shrank back behind the tree, holding his breath. He couldn't see what was happening, but he heard twigs snap and a high-pitched shriek as the rabbit was caught.

"Look what we have here!" growled one of the Fierce Dogs.

Lucky risked a look around the tree and had to stop himself from crying out in fear. One Fierce Dog held the rabbit by the neck—the other had his teeth locked on Storm.

The Pack crowded around, taunting the young dog with growls and jibes.

"It's the City Rat's pet!" snarled one.

"The escaped runt!" put in another.

Storm struggled but couldn't get free.

The Fierce Dog with the rabbit snapped its neck and tossed it on the ground to an explosion of barks as the Pack descended on the small creature. Lucky could hear crunching bones, snorts, and slurps. A moment later, the Fierce Dogs fell back. All that was left were a few tufts of fur and a gristle of pink meat.

The Fierce Dog who had killed the rabbit took a step toward Storm. His lip peeled back as he snarled at her. "We'll tear you into even smaller pieces."

This was too much for Storm, who shook herself violently, broke free, and made for the dog. "Just try it!" she growled.

Lucky was sick with fear. *She can't fight them all!*

"If it isn't the pup called *Lick*," hissed Blade, appearing behind the Pack. Storm froze, her head dropping, as the others fell back. Blade sat, nonchalant. She reached out a tan forepaw and started washing it as Storm snarled and growled at her. Lowering her paw, Blade continued without looking up. "The last time we saw this pup was at the tall longpaw place. She fought ferociously, but it wasn't enough to save her Alpha, was it?" Her eyes flicked up. "Or did she *want* the Alpha to fall like that? Imagine that—a dog without a shred of loyalty to her leader."

Storm howled with anger. "I swore I'd fight you till the day I died if any of my Packmates were hurt! Alpha is dead, and I'm back to take vengeance!" The Fierce Dogs yelped in mirth, mocking her. With a howl of fury, Storm charged at Blade, but two deputies sprang in front of her. Another two snapped at her heels, one catching a hind leg with his teeth.

Why did she have to come here alone? She can't win against the whole Pack! Lucky was paralyzed, cowering behind the tree as the dogs tossed Storm between them, taking cruel bites at her flanks. Getting involved would be suicide—Lucky knew that—but how could he leave her to this torture? Lucky could scarcely stand to watch. *She's the rabbit now . . . their sport. I have to help her.*

He could hardly see her amid the tussle of glossy black-and-tan fur. The fog was also closing in again, prickling Lucky's nose with its damp touch. He squinted as it tumbled over the Fierce Dogs. There was barking, the snapping of teeth, then a shrill yelp of pain. It was too much to bear! Against his better judgment, Lucky stepped out from behind the tree and crept toward the Fierce Dogs' camp. He smacked against a bush, cursing beneath his breath, waiting for the worst of the fog to lift.

As the tendrils of fog crept back toward the bank of the Endless Lake, Lucky hurried to the place where the Fierce Dogs had been. He saw the grisly remains of the rabbit, but the Pack had disappeared, and so had Storm. He sniffed the ground. There was something odd by the rabbit's remains, something familiar . . . a bloody triangle of . . . Lucky gagged. *Storm's ear!* The Fierce Dogs had taken her, leaving her soft, felty ear discarded in the dirt. Dizzy with horror, he remembered how they'd tormented the rabbit. Tortured it . . . and *killed it*.

Heart pounding in his chest, Lucky turned on his tail and raced back up the cliff.

CHAPTER TWENTY

Lucky scrambled up the misty road, making for the abandoned long-paw building where the Wild Pack had slept through the night. As the rocky ground beneath his paws began to even out, he thought he could hear barking. Two or three voices rose on the air and he picked up his pace, panting as he rounded the edge of the building.

He was surprised to see that the dogs had spilled through the entrance and were gathered on the grass cliff top, snarling and barking. He caught a tang of fear-scent on the air and stiffened. Something was very wrong.

There was a tussle of dogs around the entrance and Lucky craned to see who was at the center. "Leave her alone!" hissed Moon, as Dart backed away a few paces, her teeth bared. Standing alongside her, Bella charged forward, throwing her forepaws against Sweet with a furious howl. Bruno and Snap flanked Bella, circling Sweet and biting at her legs. It looked like Moon and Daisy were trying to defend the swift-dog.

"Stop it, stop fighting!" yipped Sunshine in her shrill voice. "Why are you doing this? We're all the same Pack!" The other dogs ignored her.

Lucky could hardly believe his eyes. He shoved between Bruno and Snap, blocking Bella from Sweet, his tail stiff behind him. The dogs saw him and fell back in surprise. "By the Forest-Dog, what's wrong with you all? I'm gone a short time and I come back to this!" His glance trailed over the dogs. Snap lowered her gaze and Dart gave a small whine. Sweet shook her muzzle. A streak of blood ran along the dark outline of her eye. *She's injured!* His heart lurched and he longed to run to her and lick her cheek.

Instead he cast a furious look at the dogs. "Sunshine's right: We're all in the same Pack! What were you all thinking?"

Only Bella still met his gaze. "It's all very well to stand there and tell us off. Where have you been, Lucky? We woke up and you and Storm had disappeared." She threw Sweet a distrustful glare. "She made you, didn't she? Because she wanted to be the Alpha, she had to get rid of you. She just stood there and didn't say anything—didn't even have the good sense to deny it!"

Poor Sweet! *She tried to cover up for me, and this is what happened.* He turned on his litter-sister angrily. "No one told me to go. I went because Storm's in trouble. Listen to me. The Fierce Dogs have captured her!"

Whimpers of shock rose from the Pack.

"Are they here?" yipped Sunshine, starting to tremble.

Daisy barked in alarm and Bruno's hackles rose.

"Not here," said Lucky quickly. "She went down to their lair. She wanted to make sure that we weren't being followed, but they found her."

"Well, I'm sorry Storm's gone," said Bella, not looking too sad about it. "But we didn't know what was going on, and Sweet wouldn't tell us."

Lucky shook his ears in frustration. "And I suppose you voted for this?"

"Of course we did!" replied Bella, at the same time as Daisy yapped, "No, not really!"

Thorn padded toward Lucky. She looked like a miniature version of her Mother-Dog. Her fur was fluffy and long, almost completely white but for her pointed black ears and a black patch that covered one side of her face. Like Moon, her eyes were blue. "There was a vote," she said in a small but confident voice. "The vote was whether to punish Sweet until she admitted she'd forced you out of the Pack. Bella, Snap, Dart, and Bruno voted yes, but Sweet started her own vote and got four nos. That's when the fighting started."

Lucky's belly churned with guilt and disappointment. His own voting system had failed. And because he'd gone after Storm—because he'd made Sweet promise to keep the truth from the Pack—she'd been injured.

Bella looked unrepentant. Her muzzle was high and her jaw was set. "All that Four Paws stuff was a nice thought, litter-brother, but it didn't work. The Pack needs leadership, not complicated decisions that lead to bickering and fights. We need an Alpha, and I think that should be me." She held Lucky's eye, challenging him to contradict her. "I've done it before, and I can do it again. Dart and Snap think I should be leader too. Don't you?" She turned to look at them, but they had backed away, tails between their legs.

Lucky's lip twitched over his fangs. *Am I surrounded by spineless cowards?* At least no one could accuse Storm of that. His chest tightened when he remembered her, and he started to protest that they should go after the Fierce Dogs. Before he got the words out, Sweet stumbled forward.

"I want to be Alpha," she spat. There was blood on her tongue. The wound near her eye had left a long red track down her muzzle.

"You must be kidding!" Bella barked in amusement. "Look at the state of you! Do you really think you could beat me in a fight? Well, that fits your lack of judgment." Bella puffed out her chest, her yellow ears rising. "Don't confuse fear with loyalty or affection. You threw in your lot with Alpha, and now he's gone. The other dogs might've been too afraid to say it, but he was a bully and we're better off without him."

There were shocked murmurs from the dogs. Even Lucky trod awkwardly from paw to paw. He had been no fan of Alpha's, but it didn't seem right to be speaking of the dog-wolf like that now that he was dead.

Bella sauntered toward Sweet, her lip raised provocatively over her fangs. "Your time as Alpha's sidekick is over. You're no better now than any other dog now. You should be down there with Sunshine, taking orders."

"There's nothing wrong about being Omega!" whined Sunshine, but Bella ignored her.

Snap raised her head, lapping her nose with her tongue. "If we're . . ." She paused. Lucky waited for her to continue. "Well, if we're not doing the Four Paws thing anymore, and we're following the laws of the Earth-Dog again, then the challengers have to fight it out."

"That's true," agreed Moon. "Alpha didn't just *say* he was our leader. He wasn't just given that name. He had to prove his worth by fighting off a challenge from that ginger-and-white boulder of a dog."

"Yes, Black Eye. I remember," said Snap. "He had a—"

"Let me guess," Lucky interrupted. "A black patch of fur around one eye?"

Snap cocked her head, perplexed. "How did you know?"

Lucky sighed. "Never mind." He was thinking about Alpha as a young dog. It was hard to imagine him in a challenge, or as anything other than the leader of the Pack. "So what happens in this fight?"

"It's just like challenging for position, but tougher. No one else gets involved—the two dogs fight it out."

"Until the death?" gasped Sunshine.

"Until one of them submits," said Moon, as Snap's muzzle twitched in amusement.

Lucky tapped his forepaw impatiently. "Storm is in terrible danger. If you both really want this, we shouldn't waste any time." He looked meaningfully at Sweet and Bella. "The Fierce Dogs . . . They tore off a piece of Storm's ear."

Martha, who had been hovering in silence at the doorway,

took a step forward and howled in distress. "Her *ear*?"

Bella stiffened, dropping her forepaws, her haunches raised. "Then we have no time to lose. Let's name me leader, once and for all. Then *I* will choose what we should do about Storm and those attack-beasts!"

Lucky didn't like his litter-sister's tone. *What if she, like Alpha, decides that Storm is too much trouble and leaves the pup to that vicious Pack?*

He glanced at Sweet. The blood was still running along her muzzle and one of her eyes was half-shut. *She shouldn't have to fight when she's injured,* he thought. *Can't they save this for later, after we rescue Storm?* He knew they would never agree to it, though. And maybe what they were saying was true—perhaps the Pack needed certainty and clear leadership. Tail creeping toward his flank, Lucky had to admit that his Four Paws idea hadn't gone as he'd hoped.

Snap trotted out between Bella and Sweet. The Pack fell silent as she closed her eyes, raising her snout to the sky. "Sweet the swift-dog and Bella the hunter both challenge for leadership of the Pack. The decision is in the paws of the Spirit Dogs now. Choose wisely, guardians of the earth and air. May our true leader win!"

She finished to a chorus of excited howls. The dogs backed away, giving the contenders space. Lucky slipped behind Mickey, hardly able to watch. *Let's get this over with.* He felt fiercely protective of Sweet. She had proven her loyalty to him and been injured in the process. She was his friend from the Trap House, and she was a strong, noble dog. But Lucky couldn't help worrying about his litter-sister. He remembered her as Squeak, a bouncy, bright-eyed pup. He knew that behind her worldly confidence, there was something of Squeak still inside Bella. *Please, Spirit Dogs, keep my litter-sister safe.*

With a snarl, Bella launched herself at Sweet. The swift-dog twisted out of her reach, springing back on her hindpaws and boxing her forepaws at Bella's head. Bella rolled back and pounced, snapping at Sweet's muzzle.

Lucky turned away as the other dogs pressed closer. He heard Sweet yowl in pain and flinched as though he'd been struck. The Pack's chants washed over him. Some barked Bella's name, or urged Sweet on. Others yipped excitedly, not taking sides but driven crazy by the sight of the battle and the smell of blood.

Lucky wished he could cover his ears. *Sweet is in pain; she can't fight, not properly.* A howl of anguish cut through the din of the barking dogs. Lucky spun around, making for the fighters. The Pack had gathered so tightly around Bella and Sweet that Lucky had to push his way through them. As he scrambled between Snap and Mickey, he saw a flash of beige fur. Sweet was on her paws, ragged but triumphant. It was Bella who had cried out! His litter-sister lay on the ground, gasping for breath.

She twisted onto her back, revealing bleeding claw tracks on her belly. "I submit!" she panted.

Sweet sat with a deep sigh as Bella rolled onto her paws with a wince of pain and limped up to her. The golden-furred dog dipped her head, stretching herself before Sweet. "You win, Alpha," she breathed to several yips from the Pack.

The swift-dog was good enough not to humiliate Bella further. She touched her nose lightly. "Thank you for a good fight," she said.

Bella nodded, already rising. She limped next to Bruno, who helped her to lick her wounds. The other dogs hurried to Sweet, ears erect and tails wagging. They promised their allegiance to the new Alpha as she thanked them with a satisfied gleam in her eyes.

Lucky was happy for Sweet, but he felt sorry for Bella. And it still stung that his efforts to get them to work together had failed. *I guess we need a hierarchy after all,* he thought sadly. He padded away from Sweet and the dogs who were jostling around her. He shook his head with a frown. *All this feeling sorry for myself,* he thought with a stab of guilt. *And Storm's still missing!* He spotted a long wooden longpaw seat outside the building, overlooking the cliff face. He pounced onto it and addressed the dogs.

"We need to find Storm. She's all alone with the Fierce Dogs; she's in terrible danger."

Sweet shrugged past the Pack and hopped onto the seat by Lucky's side. Her injured eye was almost completely closed, but she didn't seem to notice. Ever so gently, she nudged Lucky to one side, so she was standing on the middle of the seat. Then she spoke loudly, so the Pack could hear her.

"Thank you, Beta." She gave Lucky a lick on the nose and he stared at her, shocked. They had discussed it, of course, but he didn't expect her to choose him just like that. *Don't I need to do anything? Fight some dog . . . ?* He looked about him. The other dogs seemed to accept the news without surprise.

Sweet went on. "The Fierce Dogs have Storm. We've wasted enough time already—we need to get back to their lair and track her down. Beta, you found them before. Can you lead us?"

Lucky dipped his head gratefully. *Alpha would never have asked for my help like that. He would have acted out of pride, even if it harmed the Pack.*

"Thank you . . . Alpha," he murmured. The word sounded strange on his tongue, but he didn't have time to consider it now.

He hopped off the seat and started tracking Storm's scent. The trail was already fading. "Quick!" he barked, scrambling through a burst of low shrubs. He heard Sweet's footfalls behind him and his fur tingled with hope.

Lucky retraced the route along the cliff road down to the abandoned town. As the Pack scampered after him, the Sun-Dog climbed higher in the sky. His golden tail brushed away the fog to light their path.

CHAPTER TWENTY-ONE

The dogs gathered at the outskirts of the town. The cool wind lifted the sand that dusted everything, and Lucky shook his fur, trying to get clean.

He turned to Sweet. "The camp is in a large, broken, old building just ahead. But it will be guarded. Even if there's no dog out front at the moment, the Fierce Dogs have patrols and we don't know when they're next due to come around."

Sweet's keen face was raised. "We need to get close without being seen. Maybe there's a side entrance?"

Lucky thought a moment. "Follow me." He started around the sandy street, approaching the building with the faded images of longpaws plastered over it, but this time from the back. He glanced over his shoulder to see Sweet, with the rest of the Pack edging along behind her.

Lucky padded over the sand, skirting mounds of rotting river grass and broken objects until he reached the rear wall of the building. There were no faded longpaws on this side. The wall had probably been white once, but the thin pelt of color had chipped and worn away, revealing long stretches of gray, like hardstone. Lucky beckoned to Martha, Moon, and Bella, who had been with him when he and Storm had first tracked the Fierce Dogs to their lair. "It's this one, isn't it?" he whispered.

"Yes, it must be," agreed Bella.

Lucky lowered his muzzle and sniffed deeply. A whiff of the Fierce Dogs hung on the wall, but it was faint. *The patrols focus on the big, open entrance to the building around the other side. They rarely come here.* That meant it was safer, but how could they get closer? He could hear a faint scuffling sound on the other side of the wall and his fur rose on end.

"Leave that alone!" hissed Bruno. Lucky looked up with a start. The old dog's ears were back. "Come back here; we need to stick together."

Lucky realized that Bruno was addressing Sunshine. The little dog had drifted down the far side of the wall and was pawing something on the ground, her frothy tail jerking back and forth. Lucky trotted to her and she turned with a guilty whimper.

"I'm sorry, I just wondered where these stairs go."

"Stairs?" Lucky saw that one of her dirty white paws was propped on a metal bar that ran down through the ground, through a gap in the earth. He squinted into the darkness. *She's right—there are stairs going down!*

"Well done! I think this may be just what we were looking for," he whispered, and Sunshine's eyes shone. He looked to Sweet, who hurried over to them. "There are stairs going under the building," he explained. "I think we should see where they lead."

Sweet hesitated, gazing down into the darkness. Her tail froze straight behind her. In that moment, Lucky remembered how scared she had been in the Trap House—a world away from Alpha's confident Beta, and the new leader of the Wild Pack. He was about to assure her that they could always leave if they ran into trouble, but Sweet seemed to make her mind up.

"Pack," she whispered as the dogs drew closer. "We're going in." She led the way down the metal steps into the belly of the building.

Lucky hurried after her. As he stepped down into the darkness, he could hear the soft thuds of the other dogs' paws trailing behind him. The stairs led a long way under the building. The small opening to the street was just enough to cast a thin light down there. Lucky's whiskers crinkled and he smelled the dank air as he hopped off the bottom step and followed Sweet onto the cool ground.

Martha padded past. The water-dog had hardly said a word since her fight with Storm. Lucky wondered if she had forgiven the young Fierce Dog.

Lucky heard Daisy pounce onto the ground. She pressed her muzzle to his ear. "I don't like it down here," she whined. "So dark and stale."

"We won't be here long," he assured her.

Sweet turned to them. Lucky could see her shadowy outline. "Did you hear that? Overhead?"

Lucky craned his ears. He could hear a creaking noise, then shuffling. A dog whined, but the voice was muffled. "We must be under their lair," he whispered.

The swift-dog lifted her narrow muzzle. "We need to get closer."

Martha called them in her soft, deep voice. "I think I've found something."

Sweet and Lucky followed her into the cave beneath the

Fierce Dogs' lair. Lucky noticed some chinks of light overhead. As his eyes adapted, he could just make out a knotted rope dangling down from a door in the ceiling.

"I think it's some sort of sky door," whispered Martha. "If we can pull it open, we should be able to get aboveground. That would take us into the heart of the building, wouldn't it?"

Sweet paused as Martha and Lucky waited. The other dogs crept closer and stood in silence. "Okay," Sweet said at last. "Get it open if you can. Be careful; we don't know what's up there."

Martha closed her jaws around the rope and gave it a tug. With a creak, the ceiling panel caved in and swung down to the ground, unfolding into a long ledge with steps leading upward. Dust spun through the dark air and Lucky sank down onto his haunches, covering his head with his paws, trying not sneeze. When he looked up he could see there was low light at the top of the sky door. He could smell Fierce Dogs nearby and his fur rose on end.

Sweet licked her lips uncertainly before placing an elegant paw on the wooden ledge. As she placed her second forepaw down, it creaked beneath her weight but held firm. She climbed up until her head disappeared through the sky door. Lucky waited anxiously as Sweet's tail twitched above his nose. Then she peered down.

"It's safe," she whispered. Then she climbed up through the sky door and Lucky hurried after her, the others close behind.

As Lucky reached the ground, he was certain they were inside the Fierce Dogs' camp. He could smell Blade and her Pack, and recognized the heavy red pelts that hung over the doorways. Looking around, he saw that they were in a cramped space behind one of the scarlet pelts. A passage ran behind the pelt into darkness. He lowered his muzzle, sliding his nose beneath it and taking a sniff. Storm's scent struck him and his tail gave an excited jerk. *She's alive!*

Lucky's Packmates were climbing out of the sky door and huddling together in the small space behind the draped pelts. At the front of the group, Martha, Sweet, and Lucky peered through a gap in the fabric.

Lucky strained forward. Storm seemed to be standing on her own in the middle of a raised platform. Behind her, on a lower level, he saw rows of longpaw seats, all of which faced the platform. He realized it was the same platform he had seen from the other side when he'd last been in the building—the one where the Fierce Dogs had made their camp. Peering up at the ceiling, he could make out the elaborate gold flourishes and images of winged longpaw young.

Shifting his attention back to Storm, Lucky's tail sank. She was in a miserable state, with one side of her face bloody and puckered, and a wound on her foreleg. Her trembling body was squared up, as though facing off with someone. Ripples of fear ran along Lucky's back. He could sense the Fierce Dogs had gathered along the edge of the platform, though he couldn't see them from this angle. A dog was pacing beyond the red hanging. A moment later, Lucky could see who it was: *Fang!*

The young Fierce Dog started circling his litter-sister slowly. "What a fool you have been," he snarled, lowering his head. "To think you tried to make me leave the Fierce Dogs for your *disgusting* Pack of mutts." He paused, his muzzle near her ear. "Why would I do a thing like *that?* Leave an honorable Pack for that band of rats! I should rip off your other ear for even suggesting it!" He lunged toward Storm and she cringed away. It made Lucky's heart hurt to see Storm being humiliated by her own flesh and blood. He could hear barks and snarls from the Fierce Dogs gathered along the far wall. From the sounds of it, they were all there. *Storm's completely outnumbered.*

A soft whimper behind him made him turn his head. Thorn was licking Beetle's snout. "I can't believe a brother would attack his litter-sister," she murmured. Lucky turned back to the scene that was unfolding beyond the red hanging. *I believe it,* he thought sadly. *Fang was raised by bullies. He's capable of anything.*

Storm twisted around to face her litter-brother. "You idiot dog!" Her voice rasped as she spoke and there was blood on her tongue. She spat onto the ground and swallowed hard. "You could have left! You could have done the right thing. Instead you stayed with Blade after she killed our litter-brother when he was too small to defend himself. What sort of leader does that make her? What sort of dog does that make *you*?"

"How dare you!" howled Blade, just out of Lucky's view. Fear-scent was rising from the Wild Pack and he hoped they would stay calm. If some dog panicked now, they'd be found out in an instant. What if their scent was already wafting beyond the heavy red pelts?

Blade continued. "This argument is best decided by a test," she growled. She stepped forward and at last Lucky could just see the contour of her blunt snout, her sharp fangs, and her pointed ears. Blade raised her voice, addressing her Pack but keeping her eyes fixed on Storm. "These two are no longer pups. It is time for them to undertake the Trial of Rage, the test that all Fierce Dogs must pass when they reach adulthood."

"I'm not taking any of your nasty tests!" spat Storm. "You won't bully and destroy me the way you've destroyed my litter-brother."

Lucky's heart swelled with pride for this courageous young dog.

Blade's voice was silky when she replied. "You have no choice in the matter." She turned to Fang. Now her voice was icy. "Kill her!"

Lucky's breath caught in his throat. Fang sprang forward without hesitation. The young Fierce Dog flung his forepaws against Storm's side and they toppled over, jaws snapping amid terrifying growls. Blade stepped back as they tumbled toward her, but she spoke over them calmly. "It is the Trial of Rage that makes us Fierce Dogs: Fang is to drive Storm into a violent fury—and he cannot stop, or grant any mercy, until he has broken her."

Storm froze. Lucky could see her eyes widen. She must have realized that fighting back was *exactly* what Blade wanted her to do. She pulled away from Fang and dropped to the ground, folding her forepaws around her face and curling her tail between her legs. Fang didn't let up—he launched at Storm, jabbing her flanks with his teeth and raking his claws over her back.

Sweet backed away from the red hangings and the other dogs jostled around her.

"He's killing her!" whimpered Sunshine. "What are we going to do?"

Sweet whispered urgently. "Listen closely. There is a raised area." She pointed up with her muzzle. Lucky looked through the gap in the pelts. Sweet was right: There was some sort of ledge overhanging the large room where the Fierce Dogs had gathered. Lucky could spot more rows of longpaw seats.

Sweet licked her lips. "Lucky will lead a group of dogs up there. Martha should prepare to escape around the back of the building."

The dogs blinked at her in confusion.

"What's the point of this?" whispered Bella. "We need to help Storm, not run around in circles!"

"There's no time to argue," whispered Sweet. "Just do as I say."

Lucky gave a quick nod. She had led well so far and he had faith in her.

Sweet turned to Martha. "Stay here, behind the red pelts. We're going to lead the Fierce Dogs away. When we do, it'll be your job to rescue Storm."

"But how will we get the Fierce Dogs out of here?" asked Moon.

There was a terrible howl from Storm, and Sweet tensed. "Never mind that." Her gaze was locked on Martha. "Rescue her when the way is clear. Do you understand? You won't have a moment to lose. You must be fast, strong, and ready to fight. Do you think you can do it?"

Martha raised a great forepaw. "I think I can stop a dog with one of these."

Lucky felt a pang of affection for the stalwart water-dog.

"Good," whispered Sweet. "Let's go!" She turned and scrambled through the sky door down into the dark cave beneath. Lucky scampered after her with Bella and Mickey just behind him. The darkness hit Lucky as soon as he was underground, and he staggered for a moment, almost blind. Sweet was already at the bottom of the metal stairs by the time his eyes adjusted.

She led the dogs out of the building, then turned to Lucky. "Where's the main entrance?"

"On the next street."

"I think the Fierce Dogs are all inside, which means it will be unguarded. But there's a risk . . ." She didn't finish.

"Follow me." Lucky stalked along the thin street, keeping close to the wall. He looped onto the next street and hurried toward the wide steps that led into the red-pelted building. Before entering, he paused to sniff the air. Sweet was right—there didn't seem to be any dogs around. He glanced behind to see her standing with the rest of the Pack. She ran to Lucky's side and together they bounded up the stairs and into the building.

It was cool and dark inside, with plush red soft-hides underpaw. "This way," Lucky urged, following the next set of stairs that had taken him to the huge room with the broken seats.

"We need to get to the platform at the top," Sweet told him.

Lucky didn't hesitate. Instead of breaking off on the first level, as he had the last time he'd visited the building, he kept going, climbing the stairs two at a time. *The platform must be at the top of the building.* Finally the stairs ended. Lucky sprinted along a passageway, ducked under a heavy red pelt, and found himself on the platform.

"Good work," murmured Sweet as she ran to the edge. Lucky came to her side and looked down. They were high above the huge room where the Fierce Dogs were gathered. Lucky gasped when he saw the drop down to the rows of seats below. *No dog would survive that fall.*

His gaze shifted to the black-and-tan Pack. They stood along one side of the raised wooden level where Blade had been reclining on Lucky's previous visit. Dog-lengths ahead of them, Fang was bearing down on Storm. Lucky's stomach flipped. Fang seemed to be hanging off Storm's one good ear. She gave a kick, catching his side, then drew her paws toward her once more. The Fierce Dogs jeered and howled as Storm's blood ran from bites along her back.

"What's going on?" yipped Sunshine, who was too small to see over the edge of the platform.

Lucky felt queasy. "He's destroying her." He met Sweet's eyes. "By the Spirit Dogs, tell us what to do!"

Without answering, Sweet threw her slender forepaws over the edge of the platform and barked with all her might. "Fierce Dogs! Who fights like that, so many against one? What sort of cowards are you?"

A mass of black-and-tan heads snapped up.

Blade's eyes bulged in fury as she spotted Sweet and Lucky. "Mongrels!" she hissed.

"At least we fight with honor and dignity."

"Dignity! You know *nothing* of dignity!" Blade howled. "When I'm done with you, I'll drag your body on the street and leave your guts for the birds!"

Sweet licked her lips and Lucky saw her pulse racing at her

neck, but she showed no sign of fear as she barked back. "If you want us, come and get us!"

"Fierce Dogs! *Attack!*" screeched Blade. She bounded off the wooden ledge, charging a path between the rows of seats. Her Pack surged after her like a single dark mass. They piled past Storm, who twisted out of the way just in time. Fang was caught off guard and fell beneath their pounding paws. As the last of Blade's fighters sprang off the wooden ledge, Lucky saw that the young attack-dog was lying on his side, his eyes closed. *Unbelievable. They don't even care about their own!*

The Fierce Dogs raced through the huge room and disappeared. Lucky guessed with a rush of terror that they were heading for the wide stairway. A moment later, Martha sprang out from behind the red pelt. She coaxed and jostled Storm toward the hidden room behind the wooden ledge. A jolt of elation ran through Lucky's tense limbs. *Storm's safe with Martha!*

The feeling was short-lived. Already he could hear the frenzied barks of the Fierce Dogs as they charged up the stairway.

Dart started whining. Bruno's legs were shaking, despite the tight look of resolve at his muzzle. Sunshine started running in panicked circles and Whine backed into a row of seats, panting heavily.

Lucky and Sweet shared a look. Then the new leader turned to her terrified Pack. "Get ready, Wild Dogs. Our enemies are coming. Do not be afraid—be bold and courageous. It is time to fight for our lives!"

CHAPTER TWENTY-TWO

Lucky heard the thundering of pawsteps. A moment later, the Fierce Dogs appeared. They marched onto the ledge, spreading out like a black cloud and blocking the stairs. Their muzzles were twisted with hate, their jaws stretched back and bubbled with spit. Some pounced onto seats, perching over them like strange black crows.

The Wild Pack scrambled backward, banging into one another. Lucky tripped over his own paws, his nose full with his Packmates' fear-scent. Only Sweet stood her ground, her shoulders squared and her hackles up. She dropped her head and took a step toward Blade. A growl rumbled from her lean belly.

Sweet's bravery made Lucky scold himself. *What's wrong with me? If we don't show strength now, we'll never defeat our enemies.* With a deep breath, he stepped alongside Sweet.

Blade woofed in amusement. "A skinny swift-dog as Alpha, and the City Rat as her deputy. Things must be bad!"

Her Pack snorted and barked at this.

Blade sprang toward Sweet, trying to drive her to the edge of the platform. Sweet leaped high into the air on her agile limbs, twisting out of the Fierce Dog's reach. She ducked low and scrambled past Blade to dive between a row of seats, then spun back, panting.

"Bit slow on your paws, Bully Dog," Sweet growled. "Maybe there's more fat on those bones than muscle these days."

Blade's head snapped around and she threw her bulky frame between the seats, obstructing the entrance to the row. Her look of amusement had disappeared, replaced with icy rage. But she hesitated, one forepaw raised.

She doesn't want to tread between the seats, Lucky realized. *She's worried about getting trapped.*

Lucky's fur tingled with hope. *We need to distract them long enough for Martha to get Storm to safety. Then we can make a break for it.*

That wasn't going to be easy. Mace, Blade's Beta, was already pounding toward him. "I'll get the City Rat!" snarled the thickset dog.

Lucky darted around a row of seats. Mace appeared at the end of the row, blocking Lucky's exit. The burly Fierce Dog started shunting his way between the seats, using his broad shoulders.

Lucky looked about. Dagger appeared at the other end of the row, gnashing his jaws. Lucky's pulse thumped in his ears. *I'm trapped!* He rose up on his hindpaws and caught a glimpse of the next few rows. He'd have to make a jump for it. With a deep breath, he sprang over the top of a seat and landed between Sweet and Blade in the next row.

"You won't escape me, Mutt!" howled Mace, bounding after him. The huge attack-dog threw his paws on part of a seat. It swung down beneath his weight, sending him tumbling onto the other side of the row. He smacked his muzzle and thumped onto the ground, whining in pain.

Lucky's ears flicked back in satisfaction. *Call me Mutt, will you?*

Blade started muscling between the chairs. They creaked as she shunted against them, though they didn't move aside. Then Lucky realized, *The rows of seats are attached to the ground somehow.*

"Get out of the way," hissed Sweet. "This is my fight."

She was right behind Lucky, blocking the exit to one end of the row while Blade stalked closer along the other. He couldn't go the way he'd come—Mace was on the other side of the aisle, snarling with fury. Instead Lucky vaulted over the next row of seats. His heart skipped a beat when he caught sight of Dagger, who had squared up to the exit.

"This way!" yipped Sunshine. Lucky turned to see her at the far end of the row of seats. Mace had just managed to clamber over the previous row and was jumping up and down behind the seats, barking furiously. The attack-dog's mouth was bleeding where he'd hit it on the seat back and one long fang hung at a painful angle.

"I'll get you, Mutt!" he spat as he bounced up and down, his voice gurgling with blood.

"Hurry!" whined Sunshine.

Lucky darted toward her and she shrank back to let him pass, running to Bruno's side. He could hear Blade and Sweet sparring, but could no longer see what was going on. Most of the Wild Pack was pressed against the edge of the platform as the Fierce Dogs closed around the rows of seats. He hardly noticed—his attention was focused on a gap that had formed on the top of the stairs as the attack-dogs ran to the seats.

Mace took a step toward Lucky. "You'll be sorry!" The huge attack-dog pressed onto his haunches, about to pounce, and Lucky bolted toward the stairs. Mace was just behind him, snapping at his tail. Lucky shoved a surprised Fierce Dog out of the way with his shoulder. Just as he reached the top of the stairs he slammed down his paws and threw himself against the balcony wall. Mace was moving too fast to stop, and he lurched down a couple of stairs before spinning back.

The Fierce Dog's eyes blazed with contempt. "Now you're blocked, Idiot Mutt." His lips wrinkled back and his bloody teeth looked monstrous in the half light.

Lucky raised his muzzle, standing over Mace at the top of the stairs. "Oh really?" He jabbed his paw at Mace's eyes. The Fierce Dog blinked rapidly, his head jerking back. He snapped at Lucky's paw, but wasn't quick enough to catch it.

Standing above him, Lucky had the advantage. Again he jabbed at Mace, this time daring to smack his nose. Mace chomped at the air but couldn't land a bite. "Fight fair!" he snarled. "You cheating rat!"

"Afraid of being beaten by a City Dog?" growled Lucky. "Look at the *big*, *scary* Fierce Dog. We should call you Dumb Dogs!" His taunt was cut short by a sharp yelp from within the rows of seats. Sweet was in trouble! Lucky glanced back. Through the gaps between the seats, he could just see Blade standing over her, pinning her to the ground.

Blade howled triumphantly. "The swift-dog will pay for trying to get the better of *me*!"

A howl—at once plaintive and ferocious—echoed from

beneath them on the platform. Both Packs seemed to freeze instinctively, ears pricked.

It was Storm!

"*Please* come with me!" she barked. "You don't need to stay with them!"

Fang growled back defensively. "I'm where I belong, and I'm not going to join you and your band of misfits! It's *you* who should stay *here*! We belong with our own kind."

Every dog's head turned toward the barks and they started crowding to the edge of the platform. Lucky nosed through them, forgetting Mace for a moment. Storm was standing at the center of the platform, pleading with Fang, who was sitting a short distance from her. Martha was nudging Storm with a great webbed paw, urging her to leave, but the young attack-dog ignored her. Lucky's tail drooped in despair. *All this to protect Storm—and now the plan is ruined! She must have run back to the platform.* Despite everything that had happened, she loved her litter-mate. She had risked everything to save him.

"We've been tricked!" barked Blade. "Fierce Dogs, to the camp, *immediately*!"

The dogs sprang to attention, bounding toward the stairs, colliding with the rows of seats and smacking into one another clumsily. Lucky watched in terror as they coursed over the stairs.

"I'll be back to finish you off!" spat Mace as he turned to join the rest of his Pack.

Sweet burst out of the aisle between the seats. "Hurry, Wild Dogs! We can't let them catch Storm!" She led the charge down the stairs. Lucky and the others dashed after her, scarcely realizing that now *they* were chasing the Fierce Dogs.

Sweet reached the bottom of the stairs and led the Pack through an open door. Lucky recognized the cavernous room with the gold flourishes and the soft-hide pelts. He followed Sweet to the base of a short set of stairs. She started climbing them to the platform where Blade had made her camp, but Dagger loomed over her. He snapped at Sweet's ears and she flinched. Lucky knew from his recent experience with Mace that, this time, the Fierce Dog had the advantage. Sweet parried Dagger's nips as the other Wild Dogs huddled beneath her.

"Beta!" she called without looking back. "What's going on up there?"

He sprang off the back stair and ran back along the soft-hide floor, far enough so he could see what was happening on the platform. Fang had rejoined his Pack. The attack-dogs had Martha and Storm surrounded and were looping around them ominously.

Just then, Lucky caught a familiar scent. It had wafted past him as he'd run from the platform. An acrid tang that brought back images of flashing teeth, thick fur, orders snapped from a heavy jaw. It reminded him of . . .

No, it can't be. I saw him die.

Sweet raised her snout and her tail gave an anxious jerk. She must have smelled it too, though she couldn't see what he could from his vantage point. He watched, disbelieving, as a wolfish shadow appeared on the platform behind the Fierce Dogs. Alpha, the Wild Pack's former leader . . . *alive!* Sweet threw a glance at Lucky. He knew she was waiting for him to tell her what was happening on the platform, but he couldn't find the words. What was Alpha doing here? He must have somehow survived the Endless Lake. Had he come to help them?

The dog-wolf stepped forward and the Fierce Dogs noticed him. They stopped circling Martha and Storm and watched as Alpha lowered his snout and started charging at them.

No! Not at them! Past them . . .

"Sweet, look out!" Lucky barked a warning just as Alpha bounded to Dagger's side. He sprang onto Sweet, catching her by surprise. He threw her onto the floor at the base of the stairs and clamped his jaws around her throat before she could twist from his reach. She howled with terror as he tried to shake her like a prey-creature.

Lucky's mind flooded with panic. He couldn't see, think, or feel. Then, in an instant, his thoughts returned and he was charging toward the dog-wolf with a howl of rage on his tongue. The Wild Dogs jumped out of the way as Lucky launched himself at Alpha. He slammed his head into the dog-wolf's belly, knocking him to the ground as Sweet scrambled free. Alpha rolled onto his paws and snapped at Sweet again, but this time the swift-dog was ready. She sprang out of the way and landed a kick against his hindquarters, sending him spinning.

"He makes a good addition to the Pack, don't you think?"

Lucky's eyes leaped to the platform. Blade was staring down, the Fierce Dogs gathered around her. "A fine Omega, this one."

Lucky was astonished. Alpha had joined the Fierce Dogs *as Omega*.

Sweet's jaw dropped. "Alpha, why have you joined them? You hate them more than anyone!"

"I hate weaklings!" he hissed. "The mutts and Leashed Dogs you scavenge alongside. You were useful for keeping these idiots in line, but you aren't cut out to be leader."

Sweet's muzzle was a crisscross of wrinkles as her lips peeled back to reveal her teeth. "At least I'll *never* be anyone's Omega!" she spat.

Alpha's eyes flashed and he sprang at her. He smacked her right foreleg and sent her rolling on the ground. For an instant, the two dogs were a whirl of fur and teeth.

"Get her, Omega!" howled Blade to a chorus of barks from her Pack.

Lucky threw himself into the fray, snapping at Alpha's ankles. He found his litter-sister, Bella, by his side. Together they overpowered the half wolf as Sweet sank her teeth into his flank. With a yowl, he backed against the platform.

"You're welcome to lead these rats!" he panted. "See what good it does you!"

The Wild Dogs barked in shock and fury at Alpha's betrayal.

"How could you!" snarled Bruno. "We trusted you!"

"And after we stood by you!" whined Dart, wide-eyed. "All this time, carving up food, letting you control everything, doing whatever you said!"

"The coward, siding with the Fierce Dogs!" barked Bella. "His treachery is a disgrace to everything dogs stand for!"

Alpha raised his muzzle in arrogant triumph and Lucky's forehead pulsed with rage.

Traitor! He'll pay for this!

He pressed back on his haunches, about to charge.

"Enough!" Lucky's eyes shot up to the platform, where Storm was standing, injured but proud. "Don't fight him! It's what he wants—what they *all* want," she barked. "Even if you beat Alpha, the Fierce Dogs outnumber us." She turned to Blade. Her jaw was still set but this time she spoke quietly. "I will do it," she murmured. "I will fight my litter-brother. I will fight him to the death, so only one dog is left standing. But you must let my Pack go free."

CHAPTER TWENTY-THREE

Blade's eyes glittered and she threw back her head. "Dogs, prepare for the Trial of Rage!"

Alpha didn't seem to hear her. He bounded up the stairs onto the platform and stalked toward Storm. He pressed his muzzle close to her, a menacing growl escaping his throat. "Back down, Savage. Before I make you!"

Blade turned on him angrily. "Know your place, Omega!"

The half wolf bowed his head. "Sorry, Alpha."

"Sit!" she commanded, her jagged teeth revealed in a wicked smile.

Lucky watched in amazement as his former leader obeyed immediately. It dawned on him that the wolf-dog had meant what he'd said—he truly believed that he had joined the winning Pack, and that the Wild Dogs were doomed. Tension crept along Lucky's spine, and an image of whirring snow leaped in front of his eyes. *The Storm of Dogs.* What if Alpha was right?

His dark thoughts were interrupted by Blade. "All of you, off the stage!" she barked. The Fierce Dogs hurried down the steps and the Wild Pack shrank back. But the attack-dogs weren't interested in them—not for the time being. Lucky watched as Blade's army shunted between the rows, pressing their forepaws up on the seats in front so they balanced on their hind legs and could see over the platform—the *stage*, as Blade had called it.

Only Martha, Storm, and Fang were left up there.

"Get down!" hissed Blade at the water-dog.

Martha ignored her, whining softly to Storm. Lucky couldn't hear her words, but he knew she must be urging the young dog not to fight.

Storm shook her head. "It's okay, I have to do this," she assured her. Dipping her head sadly, Martha turned and climbed down the stairs.

The Wild Pack gathered at the edges of the seat rows, glancing nervously at the Fierce Dogs. Some of them hopped onto chairs, or pressed up their paws to get a better look as Blade slunk onto the stage. Both Packs fells silent as she stepped between the littermates with an imperious grin.

"Storm will take the Trial of Rage," she announced. "If she

fails to give in to her true nature, she can crawl out of here with her mongrel Pack and good riddance to her. But if she *does* show herself to be a Fierce Dog . . ." Blade smirked. "Then she will have to fight Fang to the death, and she will belong to *us*!"

Mace and Dagger howled at this and Lucky flinched, feeling queasy. Storm was so battered, with deep wounds in her fur and a swollen cheek. She didn't stand a chance.

Blade turned to her Pack. "Let's make things more interesting! I want to hear who you think will win this blood battle. Say it loud, Fierce Dogs. Show the fighters who you believe in!"

The attack-dogs started calling Fang's name, barking at the stage in their fearsome voices. As Blade jumped off the stage to join them, the barks fell into a vicious chant: "Fang! Fang! Fang! Fang!"

The young Fierce Dog started circling his litter-sister, jabbing at her with his forepaws and snapping at her flanks with his teeth. Lucky jumped onto one of the longpaw seats to get a clear view of the stage, though he could scarcely bear to look. The dogs would have been evenly matched, but Storm was already injured, while Fang looked fit and strong. It wasn't fair.

Fang flew at Storm with a snarl and sank his teeth into a cut in her leg. She howled and the Fierce Dogs barked with feverish excitement: "Fang! Fang! Fang! Fang!"

Storm scrambled from her litter-brother's grip and limped back a few paces. Fang paused only a moment before launching another attack. This time he managed to throw his forepaws around her neck, and snapped at her ears as she squirmed wildly, trying to protect her throat. She twisted and head-butted Fang, who fell back, and Lucky was proud to see that she didn't take the opportunity to bite him. *She's not rising to the challenge. She's trying not to hurt him.*

Lucky felt a nudge on his paw and looked down to see Sunshine gazing at him from the red soft-hide floor.

"What's going on? Is Storm okay?" She was too small to jump on a seat.

Lucky glanced back at the stage. Fang was slamming against Storm with his side. She rolled, scrambled to her paws, but she was panting badly.

Lucky looked down at Sunshine. "She's trying really hard, but she needs our help."

"What can we do?" asked the little dog, her eyes wide.

"We can call out our encouragement!"

Sunshine nodded with understanding. "Storm! Storm! Storm!" she yelped. Her voice was lost beneath the chants of the

Fierce Dogs, but she tried again and Lucky joined in. Bella noticed and added her voice to theirs. Soon most of the Wild Pack was chanting Storm's name.

The young Fierce Dog seemed to hear them. With a burst of energy, she pressed back on her haunches and sprang at her litter-brother, pinning him to the stage floor.

Lucky's eyes trailed to Sweet, who was tall enough to see the action without leaning on a seat. But she wasn't looking at the stage. Her eyes were fixed on Alpha, a look of shock and fury on her face. *She was his Beta. . . . She put her trust in him. He's betrayed her even more than the rest of us.*

When Lucky turned back, he could see that Fang was beginning to froth at the mouth. The Fierce Dog was jabbing, charging, and attacking without pause, his eyes frenzied. At first, it seemed to give Storm the advantage as Fang wasn't bothering to defend himself. She thumped him back with her forepaws and snapped at his flanks, but this only made him angrier. He flew at her, tearing at her neck fur till she howled. She shielded her eyes with her paws as he rained down a flurry of bites and raked his hindclaws over her belly.

"She needs to fight back," Bella whined through the din of the barking dogs. "If she doesn't, she'll be killed!"

"But what if she fights too viciously?" yapped Beetle, leaning up on a seat. "She'd fail the test, and have to stay with Blade."

Martha barked louder, her voice fierce with a Mother-Dog's protective rage. "It doesn't matter what happens as long as she's alive! We *can't* lose any more dogs." She raised her voice. "Fight, Storm!"

Lucky's belly churned with tension as he saw the young Fierce Dog parry her litter-brother's blows. *If she fights back, she risks giving into the rage. She has to hang in there till he tires himself out.*

But Fang showed no sign of tiring. He chased Storm around the stage, gnashing his teeth, throwing back his head, and barking in fury. With a rumbling snort he launched another attack, but this time Storm was ready for him. She blocked him with her side, threw him down with her forepaws, and sank her teeth into his exposed belly. Fang's agonized yelps rose over the baying dogs, and Lucky caught his breath. Storm was boring her teeth into her litter-brother's belly, tearing at his flesh with rage in her eyes.

A shocked silence fell over the Wild Pack. *Has the Trial of Rage broken Storm?*

Fang's head rolled back in exhaustion and his body went limp. Storm's teeth brushed his throat. She could kill him with one bite.

Blade and the Fierce Dogs rushed up the stairs to the stage.

They jostled around Storm as she pummeled Fang.

"Kill him!" hissed Blade. "He deserves it after what he's done to you!"

"Your litter-brother is weak," goaded Mace. "Prove you are strong by putting an end to all this!"

Sweet started for the stairs but Lucky ran to block her. "It won't help," he barked. "All the noise will just drive her to aggression."

"Then what can we do?" asked Mickey, who had overheard.

Lucky looked back at the stage as the rest of the Wild Pack squeezed closer. "Nothing. We have to trust her. We have to believe that she'll do the right thing." He added a silent thought to the Spirit Dogs. *Please show her right from wrong. She's a good dog. If she searches her heart, she'll know what to do.* Lucky hoped this was true.

He could hardly see Storm on the stage—the Fierce Dogs were closing around her, their sleek, dark bodies masking his view. He caught a glimpse of her trembling fur. A moment later a couple of the Fierce Dogs moved back as Storm shunted them out of the way.

"What do you think you're doing?" snarled Blade. "The Trial isn't over! You must destroy your litter-brother for the honor of the Pack."

Storm turned to her with contempt. Her face was bloodied; one paw was limp and badly wounded. But her head was held high. "Whose Pack?" she spat. "I *reject* your Pack. Not all Fierce Dogs are vicious. The Wild Pack is where I belong. I have beaten the Trial of Rage—I won't kill my own litter-brother."

Lucky's heart soared with pride. "She did it!" he murmured.

Storm hobbled between the Fierce Dogs toward the steps with as much dignity as she could muster. Standing at the bottom of the stairs, Alpha tensed to pounce on her, but Lucky jumped into his path. "You disgust me!" he howled at the half wolf, all the built-up rage surging through him. "You despicable traitor. You turned on your own Pack after they mourned for you, taking you for dead!"

One after another, the Fierce Dogs became still as Lucky let out a torrent of anger. "Dishonorable beast! Even now, you show contempt for the laws of the Spirit Dogs! Blade promised that Storm could go free if she passed the Trial, that she would not be harmed!" His eyes shot from the dog-wolf to the leader of the Fierce Dogs, who glared down at him from the stage.

Sweet took a step alongside him and nodded gravely. "If you care at all for your honor, you have to let us go."

Blade's eyes grew dark and she stood in silence for several

moments. Finally she raised her muzzle. "Very well. You may go, City Dog, and take Storm with you. Run fast and hard. Because one day soon, my Pack will find you. And when we do, there will be no mercy."

Moon and Martha helped Storm off the stairs, propping her up between them. The Wild Dogs pressed around her protectively, giving her encouraging licks.

Standing at the edge of the stage, Blade was watching them with vengeful eyes. The rest of her Pack was stony-faced. There was a scratching sound and the scrabble of paws. Fang staggered into view, glaring down from the stage until he spotted Storm between the Wild Dogs.

"I will never forgive you for this!" he howled.

She turned back, shocked. "I spared you!" she yelped.

His body trembled with fury. "You should have killed me. I would rather have died bringing you back to your rightful Pack than live through your weakness and pity."

Lucky noticed Blade tapping her forepaw, becoming impatient. *We need to get out of here, before she changes her mind.* He pressed close to Storm's ear. "He's wrong. You showed enormous courage, Storm. You're where you belong."

"We're proud of you," agreed Sweet to an echo of supportive

yips from the rest of the Pack.

As they led the limping Fierce Dog from the building, Lucky knew it was true. Storm had proven her loyalty to the Wild Pack once and for all.

CHAPTER TWENTY-FOUR

The Sun-Dog bounded across the sky, streaming scarlet and gold from his shimmering tail. Already the Moon-Dog peeked over the cliff face, waiting impatiently for darkness to fall. The water of the Endless Lake crashed against the rocks, its waves exploding into silvery mist. Standing at the edge of the cliff, Lucky's eyes tracked over the water to the jagged outline of the town below. He imagined the Fierce Dogs pacing the broken streets. Fang's livid face raced across his mind. The young dog's words rang in Lucky's ears. *You should have killed me.* Lucky turned with a shiver. There was another young Fierce Dog to think about now.

They had reached the grassy territory with the freshwater pond and the small scattering of trees, where Lucky and the other dogs on Fiery's rescue mission had arrived after escaping the tunnel in the cliff. Most of the Pack had already taken shelter near the pond, and Lucky padded through the long grass to join them. Martha and Whine were helping to wash Storm's wounds. The pond's surface shimmered with frost, and the young dog howled at the touch of the icy water. Bella and Mickey sat nearby, sniffing the air, their muzzles raised protectively. The rest of the Pack was dotted about under the trees, huddling in twos or threes for warmth.

Sweet strode gracefully through the grass and settled alongside Storm. "Come, Wild Dogs," she called.

The Pack gathered close on one bank of the pond and waited for their new Alpha to speak.

The swift-dog met Storm's eye. "You showed self-restraint in the face of extreme provocation. Blade wanted you to succumb to your anger, but you were stronger than her—stronger than any of them."

Storm's tail gave a small wag and she dipped her battered head.

Lucky gazed at Sweet gratefully as she turned to address the Pack. "If any dog doubts that Storm belongs in this Pack, or that Fierce Dogs can be good, they can leave right now." Her eyes flashed in challenge, but no dog disagreed with her. Lucky saw Storm close her eyes. *Maybe now she can feel accepted and safe at last.*

"Of course Storm should stay," yipped Daisy in a small voice. "But what will we do? Where will we go?" She threw a nervous look over her shoulder. "We can't stay here, can we?"

"She's right," agreed Bruno with a gruff nod. "We all heard it—the Fierce Dogs swore to destroy us. So we'll have to run. Again." He shook his head, looking old and weary.

Lucky sighed. His heart sank at the thought of moving once more. But what else could they do?

"We can't move again," whimpered Sunshine, sinking onto her belly. "We've all been turned out of our homes or had territories destroyed, first by the Big Growl, then the Dark Cloud, and now the Fierce Dogs. All we want is somewhere to make a real camp for the Pack where we can live in peace."

"Alpha knows this place," Mickey murmured sadly. "He'll tell his *new* Pack. This is the first place they'll look for us."

"That traitor!" hissed Whine, his eyes bulging. "Acting like our leader all that time. And you were so close to the half wolf," he sneered at Sweet. "How do we know that we can trust *you*?"

Lucky sprang to his paws, furious that anyone could doubt her. "Every dog knows that I always hated Alpha!" he barked. "Even when he seemed to be the popular choice. Even when *others* defended him." His eyes lingered on Whine, who cringed away. Lucky raised his muzzle stiffly. "But I never doubted Sweet—our new Alpha—and neither should you."

"But they were very close," reasoned Snap.

"That doesn't mean she'd leave us for the Fierce Dogs!" yapped Dart.

Whine pawed the ground. "How can you be so sure?" he muttered.

Lucky's fur rose in alarm at this division in the Pack. *Why don't they trust her like I do?*

"Silence!" barked Sweet. "I'm as shocked by our former Alpha's treachery as the rest of you, believe me. I understand Whine's concern. If any dog wants to fight me for leadership I will, of course, accept the challenge." She didn't meet Bella's eye. "But first, there's something you deserve to know." She looked at Lucky. "Something that could affect the Pack's future."

Lucky blinked at her, confused.

She nudged him with her muzzle. "Your dreams."

Lucky stiffened. In an instant he was back amid swirls of snow, his limbs frozen to the earth as the barks of fighting dogs filled the air. He pulled himself into the present. The Pack was watching curiously. *Sweet's right. If there really is something to my visions—if they are flashes from the future, or warnings of some kind, my Packmates deserve to know.*

He cleared his throat. "I've been having strange dreams . . . about the Storm of Dogs."

The Pack broke into fearful yaps.

"Wasn't that the horrible battle between the Spirit Dogs? Back at the Dawn of Time?" barked Dart.

Moon shook her head fiercely. "No, no, it's a real fight here on earth. It's foretold to take place at the end of all things, when the sky turns white and the rivers flow red with blood. That's what my Mother-Dog used to tell me!"

Lucky gasped and his jaw fell limp. Moon's description was chillingly similar to his visions. *What if her Mother-Dog was right? The Big Growl was the warning, and the Storm of Dogs takes place at the end of all things.*

The Leashed Dogs looked to one another, confused. It seemed that only the original Wild Pack had heard of the Storm of Dogs, though no one could agree what it was.

"I'm *sure* it involves the Spirit Dogs," barked Snap.

Storm cocked her head. "Funny . . . It's sort of got my name."

Lucky watched her briefly. Her whole body was trembling. The young dog had been already suffered so much; he didn't want to upset her even more. "I think you came to that name for a reason," he said carefully. "That something *made* you choose *Storm.*"

The young dog didn't answer and the rest of the Pack became quiet.

Lucky shook his head slowly. "I see visions of Packs clashing, as though every dog in the world has come together for a terrible fight. I don't know what it means, when it might happen, *if it will happen*. But I have realized something." He licked his lips, hesitating. Saying it out loud would make it real somehow. But he couldn't deny it any longer. "The Fierce Dogs will never leave us alone as long as things aren't settled between the Packs. Eventually we will have to stop running. We will need to make a stand, to fight the Fierce Dogs and win." *Only we may not win,* he added silently. *We may not survive the Storm of Dogs.*

"We've just had a battle with the Fierce Dogs, or at least Storm has," Daisy pointed out. "How do you know that wasn't the Storm of Dogs? She outwitted Blade. Maybe it's all over now?" Her eyes were wide with hope.

"I'm sorry," he murmured, "I know that wasn't the one. I *feel* it. And the images from my dreams . . . It is even colder, and the land is white. The frost clings to fur and cracks paw." His voice trailed off. Against the deepening red of the Sun-Dog's last light, a powdery wisp drifted in front of his nose. It fell slower than rain. When it reached the grass, it settled as a tiny heap of white.

The first snow.

A stab of terror ran through Lucky's heart and he stumbled. *The Storm of Dogs is coming. . . . It's nearly here.*

He felt a warm touch on his neck and turned to see Sweet. Her eyes sparkled as she gazed at him, and his heart surged with hope. *At least I will have Sweet by my side.* Her scent lingered on his fur, giving him the courage to go on.

"Sweet's right. If the Storm of Dogs is real, if it's coming, it is better that we're all prepared," he told them. "Every last one of us has fought against hardships and learned to cope in an altered world. Soon we may have to fight once more, to battle for our very existence, perhaps for the last time. No dog here will stand alone. We are the Wild Pack; we are survivors! If the Storm of Dogs is coming, we will meet it together."

Warriors: The New Prophecy

Follow the next generation of heroic cats as they set off
on a quest to save the Clans from destruction.

Warriors: Power of Three

Firestar's grandchildren begin their training as warrior cats.
Prophecy foretells that they will hold more power than any cats before them.

Warriors: Omen of the Stars

Which ThunderClan apprentice will complete the prophecy that
foretells that three Clanmates hold the future of the Clans in their paws?

HARPER
An Imprint of HarperCollinsPublishers

All Warriors, Seekers, and Survivors books are available
as ebooks from HarperCollins.

Visit www.warriorcats.com for the free Warriors app, games, Clan lore, and much more!

Warriors Stories

Download the separate ebook novellas or read the first three in the paperback bind-up!

Paperback

Don't Miss the Stand-Alone Adventures

Delve Deeper into the Clans

HARPER

An Imprint of HarperCollinsPublishers

Visit www.warriorcats.com for the free Warriors app, games, Clan lore, and much more!

Warrior Cats Come to Life in Manga!

HARPER
An Imprint of HarperCollinsPublishers

SURVIVORS

The time has come for dogs to rule the wild.

Don't miss the new ebook novella!

www.survivorsdogs.com

HARPER
An Imprint of HarperCollinsPublishers